THE RIVER

CHERYL KAYE TARDIF

Praise for Cheryl Kaye Tardif

THE RIVER

"Cheryl Kaye Tardif has once again captivated readers in her third novel and latest suspense thriller, *The River*. Set in the wilds of Canada's north, *The River* combines intrigue, science, love and adventure and is sure to keep readers clamoring for more." —*Edmonton Sun*

"Exciting and vivid...A thrilling adventure where science sniffs harder, desperate to find the fountain-of-youth." —*Midwest Book Review*

"Superb! The River is Tardif's most exciting novel yet! Full of unpredictable twists and lurching turns, The River is a non-stop adventure into Canada's mysterious north." —Kelly Komm, author of *Sacrifice*

"Cheryl Kaye Tardif specializes in mile-a-minute pot-boiler mysteries." —*Edmonton Sun*

DIVINE JUSTICE

"Divine Justice is a powerfully-written chill ride that will give you nightmares. Best to keep the lights on with this one." —Rick Mofina, bestselling author of *In Desperation*

"This fast-paced thriller should be a runaway best-seller. Divine Justice reminds me of CSI or Medium. If you like J.D. Robb's In Death series, you'll love Cheryl Kaye Tardif's Divine series." —*Midwest Book Review*, Betty Dravis, co-author of *Dream Reachers* series

"One of those 'sitting on the edge of your seats' read as the team unravels the mystery and tries to solve the case. It is a unique blend of action, mystery...This book is highly recommended." —Margaret Orford, *Allbooks Review*

DIVINE INTERVENTION

"An exciting book from start to finish. The futuristic elements are believable...plenty of surprising twists and turns. Good writing, good book! Sci-fi and mystery fans will love this book." —*Writer's Digest*

"[An] excellent suspenseful thriller...promises to keep readers engrossed...Watch for more from this gem in the literary world..." —*Real Estate Weekly*

"Believable characters, and scorching plot twists. Anyone who is a fan of J.D. Robb [aka Nora Roberts] will thoroughly enjoy this one...*Divine Intervention* will undeniably leave you smoldering, and dying for more." —Kelly Komm, author of *Sacrifice*, an award-winning fantasy

CHILDREN OF THE FOG

"A chilling and tense journey into every parent's deepest fear." —Scott Nicholson, *The Red Church*

"A nightmarish thriller with a ghostly twist, CHILDREN OF THE FOG will keep you awake...and turning pages!" —Amanda Stevens, author of *The Restorer*

"Reminiscent of *The Lovely Bones*, Cheryl Kaye Tardif weaves a tale of terror that will have you rushing to check on your children as they sleep. With exquisite prose, *Children of the Fog* captures you the moment you begin and doesn't let go until the very end." —bestselling author Danielle Q. Lee, author of *Inhuman*

"Ripe with engaging twists and turns reminiscent of the work of James Patterson, Tardif once again tugs at the most inflexible of heartstrings...*Children of the Fog* possesses you from the touching beginning through to the riveting climax." —Kelly Komm, author of *Sacrifice*, an award-winning fantasy

WHALE SONG

"Tardif's story has that perennially crowd-pleasing combination of sweet and sad that so often propels popular commercial fiction...Tardif, already a big hit in Canada...a name to reckon with south of the border." —*Booklist*

"*Whale Song* is deep and true, a compelling story of love and family and the mysteries of the human heart...a beautiful, haunting novel." —NY Times bestselling novelist Luanne Rice, author of Beach Girls

"A wonderfully well-written novel. Wonderful characters [that] shine. The settings are exquisitely described. The writing is lyrical. *Whale Song* would make a wonderful movie." —*Writer's Digest*

THE RIVER

http://www.cherylktardif.com

SECOND EDITION

Imajin Books

ISBN: 978-1-926997-17-9

Originally published in 2005

eBook editions also available at various ebook retailers

Cover designed by Sapphire Designs - http://www.designs.sapphiredreams.org

Novels by Cheryl Kaye Tardif

Whale Song
The River
Children of the Fog

Series by Cheryl Kaye Tardif

The Divine Series:
Divine Intervention
Divine Justice

Short Stories by Cheryl Kaye Tardif

Remote Control
Skeletons in the Closet & Other Creepy Stories

Novels by Cherish D'Angelo (aka Cheryl Kaye Tardif)

Lancelot's Lady

Acknowledgements

Neil Hartling, author, outfitter, guide and owner of Nahanni River Adventures, and Lindy Laton, office manager at Nahanni River Adventures. Thank you both for helping me "keep it real"…or as real as a work of fiction can be. Without the two of you answering my endless questions and responding with such wonderfully descriptive answers, *my* Nahanni would have been lifeless! *www.nahanni.com*

Kathleen Meyer, author of *How to Shit in the Woods: An Environmentally Sound Approach to a Lost Art,* for allowing me to include the title of your book and all of its innuendoes. You are a Goddess among campers! *www.kathleeninthewoods.com*

David Miller, internationally acclaimed artist, and your wonderful wife, Nancy, for your constant friendship and support. Thanks for allowing *Lisa* to 'study under you'! *www.mauiarts.com*

Michele Jayasinha, Departmental Secretary at the Department of Anthropology and Sociology, at the University of British Columbia. Thank you for not transferring me again, and for answering my questions.

My editors: Mary, Francine, Marc and Linda. Your input and hard work is as always—priceless!

My daughter, Jessica, who designed the original cover for The River and who is now pursuing her own artistic endeavors. I'm proud of you!

To Jennifer Johnson at Sapphire Designs for creating an eerie cover that draws you into the depths of a mysterious underground river cavern. You rock, Jenn!

To Kelly Komm, who always creates the perfect book trailer videos to go with my novels. You give my writing a real dramatic flair. Thank you!

My family and friends, for your patience and understanding, for allowing me to hibernate and say 'no' to coffee, lunches and get-togethers in order to meet my self-imposed deadline.

Rus Hathaway, who dared me to write a story that opened with this first line…
"She always leads with her heart."
(Do I win anything?)

Dear Reader:

One of my mother's friends had a dream to travel along a mysterious river in Canada. When my mother told me some of the rumors of this river—the name of which she couldn't remember—I became *hooked* and a chilling story began to brew in my mind. The search was on to find *that* river.

The South Nahanni River in Canada's rugged Northwest Territories is one of the most spectacular sights in the world. It is fraught with exquisite beauty and hidden dangers. It is also filled with an abundance of plant and animal life—not to mention, woven with legends 'older than dirt', as my husband would say.

This *may* be the river to which my mother's friend was referring. Or it may not. Nevertheless, the Nahanni River holds many secrets. Decades ago headless skeletons and corpses were discovered along its banks. Over the years, people have gone missing, and I've heard it referred to as the 'Bermuda Triangle of Canada'.

Although **THE RIVER** is interwoven with fact, this novel is a work of fact…*and* fiction.

I'll let *you* be the judge of which is which.

Take the ride of your life, down…

THE RIVER

PART ONE
UNDERCURRENTS

I want to know the thoughts of God;
The rest are details.
~ Albert Einstein

ONE

"She always leads with her heart," a voice croaked.

Startled by the interruption, Professor Del Hawthorne lifted her head and gasped, shocked.

What the—?

A man stood in the doorway to her classroom, panting for breath. He was in his late seventies and wore a grimy suede jacket over a once-pristine white dress shirt. The shirt was torn and stained with what looked suspiciously like dried blood. The man's tailored black pants were ripped from the knees down.

He stumbled inside and slammed the door.

Del threw a warning look at Peter Cavanaugh, her young anthropology protégé. Rising slowly from her desk, she faced the old man.

"Can I help you, sir?"

His stringy gray hair covered part of his face and was in desperate need of a shampoo and cut. His mottled, creviced skin reminded her of weathered cedar bark. But it was the man's glazed yet vaguely familiar eyes that made her heart skip a beat.

Did she know him?

"Sir?"

The man's eyes flashed dangerously. "She always leads with her heart!"

Del gulped in a breath.

It wasn't every day that she heard her father's favorite saying—especially when it wasn't her father saying it. Instead, the words were coming from a man who looked like he had escaped from the psych ward.

How the hell did he make it past security?

She looked at her watch. *Damn!*

After six o'clock, security was reduced to two men on the

Anthropology wing. And they were probably on rounds or at the snack machine.

She glanced at Peter.

The young man was terrified. He stood motionless at the far end of the room, his head drooping against his chest.

"Campus security will be here soon," he said quietly.

The man turned half-closed eyes toward Peter. "Who's that?"

Del took a hesitant step forward. She rested her hands at the edge of her desk, careful not to draw the man's attention.

Where's the damn button?

Security had installed silent alarm buttons underneath the lip of every faculty member's desk. Times had changed. Schools, colleges and universities had become common targets of deranged psychopaths hell-bent on murder.

She pushed the button and drew in a breath, praying desperately that it wasn't the case today. "Security will be here any minute."

The old man's head whipped around, his eyes pleading. "Don't you recognize me?"

"Should I?"

Whatever reaction she was expecting to see, didn't prepare her for the one she got. Instead of answering her question, the man slumped to the floor, babbling incoherently. His right hand reached shakily into the folds of the jacket.

She stabbed repeatedly at the alarm button.

Where the hell is security?

Terrified, she saw the man pull something bulky from his jacket.

A gun?

Suddenly, two armed security guards rushed into the room.

Then all hell broke loose.

One minute, she was standing behind her desk. The next, she was on the floor—with Peter Cavanaugh on top of her.

She waited, holding her breath, expecting shots of gunfire. But there were none. Instead, she heard scuffling sounds and a few grunts.

Finally, one of the guards called out. "We got him, Professor."

She heaved a sigh of relief.

"You okay?" Peter asked, his boy-next-door face bare inches from hers.

She groaned. "Uh, Mr. Cavanaugh? Security has him under control, so you can get off me now. You're crushing me."

Peter turned a delicious shade of lobster red.

"Didn't want you to get shot," he mumbled, helping her to her feet.

She brushed herself off, then glanced toward the door.

The guards dragged the intruder out into the hall.

That's when she heard the man shout, "Delly! It's me!"

Only one person in the world had ever called her '*Delly*'.

"Wait!"

She ran toward the old man.

"I've seen it," he hissed, his eyes wild. "I've seen the future…not human…monsters!"

"Professor Schroeder?" she whispered. "Is that you?"

The old man's gaze locked on her. "You have to stop the Director, Delly!"

A shiver raced up her spine. "Director of what? Professor, we thought you were dead. You, my dad, the other men…"

Schroeder leaned closer, tears welling in his eyes. "They're going to kill your father, Delly."

"He-he's alive?"

"For now. The little bastards have him. You have to destroy the cell. I know how to get in. To the secret river. I know how to get in…*and* out."

"Professor Hawthorne," one of the guards said. "We have to take him downstairs."

Halfway down the hall, Schroeder's head whipped around.

"Follow your heart, Delly. And remember…only *one*!"

The guards half-dragged him into the elevator.

"Professor Schroeder!" she yelled. "What are you talking about?"

His dull brown eyes flared like a trapped fox, wild and feral.

"It's all in the book. Destroy the cell, Delly. Find the river and stop the Director before he destroys humanity."

The elevator doors hissed shut.

Del leaned against the wall outside her classroom. Her legs ached and vibrated. When her vision wavered, she closed her eyes and welcomed the darkness.

They're going to kill him, Delly.

Was her father really alive?

Someone called her name. Peter.

He stood beside her, clutching something to his chest. Whatever it was, he gripped it as though he were holding the treasures of the Egyptian Pharaohs.

"He dropped this," he said, handing her a book. "It's what the old guy was reaching for. You gonna be alright, Professor?"

She nodded. "See you tomorrow, Peter."

Del returned to her empty classroom, firmly closing and locking the door behind her. She made it across the room before her legs gave out. Dropping into a chair, she took a few deep breaths, then she picked up the leather-bound book that Peter had given her.

The cover was stained, partially missing. There was nothing on it except for an embossed symbol that was hard to make out.

Perhaps a cross.

She traced what was left of it with one finger.

Professor Schroeder, what happened to you?

Arnold Schroeder was a renowned genius in anthropology. Whenever he had visited Del's father, which was often, he would take Del under his wing and teach her something new. He was the reason she was teaching anthropology at the University of British Columbia. Schroeder had been her idol.

Other than Dad, of course.

Del carefully opened the journal, her fingertips barely grazing it. She flipped the pages, reading sentences here and there, trying to make sense of Schroeder's notes. Most of the entries in the journal appeared to be written in some kind of code and they were next to impossible to decipher. She was about to put the book down when a name jumped from the page.

Dr. Lawrence V. Hawthorne.

Just below her father's name, a date was scribbled.

January 2001.

Her hand began to shake.

2001?

She yanked open a drawer and rifled through it.

Finally, she found what she was looking for—a photograph taken seven years ago. Back in 1998. In it, her father and Professor Schroeder stood side by side wearing jeans, t-shirts and silly fishing hats. They had infectious grins on their faces, probably laughing at some private joke. The photo had been taken the day that her father, Schroeder and two associates had left for *'the adventure of a lifetime'*.

In the summer of '98, a new intern at Bio-Tec Canada, the company Del's father worked for, suggested a summer rafting excursion down the Nahanni River in the Northwest Territories. The intern seduced him with native legends about veins of undiscovered gold, and headless skeletons and corpses lining the banks of the river. Her father became consumed by the idea of exploring one of Canada's most spectacular sights, and he convinced Schroeder and his boss to accompany them.

The four men went missing three days later.

A search party was sent down the Nahanni, and the investigators discovered a headless skeleton a few miles downriver from Virginia Falls. Most of the flesh had been consumed by wild animals and the bones were badly decayed, but a forensics expert was able to identify the body.

It was Neil Parnitski, CEO of Bio-Tec Canada.

There was no sign of Del's father...or the other men.

A week later, the search party found a bloody shirt on the shore and scalp tissue embedded into a rock. DNA tests showed that most of the blood matched her father's, while the scalp tissue was Schroeder's. The investigators also said that based on the amount of blood found at the scene, even a doctor couldn't have survived without medical attention. Six months later, the investigation was closed, the missing men presumed dead.

Del stroked the photograph of her father.

He's a dead man.

Schroeder's words echoed in her mind, and she was unable to shake the doomed sensation that crept under her skin and invaded every pore.

She stared out the window into the darkening night sky, remembering the day her mother had told her that her father was presumed dead, months after his disappearance. She recalled the funeral a week later, and remembered standing in the pouring rain at the edge of the gaping hole as an empty casket was lowered into the muddy ground. The funeral had been three days before her twenty-fifth birthday—a birthday that came and went without any fanfare.

Del never celebrated her birthday anymore. Too many memories.

Now, staring at her father's picture, the overwhelming grief she had felt seven years ago came back with a vengeance.

They're going to kill him, Delly.

It was past eight o'clock when Del reached her small house in Port Coquitlam. Parking her car under the carport, she grabbed her briefcase and went inside.

"Honey, I'm ho-ome!"

An overweight, one-eared, brown-tinged Siamese darted toward her and anxiously rubbed up against her leg, mewing mournfully at the same time.

"Oh, Kayber! You act like I never feed you."

She had found the cat in her backyard five months ago. He was bruised and scratched, his right ear hanging by a piece of skin. He looked like he had been in a barroom brawl—and lost. She had adopted him on the spot.

Although, she often wondered if it weren't the other way around.

Tossing her briefcase on the couch, she returned to the kitchen, poured some cat kibble into a dish and set it on the floor. Then she sat on the couch, picking at a bowl of leftover macaroni casserole and sipping vanilla tea.

Her gaze drifted over the photographs on the mantle of the brick fireplace and dozens of memories raced through her mind. Memories of good times, happy times. Times when her father was alive—before he disappeared and left a dark void in her life.

She slid the bowl of half-eaten casserole onto the coffee table and pulled the journal from her briefcase. She leafed through the book, stopping when she came to a page filled with unfamiliar words, abbreviations, numbers and symbols.

NB...RESISTANT TO...≠
DC #02541-87654-18 PROV. BASE....BSC & SYN. CSF IN
V. SALINE...GN.

She found several references to her father but couldn't make out the content. A few pages in, the journal lapsed into page after page of numerical code. An hour went by and she was only one-third into it when she found an odd entry.

BIO-T CAN...KEY!

She hissed in a breath.

Bio-Tec Canada?

Her father had worked for Bio-Tec. Why was that in Schroeder's notes? Other than her father, Neil Parnitski and the intern, Schroeder had never had any contact with anyone else at Bio-Tec. He was an anthropologist. Bio-Tec was a research company exploring biotechnology.

Del was baffled.

She pushed the journal aside and flicked the remote control in the direction of the CD player. As Alexia Melnychuk's smooth voice filled the room, Del stretched out on the couch and closed her eyes.

Kayber, having wolfed down his food, immediately took this as an invitation and jumped up on her stomach. All twenty-two pounds of him.

"What is it with males jumping on top of me today?"

As she thought of Peter Cavanaugh with his Tobey Maguire-like face, a smile formed on her lips. Peter was in his first year of studies, but he had missed too many classes due to an ailing grandmother, which resulted in an '*incomplete*' on the regular one-year course. That was why he was taking her summer class.

Ten years younger, he was an embarrassingly shy kid, a bit of a loner—except when he was around Del. He had a severe crush on her. She knew it. Hell, everyone knew it. Half the faculty thought she was sleeping with him. But she wasn't. She wasn't a *cougar*. She didn't go after younger men. Unlike her mother.

Del unceremoniously pushed Kayber aside, then reached for the phone and dialed her mother's number. After several rings, someone picked up.

"Yeah? Wh-who's this?"

Ken, her mother's newest conquest and third husband, had been drinking again.

That's what you get when you marry a nightclub owner.

"Is my mother there?"

"What ya want her for?"

"Just put her on, Ken."

She listened while her mother's husband stumbled through the house. He swore loudly after he dropped the phone. She swore too as the sound reverberated into her ear.

"Hello?"

Jesus! What's taking him so long? Did he pass out?

She waited, listening to faint shuffling sounds. She was about to hang up when her mother's cool voice greeted her.

"Maureen Walton speaking."

"Hi, it's me."

"Who?"

"It's Delila, Mother."

God forbid if you forget to introduce yourself!

She couldn't believe that her mother was still playing *that* game. The woman lived for formality. Proper manners and etiquette, shaking hands, addressing elders by their surnames and owning a house that was treated like a show home. It was all part of her mother's attempt to become the next Miss Manners. Or, God forbid, Martha Stewart.

"Delila, I haven't heard from you in weeks. Why haven't you come to visit us?"

Del cringed, remembering the last time she had visited. The time Ken tried to cop a feel when she passed him in the hall.

"I've been busy."

"Too busy to visit your own mother?"

Great! Here it comes.

"When you were sick with the flu, was *I* too busy to bring you some magazines?"

Her mother's voice was tinged with disapproval.

"And when you went away with Tyler or whatever his name is, was I *too busy* to feed that filthy animal?"

Del held the receiver away from her ear and threw Kayber a rueful look. "She's never going to forgive you for peeing in her shoes."

She gave her mother a few minutes to vent, then drew the phone back to her ear.

What could she possibly say that would shut the woman up?

"Dad's alive."

A sharp gasp on the other end was followed by silence.

"Well, that worked," she said dryly to Kayber who was busy grooming himself.

She pressed her ear against the receiver.

Dead air.

"Are you there, Mother?"

"Of course, Delila. Now what's this nonsense about your father?"

"I had a visitor today. Professor Schroeder."

"Arnold? But that's not possible, dear. They found a piece of his head."

"His scalp."

"What?"

Del gritted her teeth. "They found a piece of his *scalp*, Mother. And a bit of hair. That's all."

"Well, whatever. He was dead and buried along with Neil, Vern and your father six years ago."

Del resisted the urge to correct her again. It had been *seven* years.

"Vern?"

"Yes, dear. The young man, your father's assistant or whatever he was. At least I think his name was Vern. Or maybe it was Victor…"

Her mother's voice dwindled away, lost in thought.

"Professor Schroeder says that Dad is alive. He gave me a journal. It has some strange notes in it, Dad's name—"

"Arnold always was a bit of an odd duck, Delila. I wouldn't take too much that man said seriously. God only knows where he's been."

"I'm going to bring him back, Mother."

There was a pause on the other end.

"Arnold?"

"No. I'm going after Dad."

"You can't be serious, Delila. He's dead!"

"I *am* serious. I'm bringing Dad home."

She hung up, feeling both relieved and irritated.

Why was her mother so heartless? Her parents had been married nearly thirty years. Didn't that count for anything? Didn't the woman care that her husband might still be alive? Or was it that her mother didn't want her perfect little life to come crashing down?

Del scowled.

She was the first to admit she certainly wasn't an expert on relationships. Look how long it took her to realize that TJ was screwing around on her. He had moved into her house *and* her heart.

Then he betrayed both.

She would never forget the day she came home early, barely able to walk and yearning for her bed—only to find that it was otherwise occupied.

Her neighbor, Julie Adams, had always been asking whether the rumors about a black man's libido and the size of a specific part of his anatomy were true. Now Julie knew.

Del had kicked TJ out on his ass that same day.

She shrugged off the dark mood that threatened to engulf her and gave Kayber a quick pat on the head. With the journal and briefcase in her hands, she walked to the large second bedroom that doubled as an office. She flicked on the lamp and was immediately greeted by a pile of final summer exams that screamed to be marked.

Turning a deaf ear, she nudged them aside, opened her briefcase and pulled out an empty notebook. She wrote a reminder at the top of the first page.

Find out where Schroeder is. Go see him!

Then she began to translate Schroeder's journal.

An hour later, she gave up trying to make sense of the scribbled notes and strange numerical code. When she finally crawled into bed after marking the exams, it was after midnight.

She lay in the dark, the flicker of shadows moving through her room. She pictured her father as she remembered him. Tall, with golden brown hair and rich brown eyes. He was always happy, always smiling.

She closed her eyes, her lashes damp with unshed tears.

I'm coming for you, Dad.

☥WO

Early the next morning, Del entered UBC, greeted security and headed down the hall. At her classroom door, she juggled her briefcase and fumbled with the key.

"Del!"

She swiveled on one heel and was greeted by Phoebe Smythe, president of the university. Phoebe was a tall, attractive woman with hair the color of rich, dark chocolate—except for the pure white streak that sprouted from her widow's peak.

"I just heard," Phoebe said, tucking the streak behind one ear. "Is there anything I can do?"

"About what? The fact that a dear friend whom we all thought was dead has returned from the grave? Or that he's adamant that my dad is alive?"

"Oh God! I heard about Arnold, but I didn't know anything about your father. Are you all right?"

Del shrugged. "I will be. Once I talk to Professor Schroeder. Do you know where he is?"

"They took him to Riverview. He's in rough shape, Del."

"What did the doctors say?"

Phoebe patted her arm. "He has an unusual form of Progeria."

"Accelerated aging? But Progeria is usually found in children."

"It's a mystery. That's for sure."

"Well, that certainly explains why I didn't recognize him. But it still doesn't make sense. Even with Progeria, he shouldn't look as old as he does."

"They're bringing a specialist in, Del. Someone from downtown. I heard Progeria, Werner Syndrome…they really don't know. But what they do know is that Arnold's mental capacity is irreparably diminished."

"So you're saying he could have made it up—about my dad?"

Phoebe slipped her a piece of memo paper. "Call the hospital. Tell them you're family. Arnold's wife moved to London and his sons are both married and living in another province. You're all he has."

Alone in her classroom, Del called Riverview Hospital and made arrangements to see Schroeder just before four o'clock.

It was going to be a very long day.

"In review, anthropology seeks to understand the whole picture when it comes to the study of man—Homo sapiens," Del told her summer class. "As an anthropologist, you will explore geographic space and evolutionary time so that you may understand human existence. Anthropology is a unique blend of folklore and commonplace science. It encompasses the evolution of language and the microscopic killer diseases that have wiped out entire civilizations."

She glanced at the clock. "Time's up."

"Mr. Cavanaugh, are you okay about yesterday?" she asked Peter as he scurried past. "About the man who was in the classroom?"

"I heard he's a friend of yours."

"He...is a friend of my dad's."

Although he looks old enough to be my grandfather.

The young man shifted the laptop and books in his arms. "Is he gonna be alright?"

"I hope so."

After Peter left, she peered out the window.

It was raining.

Vancouver—the city of rain.

To Del, it was perfect weather to dredge up the past. Perfect weather to revisit the dead. Or not so dead.

By the time she reached the outskirts of Riverview Hospital, an early summer storm had unleashed its fury on the entire Vancouver area, swamping the streets with water. She turned into the visitor's parking lot, snatched a ticket from the dispenser and made her way to an empty stall. Dashing through the main doors of the hospital, she was caught off guard by the slippery floor. She slid across the tiled surface—straight into the arms of a very handsome stranger.

"Well, hello," he said, rewarding her with a dazzling smile.

The man who held her was dressed in a casual suit. But he could have been wearing nothing at all as far as she was concerned. His dark brown hair was slicked back, except for an errant lock over one finely sculpted brow. The man's face was angular, with a strong jaw and ridiculously high cheekbones. He sported a closely shaved moustache and goatee. Kind of a seven o'clock shadow look.

Regardless, Del liked it. Hell, what wasn't there to like?

If he lets go, I'll melt to the floor.

"Sorry. I-I…slipped."

"Good thing I was here to catch you then."

His voice was warm and inviting, like comfort food.

"Yeah, good thing," she murmured.

"You don't look sick."

"I'm, uh, visiting a friend."

"Hmm…lucky friend."

Her mouth dropped. *Oh my!*

He released her and she was suddenly cold.

"Well, uh…thanks for, uh, catching me."

She could have kicked herself. Could she possibly sound more dim-witted?

Deep blue eyes swept over her. "Anytime."

Mesmerized, she stared as he walked away. Then she turned toward the elevator and made it inside before she caught sight of him again. He was standing at the receptionist's cubicle. Before the elevator doors closed, before her raging hormones kicked into overdrive, the man turned and winked.

Cursing under her breath, she jabbed at the button for the third floor—the secured psychiatric wing. When she reached the main nurse's station, she signed a form and was escorted through a set of locked doors.

The nurse placed a hand on her arm. "I'll warn you, Miss Hawthorne, we had to sedate him. When he was admitted, he was hallucinating…and he's in a lot of pain."

Del forgot all about *Mr. Tall, Dark and Oh-So-Sexy* the instant she stepped inside Schroeder's room—a room lit only by a small night-light glowing in the far corner. Someone had pulled the curtains partially open but it made no difference. Outside, the raging black sky held the sun at bay and unleashed its wrath.

Schroeder was lying in the bed, one wrinkled hand strapped to the rail while the other was swathed in thick cloth bandages. An IV ran from his hand to a bag of clear liquid suspended on a pole, and near the bed, a heart monitor beeped steadily.

Del watched the heart blips.

Schroeder was still alive.

"Professor?"

He didn't move.

Stepping closer, she stared in shock.

Arnold Schroeder's face had severely aged. The skin under his chin hung in loose folds across his neck. Every inch of his spotted flesh was withered and scaly. His lips were cracked, peeling.

Yesterday, in her classroom, the man had looked about seventy.

Now he looked like he was nearing his nineties. Nearing death.

What could have happened to make him age so rapidly? Progeria?

Del reached forward and brushed the hair from Schroeder's face. When she withdrew her hand, the hair went with it. Appalled, she shook the tuft into the garbage can next to the bed.

The man's rheumy eyes opened slowly.

"You're in the hospital," she said, stroking his arm.

"Delly?"

"I'm here, Professor."

"Aw, isn't it about time you called me Arnold?"

His question ended with a ragged coughing spell.

She picked up a glass of water that was sitting abandoned on a cafeteria tray. She brought the straw to his mouth and was shocked by the sight of his bloody gums and missing teeth.

After a few weak sips, he waved the glass away.

"Did you find it, Delly?"

"The journal? Yeah."

"It's all in there. Everything you need to know. Follow your heart. Find the key first. But, Delly...don't tell anyone! If you tell the police that you know your father's alive, you'll both be in danger."

He groaned as a spasm of pain wracked his body.

Del gripped his hand. "Do you want me to call a nurse?"

"No, it's too late for me. It's only a matter of time now. But you, Delly...you have to go, find the key."

He coughed sharply, spewing up blood.

"Leave no stone unturned. Remember...that. Take care again—"

Suddenly, the heart monitor raced and an alarm pierced the air.

Del watched, helpless, as every muscle in Schroeder's body convulsed. The veins in his forehead and scalp protruded, his eyes rolled back into their sockets and he let out a horrific scream of agony. Then he collapsed—silent, unmoving.

A tall Asian doctor rushed into the room. She was followed closely by two men pushing a crash cart.

"I'm sorry, but you'll have to leave."

Del's pulse raced as she stepped out into the hallway. She peered through the small window in the door while the doctor held the paddles over Schroeder's bare chest. When his body arched in response to the electrical current, Del pulled away from the glass.

Depressed, she wandered into the small sitting area, with nothing to do but gaze at other visitors, their faces drawn in sorrow as they waited to hear news of a loved one. How she hated hospitals! She hated the smell of death and illness, the taste of decay. She abhorred the poking and prodding by doctors, nurses. And the endless tiresome tests.

Yeah, she and hospitals were intimately familiar.

She shook her head.

No time to dwell on that now. There was Schroeder to think about…and her father. Something terrible had happened to them, and she was determined to find out what.

The doctor exited the professor's room and approached with an apologetic look on her face.

"You're Arnold Schroeder's family?"

Del remained silent.

"I'm Dr. Wang. He's stabilized at the moment but I have to tell you, I think it's only a matter of time."

Exactly what Schroeder said.

"We have a specialist on his way. In fact, he arrived about thirty minutes ago."

Del was shocked. *What's taking him so long?*

Dr. Wang suddenly smiled. "There he is now. Excuse me."

Standing at the counter, the specialist turned his head and Del recognized him immediately.

The man from the hospital lobby.

Dr. Wang greeted him. They exchanged a few words and the doctor shook her head. Minutes later, they disappeared into Schroeder's room.

Del's shock quickly turned to anger.

Mr. Tall, Dark, Oh-So-Sexy *and Selfish* had certainly taken his sweet old time. He should have been checking on Schroeder, not flirting with her.

She left the hospital feeling pissed off and disappointed.

At the handsome specialist…and herself.

An hour later, she was sitting in her living room with Lisa.

Lisa Shaw had been her best friend since high school. They were like sisters, although Lisa was the complete opposite of her in almost every way. Six inches shorter than Del's five-foot-nine frame, Lisa was a brunette with a figure made for modeling. Her eyes were hazel in comparison to Del's pale blue.

"So exactly how cute was this guy?" Lisa asked between mouthfuls of pizza. "I mean, was he Orlando Bloom cute or Harrison Ford cute?"

"More like Johnny Depp cute."

"My God!"

"Well, he thinks he is."

Lisa threw her a knowing look. "You think he's a God too, Delila Bea Hawthorne. I know it."

Del felt the heat rising in her face. "Shut up and eat your pizza."

"So, you gonna show me this book?"

Del grabbed the journal and set it on the table.

Lisa opened it carefully. "What's with all these numbers?"

One line read *233253 = 3132218142!* And one number was repeated throughout the book. *233253.*

"I have no idea."

Lisa scowled. "He's not much of an artist."

"Just because you studied under David C. Miller doesn't mean everyone had that honor."

Miller was an internationally acclaimed marine artist from the United States, and he had taken Lisa under his wing. In two weeks, Lisa's newest collection of giclee canvases would be shown at *Imagine*—one of the most prestigious art galleries in Canada. There was already a buzz amongst the media, and some influential people planned to attend. Even Miller and his wife would be there for the big reveal.

"This looks like a tree, Del. With two main branches. See? And this *N* shows that he was looking north through the trees."

"How the hell am I supposed to find my dad with this?"

"The professor said everything was in this book, right? Well then, you'll figure it out. When are you leaving?"

Del's shoulders slumped. "I'm not sure. I have to make flight arrangements, but I can't even do that until I find some people to come with me."

"You know I'd go…if I didn't have this—"

"I completely understand, Lis. I'll find someone to help me bring my dad back. You just make sure your show is a smashing success."

"What about TJ?" Lisa asked hesitantly.

Del arched a brow. "What about him?"

"You know he'd do anything for you. Plus he's an expert rafter."

"Yeah, and an expert liar."

"Have you seen Julie lately? She's an elephant."

Lisa mimed a huge pregnant belly, then noticed Del's expression.

"Oh, crap, Del. I'm sorry."

"Don't worry about it. TJ made his bed—well, mine actually—and he doesn't seem to mind lying in it. I hope he's happy with her. And the kid. He always said he wanted a large family."

She closed the journal, signaling the end of the conversation.

"Do you want butter or cheese popcorn, my friend?"

Lisa gave her a wide-eyed innocent look. "Why not both?"

Del snorted.

If there was one true gift that her friend had, it was the ability to make her laugh.

"Comic relief. That's what you're here for, Lis."

They watched two Jackie Chan movies back-to-back, pigged out on popcorn and finished off two six-packs of beer. Then Lisa passed out on the couch, snoring softly and fighting for space with Kayber.

When Del crawled into bed, she wasn't feeling any pain either.

A million thoughts raced through her mind when she awoke.

How could she possibly convince anyone to join her on a crazy trek down the Nahanni River? People would think she was nuts if she told them she was searching for her presumed-dead father. And who in their right mind would go with her, knowing that she had no idea where her father might be and no proof that he was actually alive?

Maybe I should ask TJ to go with me.

Frustrated, she whipped the blankets aside and listened for the familiar clanging of pots and pans that always followed one of Lisa's sleepovers.

There were no sounds of life from the kitchen.

Del's stomach growled rebelliously.

Groaning with hunger, she clambered out of bed. She threw on an old blue robe, stuffed her feet into Tweety slippers and plodded into the hallway.

"Hey, Lisa!" she hollered, raking her fingers through unruly, short blond curls. "Is breakfast ready?"

No one answered.

She reached the kitchen, expecting the aroma of bacon and coffee to assault her senses.

What she got was a note stuck to the fridge door.

> *Mrs. Johnny Depp,*
> *I left you some herbal tea. It has some kind of root bark from Africa in it. Supposed to give you energy, ward off the effects of alcohol.* ☺
> *Love Lisa. XO*
> *P.S. I called TJ. He said of course he'll go.*

"Traitor!" Del muttered.

She looked around the empty, foodless kitchen and spotted Kayber pacing by the door. She threw him a disgruntled look.

"The least she could have done was make us breakfast."

Lisa's tea sat on the counter, in an unmarked bag.

Sniffing the contents suspiciously, Del prayed that her house wouldn't be the target of a drug raid.

"Whatever's in here probably isn't tea."

It probably isn't legal either.

She made herself a cup, just to be sure.

Afterward, she headed for Bio-Tec.

♀HREE

It had been years since she had set foot inside Bio-Tec Canada, the company her father had worked for. The company that was mentioned in Schroeder's journal. Not much had changed. Even Annette Taylor was still there.

The receptionist's eyes widened as Del approached.

"Delila, what a surprise. What are you doing here?"

"I'm not really sure, Annette. Who's in charge now?"

"Edward Moran."

Moran had been one of her father's associates, a man with a hard edge and a way of looking at her that made her cringe. She had always avoided him whenever her father had invited her to social events.

"Do you want me to buzz him for you, Delila?"

"I guess so. To be honest, I'm not even sure why I'm here."

She was starting to sweat and her legs were beginning to shake.

Damn! Not now!

Annette returned with a glass of water. "Mr. Moran will be down shortly. Can I get you anything else?"

"No, I'm fine, Annette. Thanks."

Ten minutes later, Edward Moran strutted through the doorway, his chest puffed like an old rooster. He was a heavy-set man with a round, pudgy face. Small, squinty brown eyes were framed by copper-rimmed glasses perched atop a thick nose. Dark, curly hair receded from a wide forehead and settled into gray streaks above his ears. On some men it would look distinguished but on Moran, it just made him look old.

The man's navy-colored suit strained across his stomach as he approached. It was at least one size too small. The black buttons on the jacket were fastened…barely. One sneeze or cough would likely send them flying like shrapnel, and Del pitied whoever was in the line of fire.

"Delila Hawthorne, is that really you?"

"Can we talk somewhere private?"

Moran shrugged. "Of course. This way, please."

She followed him down a narrow corridor to a door that read *Edward T. Moran, CEO.* He opened it and allowed her to pass.

"You're looking as lovely as ever, by the way."

It didn't take Del long to remember what she had always disliked about the man. He had a habit of licking his lips every so often, especially whenever his eyes landed on a woman. His fat pink tongue would sweep around his mouth in a full circle, leaving a trail of saliva behind.

Yeah, maybe Moran had chronic dry mouth, but it probably had something to do with what he imagined when he watched her. His gaze never seemed to fully meet hers. Instead, his eyes constantly drifted toward her cleavage. He made her feel dirty, violated.

I'll need a bath after this.

Moran beckoned toward a couch in his office.

She moved toward the armchair instead and self-consciously folded her arms across her chest.

Lick. "So what can I do for you, Delila?"

"I'm here about my dad," she said.

Moran sat down across from her, leaned forward and patted her knee, lingering far too long.

"Your father? Yes, well, it was a sad event. We were all very sorry."

She brushed his hand away. "Mr. Moran, haven't you heard? Arnold Schroeder, my dad's friend, is alive."

"Really?"

His face went pale and his tongue slithered over his lips again.

"So, why have you come to see me?"

"I thought perhaps you knew where they had been heading. Before they disappeared, I mean."

Moran shook his head. "Why don't you ask the professor?"

"He's in the hospital. Dying."

He gave her a sympathetic look. "I'm sorry but I can't help you. I wasn't included in their plans. Besides, it's been seven years now. I'm sorry to hear about your friend and I'm sure that you didn't need a reminder of your father's death. If there's anything I can do for you…"

His eyes drifted to her blouse again.

She bolted to her feet, desperate to get out of the man's office, into some fresh air.

"My dad is alive, Mr. Moran!"

As soon as the words were out of her mouth, she recalled Schroeder's warning.

Edward Moran's jaw dropped and his face lost all color.

The last thing she saw before slamming the door behind her was a small black button springing free from the man's jacket. She heard the soft *ping* as it hit the floor.

Heading for the parking lot, she climbed into her car, pulled out her cell phone and called TJ.

He picked up on the first ring. "Yeah?"

"Meet me at the Starbuck's, near my place."

She hung up.

Lisa was right. TJ really was the perfect choice. He was skilled in canoeing and rafting, and he was great at organizing outdoor events.

He was great at a lot of things, Del realized.

Including lying, cheating and deceiving.

And being late, she thought twenty minutes later.

TJ was running on Tyrone Jackson time. As usual.

She was about to call him again when she heard her name. She spotted TJ weaving his way through the coffee addict crowd, carrying two venti cappuccinos.

He put the coffees on the table, then grinned. "Long time no see, Del? I missed ya."

He enfolded her in his arms, kissing her soundly on the lips.

She pushed him away, gaped at him. "What, no more dreadlocks? What happened to you?"

TJ ran a hand over his short black hair. "Julie happened."

Del flinched, her eyes drawn to the gold-plated dog tags she had given him.

Was that only two years ago?

It had been seven months since she had booted TJ out. Seven long months of lonely nights and an empty bed.

Damn! He looked good—real good.

Suddenly, she stopped herself. What was she thinking? TJ had a girlfriend. A very *pregnant* girlfriend.

Crossing her arms, she flopped in the chair. "How is Julie?"

TJ slid into the chair across from her. "She's good. Baby's doing fine too. Due in six weeks. So what's going down, Del? You wanna go way up north in the middle of nowhere?"

She nodded, not trusting her voice.

"You really think your dad's still alive?"

"Yes."

"But how do you know for sure?" he asked. "Your dad's friend could've been hallucinating, making it up. Who knows what happened to him out there? Don't you think if your dad was alive, he'd try to contact you, somehow?"

"What did Lisa tell you?"

His warm brown eyes locked on hers. "That you needed me."

She scowled.

It would be a cold day in hell before she needed TJ again.

Well, other than on this trip anyway.

TJ let out a frustrated sigh. "She said you think your dad's alive, lost somewhere up north. And that you have a map or something."

Or something.

"When you wanna go, Del?"

She held her breath. "Two weeks?"

"That soon?" His brow arched in shock. "Doesn't give us much time to get organized. We're gonna need a tracker. Someone good in the mountains. We'll also need a couple more people, that's for sure. Someone to work on the code and someone who can handle a canoe. Know anyone?"

"Peter Cavanaugh. You remember him?"

"Ain't he the kid who's got a crush on you?"

Del blushed. "He told me he took a whitewater course last summer. Says he's pretty good, and he seems really excited about going. In fact, he insisted."

"Man! He's got it bad. You asking some others or you want me to?"

"No, you go ahead. Ask anyone you want. Whatever it takes to get my dad back."

They finished their cappuccinos in awkward silence.

When she rose to leave, he restrained her. He opened his mouth as if he wanted to say something. Then he let go of her arm, without saying a word.

"I can't wait around for you," she warned. "So if you're going to do this—"

"Call me Monday," he said, cutting her off. "I'll check around, see who I can find to come with us."

He followed her to the door and she stared at him as he crossed the street. On the other side, he held a closed fist up to one ear, extended his thumb and pinkie, wiggling his hand. "Call me!"

Walking home, Del felt a burning in the back of her throat. She squared her shoulders, fighting the urge to break down. There was no time for tears. Her father's life depended on her strength and resolve. She would not let him down.

Secure in the familiarity of her small two-bedroom house, her eyes searched the fireplace mantle, lingering on a photograph of her father. She recalled his contagious laughter and corny jokes.

And the dam finally broke.

She wept for her father, a man who was taken away from everything and everyone he loved. A man who was waiting for God-knows-what as his fate. She cried for the lost years, for the young woman who had stood at his graveside believing that her father was gone forever. When her tears subsided, she sunk into a dark depression. She ached for her father, terrified that they'd be too late.

"Dad?" she called out to the empty room. "I'm coming for you."

Exhausted and emotionally drained, she fell asleep on the couch, dreaming of her father—young and full of life. In her dream, he feigned annoyance when she beat him and his poker buddies one night, even though she knew he was secretly proud. Then the dream flashed to the night she had invited her parents for dinner in her small one-bedroom apartment. Her father had teased her about her hockey puck Yorkshire puddings. He called them *doorstoppers*.

In her sleep, she smiled.

Until the brash ringing of the telephone jolted her awake.

"Y-yeah?"

"Delly?"

She sat up immediately, gripping the phone tightly.

"Professor Schroeder? How did—"

"Delly, I don't...time. You need...follow your heart. And remember, leave no stone...care...Bio-Tec."

"Professor, I can barely hear you! I already went to Bio-Tec. They don't know anything."

"Go back! Take care again—"

The line went dead.

Spurred by panic, she dropped the phone, snatched up a notepad and scribbled Schroeder's words on an empty page.

Damn! She had to pay Bio-Tec another visit in the morning. And sure as hell, Edward Moran—with his slimy wet lips—would be there to greet her.

Edward slammed an angry fist down on the desk.

"Where the hell are they, you sonofabitch?"

It was early morning and he was in the main NB Lab, typing furiously at the keyboard in front of him. The monitor kept flashing him the same message.

No such files exist!

It had been seven years since Lawrence Hawthorne went missing and was presumed dead. In that time, Edward had taken over most of Lawrence's research, but he was positive there was more. He suspected that the man had enlisted the aid of an encryption expert, encoded his files so that they were virtually invisible. But they were there. Somewhere. It was only a matter of time before he found them.

Hawthorne had been researching something big before he disappeared. And someone else obviously knew about it. Four years ago, the NB Lab was broken into and tossed. Whoever was responsible for the break-in walked away with a number of files, notebooks...and Hawthorne's laptop.

"Looking for something in particular?"

Edward cast a sharp look at a white-smocked doctor standing in one corner juggling test tubes. "Pardon me, Jake?"

The doctor edged closer while Edward tapped the keyboard and hastily exited from the lab directory.

"Just wondering if you were looking for something specific."

"I'd appreciate it if you would finish doing whatever it is that you were doing and leave me to my work." *Insolent ass!*

Edward struggled to remember the doctor's surname. Nothing came to mind. Jake whatever-his-name-was had been with Bio-Tec for almost ten years, just two years less than he had, but they had never worked together. When the board had voted for a new CEO after Lawrence's disappearance, Jake had come in a close second, but Edward's seniority had won out in the end.

Edward hid a furtive smile.

The lab exuded power and success with its state-of-the-art equipment and leading technology. Countless lab workers surrounded him, busily nattering to each other about test results. To Edward, it sounded like some kind of classified code operated by a secret club.

My invitation must have gotten lost in the mail.

As CEO of a leading corporation like Bio-Tec, he basked in the glory of astounding discoveries and technological advances that only *his* research team had accomplished. As far as he was concerned, he *was* Bio-Tec Canada. The many doctors and experts were simply the mice in his lab, running the maze and searching for results. He was the one handing them the reward for work well done. Of course, he'd dip into those rewards too—whenever he could get away with it.

He strode past Jake. His eyes narrowed when he saw the doctor cast a hasty look toward the main computer terminal. The last thing he needed was Jake snooping around in the files.

Relax. He's a doctor, not a computer whiz.

Reluctantly, Edward strolled through the automated doors. He was about to head for his office when his pager beeped. Perturbed by the message, he swore loudly and hurried toward the main reception area.

He saw Delila before she noticed him.

Lawrence Hawthorne had created a real beauty, but there was something about the woman that Edward didn't like. Not only was her confidence intimidating, she was also seemingly immune to his charm.

What in blazes does she want now?

He caught the glimmer of fury in her blue eyes as they fastened on him. His tongue flicked over his mouth, this time from sheer nervousness. He'd have to be very careful around her.

"Did you forget something yesterday?"

"I have a few more questions, Mr. Moran. Your office?"

Edward did not like her curt manner one bit. He stomped into his office, huffing indignantly. Then he closed the door behind them and got right down to business.

"While I can appreciate that you're having difficulty accepting your father's death, I hope you can appreciate that I'm a very busy man. We're in the middle of a huge research proj—"

"I'm not here to talk about your research. I want to know where my dad's files are."

He couldn't believe the woman's audacity.

"That's Bio-Tec's property! Anything your father did here we own. You should know that."

"It might be the only way I'll find him."

What could he possibly say to get her off his back and off Bio-Tec grounds?

He stood abruptly. "Follow me."

When they reached the NB Lab, he swiped a small card through a keypad, pushed a button and beckoned her inside. He took her arm, steered her toward the main computer terminal.

"This is where your father worked seven years ago. A lot has changed since then."

Shit! Jake—the obnoxious moron—was sitting at the monitor, with his back to them.

Edward paused. "The lab was broken into a few years ago. Most of your father's stuff was stolen. His files were deleted."

The woman eyed him suspiciously but said nothing.

"Of course I knew you wouldn't believe me so I brought you here to show you. Once I do, I expect you to stop coming here. Do you understand, Miss Hawthorne?"

"Oh, I understand perfectly."

The intensity of her glare burned a hole through his skull, and he was the first to look away.

Del battled a multitude of thoughts, furious at Edward Moran's demeanor. Her father's files may have been deleted, but Schroeder had tried to tell her that there was *something* at Bio-Tec. All she had to do was find out what.

Moran tapped the shoulder of the doctor sitting at the computer, then he leaned down slightly and said something, motioning the man to stay seated.

"Delila Hawthorne, this is Jake. He'll be happy to show you the folder that your father used."

When the man in the chair turned, she found herself ogling the attractive blue-eyed doctor from Riverview. Schroeder's specialist.

Mr. Tall, Dark and Oh-So-Sexy.

She struggled to catch her breath. *Oh crap!*

The man appeared equally as stunned. "We've met. Well, sort of." He held out a hand. "Jake Kerrigan, scientist and doctor. How are you doing today?"

She slipped her hand in his, then pulled back quickly, feeling a bit lightheaded from the electrifying contact. "I'm fine."

"Yes, you are," the doctor said boldly. "Grab a chair."

"Thank you, Dr. Kerrigan."

As soon as the words were out of her mouth, she paused.

Kerrigan. Why did that sound so familiar?

In the hospital, Schroeder's doctor had never mentioned the specialist's name. She was sure of it.

"What kind of specialist are you exactly?"

A smile formed on the man's lips. "I specialize in youth. Actually, in layman's terms, I'm researching the aging process and aging diseases such as Progeria. We've made some fascinating discoveries in the past ten years."

"Is that why you went to see Arnold Schroeder?"

"I've run some tests on your…friend."

"Professor Schroeder was my dad's friend. And my mentor."

There was a look of surprise on the doctor's face. "You're an anthropologist? I never would have guessed."

Behind her, Moran let out an impatient huff.

She clasped her hands tightly. "Dr. Kerrigan…"

There it was again, that faint recognition.

"Jake," he insisted. "I'm not one for formalities."

My mother would hate you then.

Del saw Moran move closer, until his vast stomach pressed against the mahogany desk. He observed every move Jake made on the computer. When the doctor made a data entry error and had to backtrack, Moran's beady eyes flicked him a look of disdain.

"I'll leave you two at it then," he said after a while. "Remember what I said, Delila. I don't expect to see you back here again."

He made his way toward the doors.

As far as she was concerned, Edward Moran hadn't left soon enough. Something about the man made her feel as though an army of fire ants were crawling over her body.

"There you go," Jake said, angling the monitor toward her.

He pulled up a folder labeled with her father's name.

It was empty. Nothing. Not one file.

Moran was right. Someone had deleted all her father's work.

But why?

She stared at the screen, willing it to change.

"Can you do a search? See if he had files stored someplace else?"

"Let's see what comes up if I search for one of your father's research topics." He glanced up from the keyboard. "Do you prefer Miss Hawthorne or Delila?"

"Call me Del. Everyone does."

"Ok, Del. It could take a few minutes for the computer to scan all the files. Why don't we head for the lounge, grab a coffee?"

They swiveled in their chairs simultaneously, their knees knocking together.

Jake gave her a rueful look. "Sorry. Ladies first."

She stood, then followed him.

"Did you know my dad?"

"Yeah, he was a great guy. We worked on a few projects together. You're a lot like him."

"Is that a good thing?"

He flashed her a wicked smile. "Uh-huh. *Very* good."

Embarrassed, she looked away.

"So, are you going to tell me why you're here, Del?"

She thought of Schroeder's warning. *No police.* Well, Jake wasn't the police, but could she trust him? She had already let it slip to Moran that she thought her father was still alive. That could prove to be a huge mistake.

Thankfully, the lounge was empty. The pastel beige walls of the room were bare, except for a set of brightly colored prints that someone had hung in an attempt to make the room cozier. Coffee-stained laminate counters held a variety of small appliances, including an ancient microwave—maybe the first ever built. In the corner, an old refrigerator rumbled and coughed, probably on its last legs too.

So much for advanced technology.

"You need a visit from the *While You Were Out* gang."

"Hey!" Jake scowled. "I decorated this room myself."

"Don't give up your day job."

"Ha, ha," he said wryly. "Has anyone ever told you you're like Samson's Delila? Chop off a man's hair or chop him off at his ego, it's all the same."

She laughed at his wounded expression. "So what are the pictures of?"

"Nanomachines."

She stared at him blankly.

"Extremely minuscule electromechanical devices. Computers. Programmed with different functions, like repairing molecular anomalies or malfunctions. They're manufactured on the nanoscopic scale, so they're invisible to the naked eye."

"It's hard to imagine a computer that small."

"Your father was working on a few projects involving Nanotechnology. But he was especially interested in genetic diseases. I was very sad to hear about his death. We all were."

She flinched.

But he's still alive!

"Were you here when the lab was broken into?" she asked.

"Yeah, but I was working in another part of the building. It was late, probably close to eleven o'clock. I still don't understand how anyone could have gotten past security. All the doors are locked and coded at night."

"So the only people who can get in are those with the codes?"

"Or an ID pass."

Jake held up a small card identical to the one Moran had used.

"Didn't security spot anything?"

"Yeah, a ghost."

Her head shot up in shock.

"Just kidding," he said. "There was a glitch in the computer system. It showed that Neil Parnitski had logged in."

"Parnitski? But that's not possible. They found his body when my dad went missing."

"Someone could have taken his pass card…if he had it on him at the time. Although, there are no markings on our cards. They don't even say Bio-Tec. A stranger in the woods wouldn't have a clue what the pass card unlocked."

Del bit her lip.

But someone traveling with Parnitski would.

The thought troubled her. If her father was alive, why would he break into the lab and steal his own files? And why would he go back to the Nahanni, put his life in danger? Nothing made sense.

"The computer should be done," Jake said quietly. "Let's see what it has to say."

Following him to the lab, Del read the message on the screen.

No such files exist!

She wanted to cry. The empty folder with her father's name on it was the only sign that he had even worked at Bio-Tec. It was almost as if he had been…erased.

Jake's mouth tightened. "Sorry, Del."

"I was so sure that there was something here. Arnold Schroeder said there was."

"What exactly did he tell you?"

"He was rambling on about Bio-Tec. About…I don't know."

Frustrated, she reached for her handbag and pulled out the notepad. She flipped the pages until she came to the note on Schroeder's call. She showed it to Jake.

"You need…care…Bio-Tec," he read. "Go back. Take care again."

Del slapped her forehead.

Of course, you idiot! Take Kerrigan!

Her head snapped in Jake's direction. He had a bewildered expression on his finely chiseled face.

"Jake, Schroeder says my dad is alive, somewhere on the Nahanni River."

"After all this time?"

"I know it seems impossible but I believe him. Didn't Schroeder say anything to you when you went to see him in the hospital?"

"Not a word, Del. By the time I finished reading his files and made it to his room, he had already coded. And when I left, he was unconscious. I've been running his blood work from here."

"How close were you to my dad? I mean, there must be some reason why Schroeder thinks I should take you."

His eyes flickered nervously. "Take me where?"

"To the Nahanni River. To find my dad. Schroeder thinks you should go with me. Probably because my dad trusted you."

She paused for a moment.

Maybe she was wrong.

"He did trust you, didn't he?"

Jake's jaw dropped. "You can't be serious, Del! How the hell do you expect to find him after all these years? If he's really alive."

"I know he's alive! I can't explain how, but I know it. I've always known it. When my mother and I buried him, I knew the coffin was empty for a reason. Not because they hadn't found his body, but because I knew there *was* no body. At least not a dead one."

"Wait! I don't understand why you need me. I don't know anything about your father's disappearance."

"Maybe not, but you knew my dad, how he thinks."

Tension invaded the air, sucking out the oxygen as Del waited for his answer.

"I'm sorry," he said quietly. "I can't possibly leave right now. Especially to go on some wild goose chase up north. I'm in the middle of a huge research project and—"

"Forget it!"

Snatching the notepad from his hand, she hurried to the exit.

As the doors parted, she threw him a withering look. "The professor was in perfect health before he went to the Nahanni."

When he said nothing, she huffed in exasperation. "Doesn't it make you the least bit curious about how he could've developed Progeria?"

She stalked out of the lab.

Bastard!

FOUR

Two weeks later, Del was anxious to set off for the Nahanni River, but the stress of seeing Arnold Schroeder's rapid deterioration made her second-guess herself. What if he *had* been hallucinating? What if he had simply been separated from the other men?

What if—?

"Morning, Del," TJ greeted.

It irked her to see him enter her house so nonchalantly.

"Ever hear of knocking, TJ?"

Ignoring her, TJ's eyes grazed over the living room. It was clear from his wounded expression that he noticed the empty space on the table by the window, the space where his photograph had been. She wasn't about to tell him that the photo had been shredded into tiny pieces.

Or that she had used it to line the kitty-litter box.

"Play nice," Lisa whispered in her ear.

TJ slid his long-legged body into a kitchen chair. "The others'll meet us at the airport. You ready?"

Del jerked her head toward a large backpack propped up beside the door. Her bags had been packed, ready to go for hours.

"Let's go."

Hefting the heavy pack over one shoulder, she motioned toward the door. TJ and Lisa followed her outside to the taxi that was waiting in the driveway.

"Have any problems getting a charter?" she asked, stuffing her bags into the trunk.

"Nope," TJ said. "Got us a twelve-seater. We'll West Jet it from here to Edmonton, take the charter from there to Yellowknife and Fort Simpson, and a seaplane to Rabbitkettle Lake. Got us a guide too."

Del had to give TJ credit. He had certainly done his part.

She gave Lisa a quick hug. "Thanks so much for looking after Kayber for me, Lis. Don't let him eat you out of house and home. And don't leave your coffee on the counter either. The pig'll drink it all. He's such a caffeine addict."

Wiping away a few tears that had gone AWOL, she climbed into the backseat of the taxi. TJ folded himself in beside her, his knees pressed awkwardly against the back of the passenger seat.

"Why don't you sit up front?"

"Naw, it's cool," he said.

She closed her eyes and leaned back against the seat, thankful that TJ had made all the arrangements. She wouldn't even have known where to begin.

"Isn't a twelve-seater kind of big for the four of us, TJ?"

"Six."

Her eyes snapped open in surprise. "Who else did you invite?"

TJ stared at her, bewildered. "Not me—*you!*"

"I didn't invite anyone else."

"Yeah, you did. The doctor from Bio-Tec?"

"Jake Kerrigan?"

She was floored.

Why did he change his mind?

TJ gave her a strange look. "He called your house when you were out. Lisa answered. Didn't she tell you?"

"No, but then Lisa's been going behind my back a lot lately. What did she tell him?"

"To call me. When I told him the details, he said he was in. He's bringing someone with him too."

"Who?"

"His research assistant."

Arriving at Vancouver International Airport, she spotted Peter Cavanaugh wearing an Edmonton Oilers t-shirt. He was at the West Jet baggage counter, standing next to a young Japanese girl.

"Peter, are you sure you want to do this?" Del asked nervously.

The young man straightened. "Yeah, I'm sure, Professor."

"Call me Del. Please. We're all on a first name basis here."

She smiled, noting the faint reddening of the young man's cheeks. Then she turned to the girl at his side. "And you are?"

"Miki Tanaka," the girl said in a soft, accented voice.

Miki was young—*very* young. She was maybe five feet, two inches tall, with shimmering black hair that draped sleekly over her shoulders. Her expression was serious and there was no hint of a smile in her dark eyes.

Del cursed under her breath. She didn't need the burden of worrying about a kid on the trip. She had enough to deal with.

What was Peter thinking?

She took his arm and steered him a few feet away.

"Your friend looks like she's barely out of high school, Peter."

"Miki's majoring in math and, uh, botany."

She glanced over at Miki Tanaka who gave the impression that one sneeze would snap her in two.

"This is going to be a grueling few weeks, Peter. We need people who can keep up."

"She's tougher than she looks, believe me. And you said you needed someone to decode that book. She's not just majoring in math, she's a math savant."

Del studied the girl again.

A math genius who may be able to break Schroeder's code? Well, that certainly puts a spin on things.

"Okay, but you're in charge of keeping an eye on her."

TJ tugged on her arm. "Hey, isn't that your doctor friend?"

When Del turned, she was caught off guard. Jake Kerrigan's eyes engaged hers and she saw him release an uneasy breath.

"We've got to stop meeting like this," he said.

She stared at his lips as they curled into a slow smile. Abruptly, she lowered her gaze, praying that he wouldn't see how glad she was to see him again. The man had the strangest effect on her. She felt it in the quivering of her stomach, right down to the tingle in her toes.

TJ possessively draped an arm across her shoulders. "You gonna make some intros, Del?"

"Dr. Jake Kerrigan, this is Tyrone Jackson. My…friend."

Her ex-boyfriend gave her a miffed look. "Actually, Jake, everyone calls me TJ."

The men shook hands briefly, then Del introduced Peter and Miki. She was about to ask Jake whether his assistant was still coming when she heard TJ's sharp whistle.

Four heads turned in unison.

Del watched a strikingly beautiful woman move toward them, long auburn hair bouncing with each step. She looked like she had just stepped out of an Eveline Charles spa—or a photo shoot. Even her skin was flawless. Hell, there wasn't an imperfect cell in her body.

"Thank you, Jesus!" TJ grinned, rubbing his hands together as the woman approached. "Please be on our flight!"

"Francesca Baroni," Jake said dryly. "My assistant."

Jake's *assistant* wasn't dressed for an adventure trek in the wild north. The woman wore tight-fitting designer jeans and a black lace blouse that was cropped above her midriff. A crystal necklace played hide and seek between the low neckline and Del caught TJ vying for a glimpse when the woman adjusted her handbag. It wasn't the necklace he was trying to see.

Francesca seemed in a hurry to get through the introductions. She barely acknowledged Del. Or the rest of the group. In fact, she only had eyes for one person—Jake Kerrigan.

Jake leaned down and picked up Francesca's bag. He tossed it on the counter as if it weighed nothing, yet Del suspected the woman had packed enough for a two-month luxury vacation. Her suspicion was confirmed when an airport attendant wheeled a cart behind them, unloading a second bag.

Jake whispered something in Francesca's ear and the woman playfully swatted him. That's when Del noticed the fresh gel nails.

'A high maintenance bee-atch!' as Lisa would say.

What in God's name is she doing on this trip?

Del was about to tear a strip off Jake but he pulled her aside.

"Listen, I just want to explain. Francesca insisted on coming so we could finish our notes in our spare time, but I want you to know that my priority is helping you find your father."

"What made you change your mind?"

"The more I thought about it, the more curious I got. About Schroeder's Progeria. And I realized that I owed it to your father. He was a good man, Del."

"Is," she said quietly.

Jake nodded. "I ran some more tests on your friend Schroeder. There's no explanation, no genetic reason for his condition."

"Then what's killing him?"

"I honestly don't know."

Neither did Del. Schroeder must have been wandering around in the woods without food or water. *How'd he survive?*

"Could it be something he ate?" she asked.

"Normally, I'd say that was impossible. He's experienced rapid aging, his organs are shutting down and we can't find the cause. Or the cure."

Del blinked back the tears that threatened to escape.

"Maybe when we get back?"

Jake shifted uncomfortably. "He may not be alive when we get back. All we can do now, Del, is make Schroeder as comfortable as possible."

And wait for him to die, she finished silently.

Boarding the plane, Del noticed that TJ had already confiscated the aisle seat next to Francesca. She was positive that the woman would make TJ move, but nothing was said. Sliding into the row across from them, Del was startled when Jake took the empty seat next to her.

She arched a brow. "You sure you don't want to swap with TJ?"

"Nope, I like it here."

He closed his eyes and leaned back.

She shrugged, distracted by Peter and Miki, who moved to the row in front. Miki's eyes darted over the interior of the plane as if she'd rather be dragged behind a chuckwagon at the Calgary Stampede.

"Don't you like flying, Miki?"

"Last time I was in a plane was when I moved here from Osaka."

Del smiled. "I was in Hiroshima five years ago. With an international team of anthropologists and archaeologists. We were helping to identify some pottery and bones at Kusado Sengen."

"Where's that?" Jake asked without opening his eyes.

"In Japan. It used to be a medieval town, near the mouth of the Ashida River. Now it's called Fukuyama City. It was one of my favorite digs."

When Miki sat down, Del stole a peek at the man beside her.

Jake Kerrigan was the epitome of the word *'manly'*. It oozed from his very pores and was evident in the unruly lock of hair that clung rebelliously to his forehead. His dark eyebrows framed thick-lashed eyes that were a piercing shade of blue—when his eyes were open. And then there were Jake's cheekbones. The kind that some women paid for—and most would gladly kill for.

Her gaze drifted to his mouth, the fine, evenly shaped lips.

Everything about Jake was fine, right down to his strong hands and neatly trimmed fingernails.

"See anything you like?"

Her head shot up and she gulped in a ragged breath.

Jake's eyes were open a crack and he was staring at her.

Embarrassed, she ignored the sudden flash of heat in her face and snapped her head in TJ's direction. She tried to get his attention but he was busy showing Francesca a book he had bought for the trip.

Reading the title, Del let out a loud snort.

How to Shit in the Woods: An Environmentally Sound Approach to a Lost Art.

"TJ has strange taste in reading material," Jake murmured.

She scowled. "He has strange taste in a lot of things."

"Enjoy the flight, Del. Your boyfriend looks like he will."

She was so completely taken aback that she didn't correct Jake's assumption that she and TJ were together.

Maybe it was safer that way.

After a long day and three different planes, they finally arrived at Fort Simpson, a tiny town in the Northwest Territories with a population of about 1300. Climbing from the plane, Del's eyes drifted across the rugged beauty that surrounded her and she experienced a sense of familiarity. *Déja vu.*

PART TWO
Undertow

Everything you see has its roots in the unseen world.
~ Jelaluddin Rumi

FIVE

She waited for the others to disembark before following the wood-planked steps up the steep hillside. Halfway up, Del noticed a short, stocky man awkwardly juggling a bulky camera. On his head was a knitted toque—the kind that her grandmother used to make. And tucked between it and his ears were a pair of small wire-rimmed glasses that, at the moment, were halfway down his nose.

As she passed, he beamed a smile and held out a beefy hand.

"Gary Ingram from Ottawa."

Gary was in his late forties and not in the best of shape. His face was flushed, probably from climbing the stairs, and his rounded stomach spoke of too much rich food—and perhaps a few cases of beer thrown in for good measure.

"Finally!" TJ groaned when they reached the last step. "Solid ground."

He sank to his knees, kissing the weedy patch of grass.

Watching him, a smile crossed Del's tense face.

"Well, that certainly made my day," Jake said beside her.

She turned. "TJ? He's always got to be the class clown."

"I meant your smile."

She broke away, desperate to change the topic. "Gary, are you a professional photographer?"

"I'm a…computer programmer," the man said hesitantly. "My friends convinced me to get out from behind the desk. Said I needed to *experience some adventure*." He peered toward the lake. "They're a bit late. Should've been here an hour ago."

"I'm sure they'll be here soon."

"They'd better be. I paid a lot of money for this."

A tall native man motioned them forward. "I'm Hawk, your guide. Is this everyone in your group?"

"I'm not with them," Gary said. "My friends are late."

"Well, you might as well join us for the orientation."

Hawk led them to a small log cabin.

"This is our main office. We store all the gear in the buildings out back."

He handed them each a thick guidebook.

"I suggest you read up on the Nahanni if you haven't already. We're pretty strict here, for safety reasons. Who's done any rafting or canoeing?"

Peter and TJ raised their hands.

"Either of you ever attempt whitewater rapids?"

"I've done some of the big ones in Banff," TJ said. "Peter's done some of the smaller ones."

"Good. It always helps to have some experienced people in the group. The rest of you, I take it, have never done this before. That's okay, as long as you can swim real good."

Francesca's face paled.

Hawk threw her a grin. "Just kidding. But I do need to know who can or can't swim, even though you'll all be wearing the safest PFD's around."

Francesca frowned. "PFD's?"

"Personal Flotation Devices," Hawk explained. "Life jackets."

"I hope they're comfortable," the woman muttered, reaching into her handbag and pulling out a pack of cigarettes.

Hawk shook his head. "Not in here, please. You can smoke outside, but make sure you put out the butt. Once it's out, you can dispose of it in one of the garbage cans."

He turned to the rest of the group. "For any of you who smoke please make sure you throw all butts in the campfire. Don't leave them lying around for animals to eat. And make sure you don't flick them into the bushes. We've already had a few fires in the area that have started because of some careless smoker."

Del bit her lip, trying to hide her impatience. "So, when do we leave for Rabbitkettle Lake?"

"We've got to load up the floatplanes first. We'll be taking two."

His comment drew a whimper from the back of the room.

Del snickered. *Poor TJ.*

"We'll leave in about an hour," Hawk said. "We'll get all the gear packed up first. Four of you can come with me. The rest can go in the second plane with the gear."

Gary glanced nervously at his watch. "What should I do?"

"Wait here for the rest of your group, Mr. Ingram. You're guide is McGee. He'll be here in a bit. The rest of you, follow me."

Del followed Hawk to a building that was constructed of rough cedar logs. There were two small windows and a row of florescent lights on the ceiling. Plastic storage bins lined the walls, filled with an assortment of canoeing, rafting and camping gear. A long empty table sat in the middle of the large room.

"Put your essentials in this waterproof day bag," Hawk instructed, holding up a small backpack. "Make sure you leave room for water, personal items and snacks. But keep it light."

He walked to a storage bin and began pulling out large vinyl bags and tossing them on the table.

"Waterproof river bags. You need to line them with plastic first."

He held up a package of multi-colored nylon bags. "These are called stuff sacks. You can put your clothing, waterproof boots and the rest of your belongings into them. If you need any other equipment or clothing you can rent them from us."

When everyone was packed, Hawk weighed the river bags.

Del heard him grunt in satisfaction…until he came to one bag.

"This one has to be repacked. You can leave some of your stuff behind in one of our lockers in the office."

"But I need these things!" Francesca sputtered.

He ignored her and passed them each a small case. "This will keep your cameras waterproof. Ladies? Here's some info on how to dispose of your…uh…feminine products."

Del scanned the paper he passed her, scrunching her face distastefully. If her period put in an appearance while they were on the trip, she would have to burn the tampons afterward to deter bears and other wild animals. Or pack them out in a Ziploc stored in her river bag.

Neither method of disposal seemed dignified.

Hawk supervised and rechecked all the bags until they were piled in the corner beside the door. The man didn't miss a thing. Not even Francesca's sad attempt to toss in a bottle of perfume.

"You really wanna be covered in mosquitoes and flies?"

Without waiting for her to answer, Hawk tossed the perfume bottle onto the table.

"Okay, one last thing," he said. "Medications. Is anyone on anything, allergic to anything?"

Timidly, Del raised her hand.

Crap! The one question she had been dreading.

"I need you to fill out this waiver, Miss Hawthorne. Make sure you list what you're taking."

Quickly filling out the form, she handed it back to him.

Hawk read it silently, then gave her a wary look.

"You're all right to do this?"

She lifted her chin. "Yes."

"Daddy, you in there?"

The door opened and a girl of about fifteen stepped inside the building. She gave her father a slip of paper, then disappeared.

Hawk scanned the note quickly.

"Excuse me for a moment."

"I hope nothing's wrong," Del murmured.

TJ feigned a wounded look. "What could possibly go wrong? I planned everything."

Hawk slammed down the phone. "Shit!"

"What's the story?" his partner asked, rubbing a wrinkled hand over his bald head. "Got us a loner?"

"Yeah, Ingram's group isn't gonna make it. You two should come with us, McGee. It'll be a large group."

"Actually, Hawk, I was gonna call in sick today. My stomach's off. Food poisoning maybe."

Henry McGee's face *was* a bit pale.

Hawk sighed. "Go on home then. I can handle this group. Two experienced, five newbies, plus me."

McGee paused by the door. "Any of them been here before?"

"I don't think so."

Alone, Hawk flipped through the files on his desk. He pulled Gary Ingram's folder from the bottom and opened it. The man was a desk-jockey. He had probably never even set foot near a river, much less in a canoe.

"A real river virgin," Hawk muttered.

There were a couple of virgins in that group. Yeah, something was definitely going on with that bunch, something more than a fun vacation. He just couldn't put his finger on it.

He had two choices. And neither felt good. He could send Ingram packing and the company would lose the money. Or he could convince the other group to let the man join them. But he had a feeling that adding another stranger to their group was the last thing they wanted.

Someone knocked on the door.

Hawk sighed when he saw who it was. "Ah, Mr. Ingram. I was just coming to see you. I'm afraid we've got a slight problem. Your friends missed their flight."

Ingram's eyes widened in shock. "Well, w-when are they getting here?"

"They're not. Apparently two of them have the flu."

"But I'm here already!"

"There's another option. You could come with my group."

"Think they'll mind?"

Hawk shrugged. "It's my call. They signed the contract and it states we can add to their group. I'll talk to them."

Outside, they headed for the six people waiting at the hilltop.

"Miss Hawthorne, we've got a slight dilemma. Mr. Ingram's friends aren't gonna make it. He'll have to come with us."

Hawk saw a flicker of nervousness in the woman's expression, and her mouth opened as if she were about to say something. Then she snapped it shut.

"Ok," he said, relieved. "Who's going in the plane with me?"

Delila Hawthorne, the black man, the doctor and the redhead raised their hands. That left the kid, the Japanese girl and Ingram in the second plane with the bulk of the gear.

He led Ingram back to the storage building to pack.

"You sure you wanna do this?"

The man shuffled his feet uncomfortably. "My friends wanted me to have an adventure."

Hawk sighed.

He had been a Nahanni River guide for more than twenty years, and if there was one thing he knew for sure, people were always eager for adventure.

Until they got it.

Escorting everyone to the floatplanes, a strange foreboding settled in his chest. Adventure...or misadventure? Whatever it was, something was waiting for them.

He felt it in the wind.

Del gazed uneasily through the small window, swearing as the plane lurched over an air pocket. When it unexpectedly dropped, her stomach was still suspended a few feet above her head.

TJ moaned beside her. "When we get back, Del, I'm not stepping foot on another plane."

"If you all look out your window you'll see Rabbitkettle Lake," Hawk said from the co-pilot's seat. "This is all part of the Nahanni National Park Reserve. It's protected territory, listed as a World Heritage Site by UNESCO."

Del shielded her eyes against the window.

Two beige mounds came into view. They looked completely out of place, as if God had dropped two giant pancakes in the middle of the forest.

"What are those rock formations?" she asked.

"Tufa mounds," Hawk replied. "Hot sulfurous water escapes to the surface through cracks in the ground and leaves behind terraces of hardened calcium. You'll all get a chance to see them up close."

As the plane dipped and skidded along the lake's surface, she gnawed her lip and glanced at TJ who was engrossed in his *Shit* book. His face was deathly pale—for a black man.

She hid a smile.

Maybe he's waiting for Kathleen Meyer, the book's author, to write the sequel—How to Puke in the Bushes.

As they climbed from the floatplane, she discovered that her ex-boyfriend didn't need a book for that. TJ was a natural.

Once they had unloaded the planes, Del slid on a pair of sunglasses and gazed across the water. The mirror-like surface was placid, surreal. Trumpeter swans and other water birds dabbled along the water's edge, occasionally calling out to one another.

She gulped in a lungful of air.

I'm one step closer to you, Dad.

Tomorrow their adventure would begin.

Everyone had assumed that Schroeder had told her exactly where her father was, that it was just a matter of going in and bringing him back. What would they say when she told them that all she had was an old stained map to lead them to her father—a map that was written in code?

After five tents were pitched on a flat grassy area near the banks of the lake, Del rested at the picnic table, watching Hawk trek off into the bushes for some firewood. Within minutes, he returned with a stack of chopped wood and kindling.

"That was fast."

Hawk smiled wryly. "There's a woodshed back there. What? Did you really think I'd be chopping wood all night? There's an outhouse down that path too."

She took a moment to examine Hawk as he stacked the wood against a tree. A small gold loop hung from his left ear and below it, on the side of his neck, a tattoo peeked from under the collar of his jacket. His black hair was tied back into a shiny ponytail and he favored the tidy moustache and chin goatee.

Like Jake.

She shook off a sudden chill.

Hawk's eyes narrowed. "I'll get the fire going. You should put on a warmer jacket, Del. It gets cold here at night. By the way, I thought that you'd prefer a tent to yourself. Or do you want to bunk with the girls?"

"I think I'll stick with my own tent, thanks."

She glanced at her watch.

It was late, but the sun was still beaming high in the sky.

In the distance, a solitary loon crooned for its mate, and Del felt miniscule, unimportant in all the grandeur before her. Peering up at the northern sky, she realized just how small she was.

After a late supper of chili and cheddar dill bread, Del wanted to do nothing more than climb into her sleeping bag and drift off into dreamland. But Hawk had other plans.

"It's important that everyone keeps the campground free of food, litter and anything scented," he said. "All food, including candy and gum, must be stored in the food cache."

He showed them how to work the pulley that hoisted their food bin up into the highest branches of the trees.

"You might all be wondering why it's still daylight. This area is called *The Land of the Midnight Sun*. On June 21st we had twenty-four hours of daylight, but now that it's early July, it'll start to get dark after midnight. Keep that in mind when you're wandering around the woods. Predators come out to hunt at night, regardless of how bright the sun is. Oh, and in case you think you're sleeping in, sunrise tomorrow will be early, sometime after four. We'll be on the river by seven."

As everyone headed for the tents, Hawk pulled Del aside.

"I don't know much about your, uh…condition. Other than what you've listed on your form."

She waved him away. "I'll be fine. I'm in remission. As long as I take my medication and control any minor exacerbations, I'll have no health problems on this trip."

"Would you tell me if you had any?"

"Of course I would," she lied.

"If you have any complications you let me know immediately. I can use my satellite phone, call for a helicopter."

"I won't be needing a helicopter."

Del stared after him as he walked away.

Hawk might prove to be a problem, a big problem. He might put an end to the expedition if he felt anyone was at risk. She'd have to find a way to convince him to help her…when the time was right.

She turned quickly.

And slammed into Jake.

Without saying a word, he grabbed her arm and steered her toward the rock-strewn path that ran alongside the lake.

"Jake! What do you think you're doing?"

"Getting to the truth."

He stopped abruptly, gripped her shoulders. "What condition?"

She shook her head stubbornly.

His lips curled into an angry scowl. "Tell me!"

"I have MS."

"Multiple Sclerosis?"

"I'm in remission. It's been a year since the last exacerbation."

"What in God's name are you doing?" he thundered. "You're out in the middle of nowhere. There's no hospital, no doctor and no supplies. What were you thinking?"

Her cheeks burned with humiliation. "You're a doctor."

"Damn it, Del! I'm a scientist with a PhD. I don't treat people. I treat genes and microcomputers."

"What about Arnold Schroeder? You treated him."

Jake's eyes gleamed. "The only reason I went anywhere near him was because of the research I've been doing the past few years. And I didn't treat him. It was too late for that. Listen, I know how much you want to find your father but have you ever thought that maybe—just maybe—Schroeder was hallucinating? Maybe your father really is dead."

"He's alive!"

She glared at him defiantly.

"I'm willing to help you," he said stiffly. "On one condition."

"And what's that?"

"I get to stick to you like static. Everywhere you go, I go. And if you get sick, you have to tell me and we go home."

She backed away, crossing her arms in front. "Go home? Not on your life, Kerrigan. Not until I find my dad."

The humid night air made her tremble. At least she hoped it was the air and not Jake's anger.

"But it could mean your life, Del! And if there's one thing I remember about your father, he'd never want you to put yourself in danger to save him."

Glaring at her, Jake muttered something beneath his breath and stomped off in the direction of camp, leaving her alone with her thoughts.

Her eyes grazed across the sparkling lake, oblivious to the mosquitoes that feasted on her neck. The only hint of night was the looming shadows that formed between the trees and bushes.

My life is full of shadows. And I'm tired of carrying them.

That day, twenty years ago, when a specialist had called her in after a physical by her regular doctor, her world had crumbled with four words.

You have Multiple Sclerosis.

He proceeded to tell her in a dispassionate voice that she could count on losing her boyfriend, her career and her life. MS would take away her ability to walk, strip her of her eyesight, make her a liability to others. He told her she would have to get used to the idea of spending the rest of her life in a wheelchair, of having to be dependent on others for everything. The callous specialist had given her a death sentence…with no last meal.

Del had immediately phoned her parents from the hospital, but it was her father who raced through rush hour traffic to pick her up. Sitting in the waiting room, suffering from shock, she burst into tears the moment he appeared, his face pale as a ghost. It was her father's arms that comforted her. And it was her father who clung to her and promised her that everything would be all right.

He had always been her Rock of Gibraltar.

Now it was her turn.

Jake was right about one thing.

Her father wouldn't want her to risk her life for him.

"But it's my life to risk," she whispered to the shadows.

The following morning, Del awoke to the clanging of pots and the pungent aroma of campfire coffee, which for some reason usually tasted much better than anything she made at home. She emerged from her tent, fully clothed and rested.

The sun was shining brightly, and although there was still a morning chill in the air, she suspected it would get much warmer by afternoon, especially out on the water.

Jake, Gary and Hawk were busy talking while Peter and TJ tended to the bacon and coffee. Miki sat at the picnic table, alone.

Del joined her. "Is the coffee drinkable?"

"If you like it strong."

The girl looked over her shoulder. "Hey, Peter! Make the bacon nice and crisp. But don't burn it."

Peter grinned. "This from a girl who eats everything raw."

Del poured a mug of coffee, feeling strangely bereft.

So much for Peter's crush on me.

Jake sat down across from her. "Sleep okay?"

Del's stubborn streak flared. "Like a baby."

"TJ made scrambled eggs. Go eat."

"Where's Francesca?"

Jake shrugged. "She must be sleeping still. I'll go wake her up."

"You do that," she said dryly.

Minutes later, he returned with Francesca clinging to his arm.

The woman grabbed a cup of coffee, tasted it and made a face.

"For what we paid, you'd think the least we could get is some gourmet coffee."

With a quick jerk of her hand, she emptied her mug onto the grass, then lit up a cigarette, puffing on it as if it were her lifeline.

"I know this isn't exactly a four-star resort," Del apologized.

Francesca's eyes flared. "I'm certainly capable of roughing it."

"I didn't mean—"

"Anyone want to know what's on the agenda for today?" Hawk said, cutting through the tension.

TJ grinned, flashing his white teeth. "We're going skinny-dipping in the lake. Right, dawg?"

Hawk laughed. "Not unless you want to get eaten alive by mosquitoes. Actually we'll be hiking to the tufa mounds. After that we'll practice with the canoes. But first, some tips on safe drinking water."

He showed them a strange contraption.

"This is our water filter. Before drinking water from the river, you've got to pump it through this clay filter first. It'll remove most of the sediment and impurities found in the river. If you're making tea, coffee or soup you don't have to filter the water. Just make sure it's boiled. Thoroughly."

Francesca frowned. "Why, what's in the water?"

"*Giardia lamblia.*"

When everyone stared blankly, he added, "It's a parasite found in animal and human feces."

TJ groaned. "Gives you the runs."

"Yeah. It'll make you nauseous, unable to eat and you'll have a bad case of diarrhea. All after two weeks or so of ingesting the water. If you get an infection, TJ, you won't be needing that book of yours."

After Hawk's enlightening discussion, Del grabbed a plate of bacon and eggs from TJ.

"How ya doing, Del?" he asked, studying her face.

"I'm doing." She caught Miki's eye. "I have something I'd like you to look at later."

The girl nodded. "Peter told me you would."

Del tossed back a handful of vitamins and chased them with a long gulp of coffee. Immediately, she caught Jake's watchful gaze.

"They're just vitamins," she muttered.

His brow arched in doubt. He was about to say something, but Francesca grabbed his arm and pulled him into the bushes.

What the heck are they doing?

Determined to get her mind off Jake and his assistant, Del turned to Hawk. "When do we actually head for Virginia Falls?"

"Tomorrow morning. Today you all need canoe practice. The rapids are tough on newbies. Once I know how good you are, I'll be splitting you into pairs."

A few minutes later, Jake returned with Francesca in tow.

The woman leaned close and kissed his cheek. Then she whirled around and caught Del's eyes, her lips curved into a gloating smile.

"Okay, everyone," Hawk said. "You need to pack up your day bags, fill your water bottles and dress appropriately. Before we leave for the tufa mounds we've got to go over some safety rules."

Gary slid his glasses up his nose. "Safety rules?"

"The woods are home to bears and other predators. Lots of them. Wolves, coyotes, cougars, grizzlies, blacks—you name it, we got 'em. Just, please, don't ever creep up on a bear. When we're walking, make lots of noise. You can whistle, holler, sing…just make noise."

TJ elbowed Del in the ribs. "Your singing would clear the path for all of us."

She threw him a withering glare.

"Just telling it like it is, Del."

She was surprised when Jake came to her rescue.

"I'm sure she can carry a tune. You can sing, can't you, Del?"

"Singing ain't what I'd call it," TJ snickered. "Unless you'd consider the wailing of a dying cat, music."

Del scowled. "Oh, shut up, TJ!"

Six

It took over an hour to hike to the tufa mounds, and from where Del stood, she could see the Nahanni River in all its glory. The view was spectacular.

She moved to the edge of the largest mound and saw trickles of shimmering water cascade across its surface. The water was pulled by gravity into small circular pools set into the beige rock.

Hawk sat down and untied his boots.

"These are the largest tufa mounds in Canada. Over ten thousand years old, untouched by the ice age—*Mr. Ingram!* Bare feet only. The terraces are very fragile, remember?"

Gary gave Hawk an apologetic look and immediately obeyed.

Removing her hiking boots, Del followed Hawk and TJ out onto the mound. The water was surprisingly warm. The ground beneath her feet was textured, rough in spots. She walked to the edge of a deep vent in the earth and peered down into the water. It was crystal clear until it reached the murky depths several feet below.

"Water issues from the vent and flows clockwise over the tufa mound," Hawk explained. "It takes years to do a complete circuit."

TJ edged closer to the vent's lip. "This reminds me of that scene in Lord of the Rings. You know, the one where Frodo falls into the water filled with all those dead bodies."

"Usually it reminds people of a Japanese garden," Hawk said wryly. "The small pools of water you see are called gours. They're formed by rimstone dams."

Del followed the native man back to solid ground.

"Is Hawk your real name?"

"No, it's Travis. Travis Hawkins."

She chuckled. "Ah...hence the nickname."

"Nicknames are not uncommon among the Dene."

"My dad's nickname is Larry but not many people called him that.

He's a scientist. Biotechnology. That's the study of—"

"I know what biotechnology is," Hawk said evenly. "We Dene pride ourselves on keeping up with the modern world. Some of us even know how to operate computers and cell phones."

Del winced. "Sorry. I didn't mean to stereotype."

"Forget it. I get a bit touchy sometimes. Especially when I feel like someone's keeping something from me."

"I don't understand."

Hawk's eyes narrowed. "When are you gonna tell me what you're really doing here?"

"What are you, psychic?"

He smiled slowly. "I see like a hawk. Hence the nickname."

Del was beginning to like Travis Hawkins, a.k.a. Hawk. Not only was he an excellent guide, he was brutally honest.

It was time for her to be just as honest—with everyone.

"Tonight, after supper, we'll talk. I promise."

"The Dene take promises very seriously," he warned.

"So do I."

A jolt of envy surged through Jake as he observed Del and Hawk.

That's when it hit him.

He'd been flirting with the woman since he met her, and he'd never stopped to consider that maybe he really *liked* Del. Something had awakened in him, the moment he laid eyes on her in the hospital. He'd been unable to put her out of his mind. He was drawn to her, the proverbial moth to a flame. And he had a feeling things could get pretty hot with Del Hawthorne around.

"Hey, Jake," Peter said, stepping up behind him. "Is it lunch?"

"Go ask Hawk."

Jake's shoulders relaxed the moment he saw Peter steer Hawk away from Del's side. He watched her for a moment, wondering what she and their guide had been discussing. He didn't like being kept out of the loop. And for some reason, he was sure that Del was keeping something from him.

"Is anyone else besides Peter hungry?" Hawk asked.

Six hands shot into the air, including Jake's.

Francesca frowned. "What's for lunch?"

"Eagles Nest Veggie Sandwiches, followed by chocolate chip cookies and oranges."

"Damn," TJ mumbled. "Do we look like vegetarians, Hawk? Bring on the beef."

"A lighter lunch makes the hike back a lot easier."

Peter prodded Miki. "Let's go look for some berries."

"Don't go too far," Hawk warned. "And make lots of noise on the path. You don't want to be a bear's main course."

He tossed Jake a container of vegetables. "You're on salad duty. Knives are in the plastic box in my bag."

"I'll give you a hand," Del said.

Surprised, Jake watched her stroll over to Hawk's bag. When she returned with the knife box, he reached for it.

"Yeah, man!" TJ yelled. "Don't let her near anything sharp! Last time I saw her use a potato peeler, she scraped half her knuckle off."

"I'll show you some knuckle," Del growled.

TJ raised a hand to his mouth in mock fear.

Jake laughed. "You wash, I'll chop."

With a stubborn look on her face, she reached for a knife.

"I think I can handle a few sharp—"

She hissed in a breath.

He moved quickly to her side. "What's wrong?"

"Nothing."

"Liar. You're bleeding."

"It's nothing, Jake."

"Can't have wild animals catching the scent."

Without thinking, he pulled her thumb to his mouth.

Del gulped in a small hiss of air. "I-I need a Band-Aid."

Jake watched her stumble off...toward TJ.

Damn!

Del was in turmoil.

When Jake's mouth had wrapped around her thumb, she felt a sensuous yearning rise from the pit of her stomach. It was a good thing he had stopped or she would have—

Hell, she didn't know *what* she would have done, but it wouldn't have been good.

She scowled at TJ. "Got a Band-Aid?"

She knew he was tempted to give her a big *I-told-you-so*, but she raised her hand threateningly and his mouth snapped shut. Then he threw her a silly smirk and passed her a colorful strip.

Examining it, she snorted in disbelief. "The Simpsons?"

"Hey, don't knock the Home-boy! Homer's life is all about beer and chocolate. What's better than that, Del?"

How about a boyfriend who understands loyalty?

She wound Homer Simpson's face around her finger, headed back to Jake and held up her thumb for inspection.

"You've got to be kidding," he laughed.

She shrugged. "TJ has a Simpson fetish."

"What's yours?"

His soft voice sent a shiver up her spine.

"M-my what?"

"Your fetish."

Tall, dark and sexy men.

"Sharp knives," she said.

Jake's smile widened, and she turned away, trying to tamp down her straying thoughts.

Damn!

After a quick lunch, they hiked back to Rabbitkettle Lake.

"Time for your class on canoe etiquette," Hawk joked.

Learning how to handle a canoe on the lake didn't bother Del a bit. But the thought of paddling through the rapids she had seen from the tufa mounds did. In fact, the idea of canoeing down the Nahanni River terrified her. And why shouldn't it? People had mysteriously vanished from its shores.

Or been found with their heads cut off.

They gathered near the lake's edge and Hawk explained communication procedures used on the river, especially in case of emergencies. Then he showed them how to secure the spraydeck that attached to the top of the canoe, protecting the gear from getting drenched.

He held up a plastic container. "You may even need to bail occasionally."

Del was suddenly overcome by dread.

Hawk caught her worried expression. "Don't worry. It's much easier than it looks."

Somehow his words were of small consolation, and she shivered, even though the sun was scorching her skin.

"Is it always this hot?" Francesca complained.

"This is unusual weather for the Nahanni," Hawk admitted. "A freak heat wave. Just be careful you don't get burned."

When everyone was coated in sunscreen, Miki and Peter climbed into one of the canoes, and Hawk instructed them to go through a series of strokes, using Peter's expertise and Miki's lack of skill to point out the correct way to paddle.

Then he divided everyone into pairs.

"Gary, you're with me. TJ, take one of the less experienced."

"I'll go with TJ," Francesca volunteered.

Del was surprised that the woman hadn't picked Jake.

She probably thinks TJ'll get her to the end of the rapids—without dumping her and ruining her makeup.

"Guess that leaves you and me," Jake said, flashing his teeth.

Within minutes, Del was paddling away from shore. Following Hawk's directions she learned how to slap rollers on the sides to adjust weight and direction. She learned about power strokes, pry and draw strokes, back-paddling, peel outs and eddying. By mid-afternoon, her arms throbbed painfully and her chest muscles ached.

She caught Jake spying on her. "What?"

"Maybe you should take a break."

She made a face, digging the paddle deeper into the water.

"Hey, Del!" Gary shouted from the canoe in front. "Thanks for including me."

"No problem."

The man waved his paddle. "Isn't this great? If my friends could see me now. They don't know what they're missing."

Del smiled.

The programmer from Ontario was proving to be a quick study, regardless of the excess weight he carried.

At least someone's having fun.

They were a few yards from shore when Jake passed her a bottle of water. "Getting tired?"

"You can't tell me you're not tired too."

He plucked at the collar of his shirt. "Hawk's a slave driver. I'm exhausted and sweaty."

A wicked thought flashed and she smiled slyly.

Without warning, she flipped the canoe.

The cold water was a welcome shock and when the life jacket lifted her to the surface, she smiled. She loved swimming. Loved being in the water—the buoyancy, the lack of pressure on her joints.

Jake tugged on her life jacket. "Hey! You could've warned me."

"Yeah, I could've," she grinned." But that wouldn't have been as much fun."

She was about to swim back to shore when she felt a hand grab her ankle. "Wha—?"

"You flipped it, Del, you bring it in."

Jake righted the canoe, tossed in the paddles and his lifejacket, then dove under the water, resurfacing ten feet away. A few strong strokes brought him to shore, leaving her less smug and more irritated than usual.

She bit back a response, swam to the canoe and tugged on the rope tied to the bow. She made slow progress but finally dragged the canoe ashore, where Jake stood with his arms crossed.

The bastard didn't even offer her a hand.

Tossing her life jacket on a log, she plucked at her clothes. They were glued to her like a second skin. And very, very revealing.

She stole a peek at Jake and caught his admiring gaze.

He was a dangerous man. Dangerously appealing. Falling for him could only lead to trouble—and she sure as hell didn't need any more of that.

Del was stuffed.

Supper had consisted of mouthwatering cheese tortellini in pesto sauce, spinach mandarin salad drizzled with Balsamic vinegar and orange juice, followed by fresh fruit salad.

After months of skipping meals, or existing on takeout and Ichiban noodles, she thought she'd died and gone to heaven. If she wasn't careful, she'd end up gaining a ton of weight. And then she wouldn't fit into her jeans—whether the top button was secretly unfastened or not.

Under Hawk's supervision, they washed the dishes, stored the food in the cache and repacked their bags for the morning *portage*—the grueling walk along the trail to the Nahanni River. When he gave a final nod of satisfaction, they gathered around the campfire, sharing two bottles of strawberry wine.

"My wife made this," Hawk said. "It's a little potent."

Del took a nervous sip. "It's very good."

TJ nudged Hawk. "You gonna tell us ghost stories, dawg?"

"Only real ones."

Francesca threw Hawk a disdainful look. "You can't tell ghost stories when the sun's shining. It's not the same. How can you stand it being light all the time?"

"When you've lived here most of your life, you get used to it."

TJ leaned forward impatiently. "Get on with the story, dawg."

"The Nahanni National Park is filled with ghosts," Hawk said. "Especially those who died violent deaths."

Del flinched, thinking of Neil Parnitski, her father's boss. There was no doubt in her mind that having one's head sliced clean off counted as a violent death.

"For thousands of years, the Nahanni Indians, or the *Nahaa* as we were once called, lived along the shores of the MacKenzie and Liard Rivers. It was the white fur traders who called us *Nahanni*. Ever hear of the MacLeod brothers?"

Del shook her head.

"Back in the late 1800's, people were struck with gold fever. In 1904, two of the MacLeod brothers hit the Nahanni in search of their fortunes. Last time anyone saw them alive was when Willie, Frank and a young Scotsman headed for the mountains."

Hawk took a long swig of wine.

"What happened to them?" Gary asked.

"Their other brother, Charlie, went searching for them. He found them, all right. They'd been shot in the middle of the night. Willie and Frank MacLeod were still lying in their sleeping bags. Afterward, the area was named Deadmen Valley."

Del felt tiny fingers of fear slide up her spine. "What about the Scotsman?"

"They never found him. Oh, I didn't tell you the worst part."

"What could be worse than getting shot in your sleep?" Jake asked dryly.

"The MacLeod bothers were missing their heads."

Del gasped.

Just like Neil Parnitski.

TJ eyed Hawk suspiciously. "Is this for real, dawg?"

"As real as it gets. Some stories say they were found tied to trees. Some say nothing was left but their skeletons. But most legends say they were found headless. And they weren't the only ones who died mysteriously on the Nahanni. Over the past fifty years, there've been many reports of unusual deaths, headless skeletons. Just a few years back, some scientists went miss—"

Del jerked to her feet.

Sucking in an agonizing breath, she rushed toward the lake.

There was no way she was going to listen to some campfire ghost story about her father and his friends.

TJ's hand clamped down on her shoulder. "You okay?"

"Nothing will ever be okay, TJ. Not until I find him."

He wrapped his arm around her. "You'll find him."

They stood, silent, watching the glassy surface of the lake.

A few minutes later, she followed him back to the campfire.

Hawk raised his head. "I'm sorry, Del."

"What for?"

"I told him why we're here," Jake said. "His partner, McGee, was the guide for your dad's group."

Hawk nodded. "McGee's never been the same since. He said they just up and disappeared in the middle of the night. He felt completely responsible. He still goes looking for them, you know."

"I need to find my dad," she insisted. "I know he's still alive."

Del reached in the pocket of her jeans and pulled out the photo of her father and Schroeder. She passed it to Hawk, whose dark eyes remained transfixed on hers. Finally he examined the photo.

"The Nahanni goes for miles, Del. The chances of you find—"

"I've got a map."

Seven heads snapped to attention.

"My dad's friend gave me a journal. But most of it's in code."

She sat down next to Miki. "That's what I wanted you to help me with."

"I can't veer off course," Hawk cut in. "It would be irresponsible of me."

"Yeah," TJ said coolly. "And it would be irresponsible of you to allow us to traipse off on our own."

Del hated putting Hawk on the spot. But she had no choice.

"We could really use your help. No one knows the Nahanni like you do. We need you." Her eyes searched his. "*I need you.*"

Hawk was conflicted—she could see it in his eyes.

Until he closed them.

She waited for an answer, but the only sounds she heard were the crackling fire and a breeze rustling the nearby branches.

Then a rasping screech sliced through the calm.

A bird with a pale chest and rust-colored tail circled overhead.

"A Red-tailed Hawk," Hawk whispered.

The bird let out another shriek then flew away.

"The Nahanni is a mysterious land," he said, opening his eyes. "It's filled with hidden dangers and legends as old as the earth you're sitting on. To find one man may be impossible."

"Then help us *make* it possible," Jake said. "Lawrence Hawthorne is a good man."

When Hawk didn't reply, Del held her breath.

But Jake wasn't so patient. "Are you in or out, Hawk?"

"I'm in. But I'll do it because the Spirits tell me it's my destiny, not for the money."

He stood, gave Del a brief nod, then said, "Excuse me."

When Hawk was gone, she gave Jake a puzzled look.

"What money?"

"It's nothing."

She gritted her teeth. "What money, Jake?"

"I offered to double his rates."

Stunned, she stared at him, watching him move toward the lake.

Miki shifted beside her. "Can I see the journal?"

Del tore her gaze away from Jake and pulled out the journal from her day bag. "Here."

Removing the book from the waterproof Ziploc, Miki scoured the pages until she came to the one with the map. She paused at the strange rows of numbers and symbols. Every so often, she would murmur something in her native language.

"Do you understand it, Miki?"

The girl nodded. "Some of it. The early part is mostly in English, with some abbreviations. I know they made it to the first stopover down the river. Once I find the base for the code, I'll be able to read it all."

Del knew the *SOS* code, but that was it. Give her a shovel and some dirt to analyze, or some ancient bones and pottery, and she was right at home. As apparently was Miki—when it came to numbers and codes.

"Tell me about your friend," the girl said.

When Del's gaze flickered in Jake's direction, Miki's mouth curved into a knowing smile.

"I meant the man who gave you this journal."

"Oh," Del said, blushing. "Arnold Schroeder is my dad's closest friend. He's an anthropologist."

"So, what happened?"

"He and Dad came here with two other men. A few days later, they went missing. My dad's boss eventually turned up...dead."

"Let me guess. No head?"

Del nodded, unable to speak.

"I'll read this tonight, make some notes."

"Thank you."

"By the way," Miki said, tilting her head. "Do you believe in destiny?"

"I guess so."

Miki stood, then flicked her head in Jake's direction.

"He didn't just offer to double Hawk's money."

"What do you mean?"

The girl shrugged. "He offered to triple it."

Del was speechless.

That night, alone in her tent, she thought about Jake.

He was virtually a stranger. Yet he had been willing to pay a hefty sum for Hawk's services.

Why?

SEVEN

A cacophony of birdcalls greeted Del the following morning. The twittering and teasing songs of warblers, sandpipers and sparrows intermingled with the calm rippling of the lake. The sounds filtered through the thin walls of the tent.

She stretched, groaning as her calf muscles contracted in defiance. Reluctantly, she climbed from the warmth of her sleeping bag and threw on some clean jeans. Then, quietly, she headed for the lake where a light ghost mist shrouded the surface.

Rolling up her pant legs, she stepped into the cold, murky water. With hands on hips, she closed her eyes and breathed in the fresh mountain air. She felt so much closer to her father.

Suddenly, she heard footsteps behind her.

She turned and Jake gave her a nod.

"You look quite at home, Del. Almost as much as they do?"

She squinted, raised a hand to shield her eyes from the light reflecting off the lake. On the opposite bank, two black bear cubs frolicked near the water, without a fear in the world.

Taking a step backward, she slipped.

"Whoa," he laughed, pulling her close against him.

For a moment, she stared, trapped in Jake's arms.

She cleared her throat. "I-I need some coffee, Jake."

Returning to camp, she felt unsettled. She didn't need any complications right now. And Jake Kerrigan was certainly a complication.

She flicked a look in Francesca's direction. *One of them at least.*

Francesca was standing by the campfire, jabbing at it with a stick. She slowly raised her head, her kohl-rimmed green eyes intense, unsmiling. Without saying a word, she stalked over to her tent and disappeared inside.

"She's got a hate-on for you, girl," TJ breathed in her ear.

Del's mouth thinned. "Good for her."

Francesca acted as though she had dibs on Jake, as if they were an item. Yet he behaved like a single guy. *An available one.*

"Jake told me their relationship is in the past," TJ said.

"Maybe he should tell *her* that."

"You interested in him?"

She bit her lip.

Was she?

"Just be careful, Del. I don't want you to get hurt."

She raised an eyebrow.

"I know," he sighed. "I was an ass. And I hurt you bad. But I still...care about you."

"I know, TJ."

"If he hurts you—"

She shook her head. "He won't. I won't let him."

Leaning close, TJ kissed her cheek. "But if he does, tell me."

"Why? So you can string him up by his teeth?"

"I was thinking of a different part of his anatomy."

Anything else he might have had planned for Jake was interrupted by Hawk.

It was time to head for the Nahanni River.

No turning back now.

The portage to the Nahanni River was exhausting, and Del wiped the sweat from her brow, waiting for her breath to slow. They had carried the canoes back first, setting them down close to the water's edge. Then they had gone back for the bags. When everything was deposited on the shore, they divided and loaded the gear into the canoes.

Hawk gave the final instructions.

"If you respect the land in all ways, the land will reward you for honoring it. That is the Dene way. Oh, and we won't be stopping for a while, so make sure you use the facilities before we leave."

The facilities consisted of two latrine holes situated a few yards into the spruce trees—one hole for elimination, the other for toilet paper. Before leaving the area, the men would fill the holes with dirt, obliterating any sign of their presence.

Del eyed the ribbon trail that marked the path. "I guess I'll go christen the latrine."

TJ leaned toward her. "Poop and scoop."

When she made a face, he grinned. "Put a fresh scoop of dirt over, uh..."

"Okay! I get it, TJ!"

"Watch for fresh animal tracks," Hawk warned. "Bears and wolf packs like to hang around close to the river."

She peeked nervously over her shoulder.

"Want me to come with you?" Jake asked.

Before she could answer, Francesca grabbed her arm.

"I'll go with Del."

With a hesitant nod, Del followed the woman down the path into the woods. Ten yards in, Francesca opened her day bag, probably to get a cigarette, and a cell phone toppled to the ground. Hastily, she stuffed the phone in her bag, right next to a package of birth control pills.

Del hid a frown.

Francesca and Jake *must* be involved. Why else would she bring birth control pills?

"I, uh, wanted to thank you," Del said slowly. "For coming on this trip, I mean. I really appreciate it."

Francesca's green eyes glittered with amusement. "You think I came here for you, or your dad?"

Del's reply was measured. "Then why?"

"Why do you think? I wasn't going to let Jake come here without me? You're all he's talked about for the past week…Del this and Del that." Francesca's expression turned sour. "Jake Kerrigan is *mine!* If you're smart, you'll remember that."

Speechless, Del turned away, looking for signs of the latrine—anything to get out of the woman's line of fire. To her far left, she spotted a roll of toilet paper hanging from the branches of a scraggly tree. Two pits in the ground were guarded by mounds of fresh soil. A shovel stood in one.

Walking toward the pits, she unfastened her jeans, without looking in Francesca's direction. "I'll make it quick."

When there was no reply, she peered over one shoulder.

Francesca was gone.

"Well, thanks for nothing."

Cautiously, she embedded her boots into the soft ground and lowered herself over the hole. The last thing she needed was to fall into the pit.

Snap!

Something moved in the bushes to her right.

"Francesca?"

Crack!

"I'll be there in a min—"

An eerie moan cut through the air.

She froze.

A black bear ambled through the bushes.

All of Hawk's survival tips dissipated into the air, and Del was left with her jeans around her ankles, her ass hanging over a latrine pit and not one bright idea of what to do next.

Plodding closer, the bear's long tongue flicked out and snatched some berries from a nearby bush. Then its inquisitive black eyes sought her out.

Del held her breath, her eyes widening in terror. Still crouched low to the ground, she wrapped her arms around her knees to keep from falling backward into the pit.

The bear lumbered toward her.

"Oh, crap."

"Well, technically, that could be what's attracting him."

To her dismay, Jake stood a few feet down the path.

"But I think it's the chocolate bar that he wants."

He pointed to a Hershey bar that was lying on a fallen tree, four feet from the latrine.

Embarrassed, she struggled to pull up her panties and fasten her jeans without drawing the attention of *Winnie* who was slowly plodding toward the Hershey bar. Cautiously moving toward Jake, she kept the bear in her peripheral vision.

He grabbed her arm and they rushed down the path.

"You okay, Del?"

"Yeah, I'm used to getting caught with my pants down while being eyed as a lunch buffet by a bear."

The corner of Jake's mouth lifted. "He was only a baby, a cub. Just be thankful he didn't introduce you to his mother. She's probably close by."

Quickening her pace, Del peeked over her shoulder, expecting the mother bear to come crashing through the bushes.

"What happened?" he asked after they were a safe distance away. "Francesca said you were right behind her."

She weighed her options. It would have felt immensely satisfying to blow off some steam and tell Jake exactly what she thought about his assistant. But why rock the boat? She couldn't afford to let Francesca interfere with finding her father.

"A girl's gotta go, when a girl's gotta go."

Francesca fumed, watching Jake hover over Del.

The woman was becoming a rancid thorn in her side. One weak little movement and Jake went rushing over, all concerned. It made her want to throw up.

"Better watch out, girlfriend," she muttered. "Don't mess with me. He's mine!"

Her relationship with Jake Kerrigan had been on and off for the past year. Of course as far as she was concerned, he just needed time to see how good they were together. With his brains and her beauty, they'd be the envy of everyone. She and Jake were the perfect couple.

Why things had fizzled between the two of them, Francesca couldn't say. But when he had told her he needed a break, she had swallowed hard and smiled. There was no way she was going to let him know how much that had hurt. She had her pride, if nothing else. Anyway, she'd win Jake back. Certainly Miss High-and-Mighty Hawthorne could see that.

"He's mine!"

"Who is?"

Startled, she whipped around.

"You shouldn't sneak up on people like that, Peter."

Peter cocked his head. "Why? What have you got to hide?"

A hiss of breath escaped from between her teeth.

The kid was annoying and nosey.

"I'm not hiding a thing. What about you?"

Peter stared at her intently, not saying a word. Then he strode away, muttering under his breath.

Francesca glowered at his back.

Peter Cavanaugh spelled trouble. *With a capital 'T'.*

Del couldn't stop the rapid beating of her heart as TJ and Francesca shoved off and began paddling away from shore, heading for Hawk and Gary. Peter and Miki followed close behind.

"We're up next," Jake said.

Del frowned. "This life jacket is a bit tight."

"You'll get used to it. Just focus on paddling."

He pushed off, sending them adrift, and the slow-moving current wrapped around the canoe, gently lapping at its sides. It took some time to get into an easy rhythm but once they did, Del began to relax. She was comforted by the thought that Gary and Hawk were only a few feet behind. If she fell out, they'd probably catch her.

Probably.

"It's easy paddling for the next few hours," Hawk said. "Take your time and work with the river."

She heard a bird screeching overhead.

A bald eagle circled above them, its immense wingspan lifting and gliding on the breeze. It dipped low, then soared off toward some unknown destination.

"Beautiful," Jake said.

She turned and caught his gaze.

Neither of them moved.

Hawk's eyes drifted lower, to her mouth, and an intense heat enveloped her, the kind of heat that was brought on by guilty thoughts.

Dazed, she faced forward, slicing the paddle deep into the water.

The Nahanni awaits, Hawk had said earlier.

But waits for what?

EIGHT

The South Nahanni River yawned. It carved a path through alpine tundra, mountains and canyons—undulating and weaving like a serpent. The river was an ominous breathing force. A paradigm of life and death.

The boreal forests that hugged its shore were thick with wildlife. Snow-white Dall's sheep grazed on the rocks, their amber horns curled regally above their heads. Three caribou quenched their thirst at the river's edge while a lone beaver swam past them with a branch clamped between its large teeth. Farther downriver, a black bear pounded the shallows in search of lunch.

The rippling water licked the canoes as they slid silently downstream. The intruders that skimmed across its surface could sense the Nahanni River's pulsating power. It was evident in the luring water, the sheer rock faces and the lush wilderness that transcended time.

Del experienced an unfamiliar tranquility. There were no classes to rush off to, no boring long-winded faculty meetings. And no wayward students making excuses about why they hadn't done their assignments. Instead, peacefulness engulfed her.

The South Nahanni River was an explorer's dream. The nurturing woman side of her recognized the simple beauty of the land and river, while the anthropologist in her was thrilled by everything she saw, including the fluvial v-shaped valley that dated back to a pre-glacier era and the bands of light-colored sedimentary and dark-colored igneous rock.

A high-pitched whistle cut through the stillness.

"I'll lead for a while!" Hawk said. "TJ, you take the rear. We'll break for lunch in a couple of hours."

Del shifted slightly and dipped the paddle in the water, holding it in one place. The canoe turned until they were following Hawk and Gary.

"Tell me about your father," Jake said.

"What do you want to know?"

"What was he like? As a father, I mean."

She smiled. "He was wonderful. Supportive, caring...fun. When I was little, Dad took me everywhere. To hockey games, dance lessons. And he always planned something special on my birthday. He had this great adventure planned for when I turned thirty. We were going to go to Québec City, stay in the Ice Hotel."

"I've heard of that place. It's supposed to be amazing. When's your birthday?"

She stared out over the water. "February twelfth. It should have happened two years ago. But he was...gone. And I couldn't go without him."

"You should, Del. Maybe next year."

"Maybe."

She thought about her father and all the years they had been separated. She'd give anything to get those lost years back.

A ragged breath escaped and her eyes pooled with emotion.

"He was my best friend—*is* my best friend. We'll find him, right?"

Jake's mouth narrowed in determination. "We will."

"Thanks, Jake. For everything."

"You can thank me by getting us to shore," he teased. "My arms are killing me, so you'd better pull your weight up there."

By early afternoon, the sun beat relentlessly upon them and Del's back was drenched with sweat. The layers of clothing she wore didn't help. When Hawk motioned them toward the shore, she was relieved. As soon as the canoe hit the shallows, she jumped out and splashed water on her face and hair.

Lifting her head slightly, she spied Jake.

He removed his life jacket, lifted his shirt and stripped it from his back. Tanned muscles flexed, rippling as he leaned down to haul the canoe onto the rocky beach.

Del swallowed hard.

Jake stretched, and she caught sight of a small tattoo on his left shoulder.

He followed her gaze. "It's a DNA strand."

"Oh."

Self-consciously, she slicked her wet hair back from her face, and when a trickle of water ran down her upper lip, she licked it automatically.

She saw Jake's jaw flinch.

Francesca's jarring voice broke the awkward silence. "Jake! We need firewood!"

Del was the first to turn away.

After a quick bite to eat, they resumed the trek downriver, and Del kept a watchful eye on the quickening current. Especially the unpredictable boils and mini-whirlpools. Every now and then, a large wave would lift the canoe, shifting it sideways, and she would have to paddle hard to help bring the canoe around.

Her mouth curved into a smile, thinking about the small band of people who had become like family.

Well, most of them.

She swiveled in her seat, searching for TJ's canoe.

TJ and Francesca were a few yards behind, with TJ doing most of the work while Francesca dipped her paddle in the water occasionally to keep up appearances.

Del fought a sudden wave of dizziness.

This isn't the time or place to get sick.

"Can I ask why we didn't just get dropped off at Virginia Falls?" Jake asked, oblivious to her discomfort. "I mean, why did we start at the beginning if your dad and his friends made it to the falls?"

"They could've disappeared anywhere along the river," she answered, looking at him. "That's why I insisted on traveling the exact route he took."

"And to give Miki time to decipher the map and the code," he guessed.

She nodded. "There are landmarks in the journal. I know they made it this far…"

She scowled as the sun slowly disappeared behind ominous clouds that hung overhead like soiled socks. A cool, biting wind whipped across the water, making her spine tingle. She could almost hear her heart beating. Or was it the pulse of the Nahanni, like ancient native drums, that throbbed just beneath the surface?

The rain held off until late afternoon. Then the threatening skies unceremoniously dumped torrents of water on the tired travelers. Within seconds, they were drenched to the skin, racing for the shore, fighting the rain, wind and river.

All of a sudden, Del saw something that made her heart stop.

Peter and Miki's canoe had flipped.

She cried out in horror as the Nahanni bucked and eddied, creating whitewater rapids where it was once calm. The river churned beneath the canoe, while rain pounded down on the river's surface, making it difficult to see anything or anyone in the water.

Jake finally spotted them. "There!"

Del clamped a hand over her mouth, stifling a cry.

Peter and Miki waved frantically, their heads bobbing in the water, the bright orange life jackets keeping them afloat. Peter managed to make it to the overturned canoe, but Miki floundered helplessly, caught in the turbulent crosscurrents. Her head went underwater.

"Miki!" Del screamed.

She stabbed the paddle into the water, paddling until her muscles burned. There was no way she was going to lose anyone else to the Nahanni River.

"Jake, grab hold of my canoe!" Hawk yelled, ripping off his life jacket.

Jake and Gary leaned across, pinching the two canoes together, then Hawk quickly dove into the raging water, disappearing beneath the cloudy depths.

Del gripped the paddle so hard that her knuckles turned white.

"Oh my God!"

"They'll be all right," Jake assured her. "Hawk knows this river like the back of his hand."

The words were barely out of his mouth when Hawk resurfaced—with Miki beside him. The girl gagged, spitting out river water. Peter, who had managed to right their canoe, quickly reached their side, pulling them safely aboard.

"Head for shore!" Hawk hollered. "Over there!"

Del was trembling visibly by the time they reached solid ground.

Relieved, she was tempted to pull a TJ and bow and kiss the earth. Instead, she headed straight for Miki. Without a word, she grabbed the Japanese girl and hugged her tightly.

Miki let out a strangled sound.

"Am I choking you?" Del asked innocently.

A shadow crossed the girl's eyes.

"Hugging is not common where I come from."

Del chuckled, releasing her. "You're not in Japan anymore."

"We're not in Kansas anymore, Toto," TJ mimicked.

"Kansas?" she said, rolling her eyes. "Hell, you're not even on the same planet, TJ."

Miki ripped off the life jacket, threw it on the ground.

"I thought this was supposed to keep my head above the water."

"If there's a rainstorm like this, the momentum of the river increases," Hawk said, his voice apologetic. "It causes crosscurrents, undercurrents."

Miki suddenly gasped. "Thank God you had the journal, Del."

"The journal wasn't what I was concerned about."

Peter and Miki could have drowned. And she couldn't imagine having that on her conscience. The day might have ended in complete tragedy.

But it didn't. We're all safe.

"The Nahanni might flood," Hawk warned. "I know a place nearby where we can get out of the rain and get a fire going."

TJ, Jake, Gary and Peter dragged the canoes up onto the grass, away from the water's edge. Then they flipped the canoes upside down while Hawk stowed the gear safely under a low-branched tree.

"Keep your day bags and a change of clothes."

Francesca glanced in the direction of the canoes. "Won't we need the cooking supplies, Hawk?"

"Not where we're going. There's a cave nearby."

Del groaned when she heard the word *cave*.

Caves made her claustrophobic. She had a deep-seated fear that the ceiling would collapse, that she'd be buried alive.

She stared at the rocky ridge that protruded from the earth a short distance away. She could see nothing remotely close to a cave entrance.

Hawk strode toward the ridge with purpose, heading toward something only he could see. He led them to a gray and white striped rock face. One minute, he was walking in front of them—the next...he was gone.

"Where'd he go?" TJ frowned.

Hawk poked his head from behind a bush. "You coming in or are you staying out there in the rain?"

TJ and Peter immediately squeezed inside a dark, narrow crevice.

With a resolved sigh, Del followed behind Jake.

Please don't let us be disturbing some animal's lair.

Francesca's voice cut through the dark silence.

"Can't we turn a flashlight on?"

"I could smile," TJ said from somewhere up ahead. "Del always says my smile is blinding."

Del snorted. "I don't think we need to be any blinder."

A warm hand fumbled for hers. Jake's.

"You okay, Del?"

"Yeah, if you can call being squished between two rocks *okay*."

Up ahead, Hawk's voice called out a warning.

"Keep one hand above and feel for the rocks."

With her free hand, Del ran her fingertips along the jagged ceiling. She crouched low when a sharp rock blocked her path. When she stepped past it, the air shifted around her and she sensed the cave expanding in front of her.

"Grab your flashlights," Hawk said, shining a light on each of their bags.

Seven flashlights clicked on and there was a simultaneous gasp.

They stood in a large cavernous room. A room that was obviously habited...by something living.

"Welcome to my lair," Hawk said soberly.

Del's brow flared in surprise.

TJ whistled. "Check this out! Dawg! You even got a bed in here."

As Hawk and Jake lit the oil lanterns that hung from hooks on the walls, Del surveyed the room. In the amber glow, she saw large plastic containers that stored dishes and cooking pots. One bin was labeled *Food* and she murmured a prayer of thanks.

At least they wouldn't starve.

Turning, she noticed a large native blanket hung from two hooks on the other side of the room. Moving toward it for a closer look, she noticed dark rusty-colored markings on the cave wall.

"Whose artwork, Hawk?"

"My Dene ancestors. They've been there for decades."

"Have they been documented?"

Hawk threw her an uneasy glance. "No. I'm the only one who knows about this cave. Even the Nahanni Park wardens don't know it's here. The Nahanni is still mostly unexplored."

Del traced the cave drawings with one finger. As an anthropologist, she could barely contain her excitement. An unexplored cave in Canada was a real find. Especially one in an area with such rich history.

Something in the opposite corner caught her attention. Halfway down the wall, the rock receded, creating a natural cubbyhole. Rain dripped down from an unseen vent above it and dripped over a pile of charred wood and ashes.

Hawk caught her eye. "My fireplace. I drilled the flu to the outside."

"Isn't that against the rules of keeping it natural?"

"Sometimes you've got to break the rules. As long as you show the land respect and humility."

"Do you bring your family here?"

He shook his head. "I come here to get away, to think."

Goosebumps crept over Del's skin and she rubbed both arms, shivering slightly, teeth chattering noisily.

Behind her, Jake uttered a soft curse.

"We need to get a fire going and change into dry clothes," he told Hawk. "Especially Del."

She was grateful for the dim light. No one could see the slow blush that spread across her face.

Hawk grabbed dry logs from a bin that doubled as a table. Soon he had a crackling fire burning. It filled the cave with a heavenly scent.

After the men rigged a thick wool blanket over a heavy cord, Del grabbed a change of clothes from her bag. She reluctantly followed Miki and Francesca behind the makeshift curtain. Clenching her teeth to stop them from chattering, she donned a pair of fleece-lined pants and a warm sweater.

When it was the men's turn, she couldn't resist checking out the legs below the blanket. She knew exactly which naked, muscular ones were Jake's. How she knew, she had no idea.

She couldn't deny that Jake had a certain animal magnetism. Or that he had an engaging smile that made her heart skip a beat. No matter how much she tried to ignore it, she felt an undeniable attraction.

All of a sudden, she sensed she was being watched.

She turned and caught Miki staring at her. The girl's mouth curved into a slow smile.

Del looked away, mortified.

Stepping from behind the blanket, the object of her wayward thoughts strolled to the bed. When he sat down to lace up his boots, she peeked at him from beneath her lashes, her face growing increasingly warm.

TJ sidled up to her, resting an arm across her shoulders.

"Damn! Warm me up, girl. I'm freezing."

Jake's head lifted, his eyes brooding and angry.

"Problem?" she asked him.

He looked away, but not before she recognized the impossible.

He's jealous?

She stiffened.

"What's wrong?" TJ hissed.

"Nothing."

He gave her a look that told her he knew she was lying.

"I have to talk to Peter," he said, walking away.

Alone, Del sank to the smooth stone floor and rubbed her aching legs, trying to forget Jake's jealousy. But she couldn't.

Focus, Del! Put him out of your mind!

"I've been thinking about the code," Miki interrupted. "I need to know more about the professor."

Del patted the floor in front of her. "Sure, what do you want to know?"

"How did his mind work?"

"Schroeder was brilliant. He'd always been fascinated by Aboriginal cultures and secret societies…death."

"Was he trained in cryptology—codes?"

"He had an analytical mind, but I don't think he knew anything about cryptology."

"What about mathematical formulas or computers?"

"Computers?" Del laughed. "He hated them. Thought they were the end of civilization. He could barely operate a cell phone, much less a computer. My dad always tried to get him to buy a Palm Pilot, but the professor said the written word was much more accurate."

"So, Schroeder didn't think like your father."

"No, he was the exact opposite."

Miki's eyes dimmed. "Can I see the book?"

Del handed her the bag containing the journal, thankful to get her mind off the fact that she was sitting in a huge cave with only one vent for fresh air—not including the narrow passageway that cut through the rock from the outside.

"Mind if I join the two of you?" Hawk asked.

Del smiled. "Have a seat."

As soon as he made himself comfortable, Miki pushed the book in his direction. "Can you make out any of these drawings?"

The rough sketch that she pointed to slightly resembled a pyramid or mountain. On either side, two lines trailed from behind it, meeting in the front.

"I'm not sure," he admitted. "But this could be Virginia Falls. I think that's Mason's Rock. It splits Virginia Falls in half."

"Then they must've made it that far," Del said, excited.

Hawk frowned. "What are all these numbers?"

"That's what I'm hoping Miki will be able to tell us."

"Soon," the girl promised. "Very soon."

Miki scowled in frustration, scouring the rows of numbers with the flashlight. What was she missing?

Peter flopped down beside her, startling her.

"You should get some sleep. You've been at it for hours."

They sat a few feet from the fire. Everyone else was asleep in the corner by the cot. By mutual vote, they had all decided that Del should take the bed. Even Miki had noticed that her mobility seemed impaired, jerkier.

"I'm not tired, Peter. I've got these numbers in my head. He had to have a key, a base."

"Professor Schroeder?"

"Yes. If he had military experience, he might have used some kind of war code. If he was into computers, he could have used a form of common encryption. I keep trying to see what he sees."

Peter gave her a long look. "Maybe instead of seeing what he sees, you need to see what's *not* there."

She held her breath.

Could Peter be right?

"What's missing, Miki?"

"Zero," she murmured without thinking.

"Nothing?"

"No," Miki smiled, raising her head. "*Zero.*"

She shone the light over the first page.

"There are no zeros in this code."

Peter cocked his head. "And that makes it…"

"Very unusual," she said. "But it does give me a clue. Now all I need to do is figure out why there are no zeros, why he only used one to nine."

"Why couldn't he have used a simple alphabet code?"

"You mean like *A* equals one? Too easy."

She pulled a notepad from her jacket pocket and copied the code.

"I'll work on the first line tomorrow morning. Once I figure out the key, the rest is deciphering. That takes time."

"Go to bed, Miki."

She waited until Peter disappeared behind the curtain, then she quietly moved toward her sleeping bag. She was about to drift off when a rustling noise jolted her awake.

Someone sat down next to her.

Francesca.

She eyed the woman's shadowy form. "Where'd you go?"

"Had to pee. You and Petey sure seemed cozy."

Miki ignored her, snuggling into the warmth of the sleeping bag.

But she couldn't sleep.

Instead, she pictured the line of code.

No zeros. Why?

NINE

Angry shouts and thundering footsteps roused Del from a troubled sleep. Bewildered, she emerged from the cave and was startled to see Francesca standing at the water's edge puffing on a cigarette, while Miki stared across the river, her mouth gaping.

As Del approached, the young girl looked up.

"We're down to three canoes."

The girl pointed and Del shielded her eyes against the sun.

One of the canoes drifted slowly down the Nahanni. Caught by a meandering current, it rounded the bend and vanished from sight.

Jake stormed toward her. "Who moved the goddamn canoe?"

"I don't know," she snapped. "I just woke up."

He tossed her a rueful look, then raked a hand through his uncombed hair. "Sorry."

Ignoring him, she turned to Hawk. "Anything else missing?"

"No, just the canoe."

"Who would do such a thing?"

"Your guess is as good as mine. We're not the only ones out here."

She twitched nervously. "Someone lives out here?"

"The forest is home to many of my people. Some don't want trespassers on their land."

"So what do we do now?" Miki asked.

Francesca's laugh was brittle. "We'll have to go back."

Del clenched her jaw stubbornly. "I refuse to give up."

Not now, not when we're so close.

Hawk sighed wearily and rested a hand on her shoulder. "Gary can go with TJ and Francesca. I'll come with you and Jake. It'll be tight, but we can make it."

Relieved, she slipped away to the cave to pack, eager to put her suspicions out of her mind. But Hawk's word's kept returning, haunting her.

We're not the only ones out here.

Someone had tried to sabotage their trip. Somebody who didn't want her to find her father. But who? Had an intruder crept into their camp and untied the canoe, or was it someone closer—someone she trusted?

"You did it!"

Turning to face her accuser, Francesca arched her brows in surprise, then smiled mockingly. "Whatever do you mean?"

Miki's eyes were like poisonous darts. "You pushed the canoe down to the beach last night and let the current take it. Why?"

Francesca struggled to keep her composure. The last thing she needed was someone spying on her. Yeah, she could play dumb...if she had to.

Casually leaning against a tree, she lit up a cigarette, inhaling deeply before speaking.

"Hey, I had nothing to do with that. I don't know who moved the canoe, Miki, but it certainly wasn't me. Hawk thinks it was some low-life Indian—"

"He never said that! I know you did it."

"I'd watch it, if I were you. People have a tendency to go missing out here. Remember?"

Miki stepped back. "Are you threatening me?"

"No, I'm just giving you a bit of friendly advice."

She blew out a stream of smoke, her eyes resting on Miki's quivering lip.

The girl was easily intimidated. *Good.* A little fear would go a long way. At least it would shut her up.

Miki clenched her fists. "When I tell everyone that you were out of the tent last night—"

"And when I tell everyone how you came to Canada as an escort for a very influential man..."

She flashed a slow smile, noting the sickened expression on the poor girl's face. It was priceless.

"H-how—"

"It doesn't matter *how*, Miki. I did my homework before coming here. You should've done yours."

She pushed away from the tree, looking back over her shoulder.

"How do you think Peter will feel when he finds out you're nothing but a tramp? And do you really think Del will trust you with her precious book if she knew that you'd slept with men three times your age?"

"Bitch."

Francesca's mouth stretched into a catlike smile. "And you're a whore." She flicked the cigarette in the girl's direction. "We all have our titles to wear."

Leaving Miki to fend for herself in the woods, Francesca strolled down the path, confident and secure. The girl wouldn't risk having her secret exposed.

When Jake had handed her the list of people going on the trip to the Nahanni, she had asked her brother to run a background check. Sometimes it was useful to have a cop in the family. Not only had her brother dug up the sealed records on Miki Tanaka, he had discovered a few other startling facts about Francesca's fellow travelers.

Some of them were hiding secrets.

Hell, she even had a few of her own.

As for the others...secrets had a way of revealing themselves.

Eventually.

Pacing outside the cave's entrance, Del refused to think about the missing canoe. She pursed her mouth in determination and tugged on a wide-brimmed hat, pulling it low over her eyes.

Keep your eye on the goal.

"We can be at the falls before suppertime," Hawk told her. "If we paddle hard."

She bit her bottom lip. "Miki hasn't broken the code yet."

"Give her time. She's a smart girl. She'll get it."

He handed her a mug of coffee, then wandered over to a flat rock.

Standing silently in front of it, he closed his eyes. Then he reached up, grabbed his ponytail and, with a pocketknife, cut off a few strands of long hair. Placing them on the rock, he covered the hair with three pebbles.

"What are you doing?" she asked, fascinated by the ritual.

"The Dene believe that the land provides all things for us."

Hawk looked at his meager offering. "The cave was here when we needed it so I leave the land a token of my gratitude."

Without saying a word, she held out her hand. When Hawk passed her the knife, she cut off a curl, adding it to his. For a moment she stared at the two contrasting strands—one dark brown, one blond.

Two people...from two different worlds.

"We're not that different," he said, reading her mind.

Del was almost relieved to be back on the river.

Miki, however, looked like she'd rather be anywhere else.

"You okay?" Del hollered.

The girl dipped her paddle into the water and nodded solemnly. She didn't even crack a smile.

Del frowned.

What the hell was going on? Miki had been unusually quiet all morning. And she had avoided Francesca like the plague.

Francesca had done nothing but complain about the food, the sleeping arrangements, the bugs. And she never missed an opportunity to suggest they turn back. It was these things, more than the woman's interest in Jake, that irked Del the most.

I wish to God that Francesca had never joined us.

Pushing the woman from her mind, she wiped the stream of sweat from her brow as the searing sun mirrored off the Nahanni and a sticky heat enveloped them—the kind of heat that made her want to strip off her clothes and plunge headfirst into the churning river.

The pulse of the Nahanni was deceptively persuasive. Each canoe fell into an easy rhythm, growing silent with the effort of paddling. Cumulous clouds partly covered the sky, occasionally shading them from the intense heat, and the infrequent shaded bends in the river were a welcome reprieve. They paddled for hours…but it seemed like days

Del tugged at her life jacket.

The thing was on so tight, she swore she felt her ribs snapping when she inhaled.

"Keep it on," Hawk scolded lightly.

With a streak of stubbornness, she slid the zipper a few inches lower. "A girl's gotta breathe, you know."

Jake threw her a worried smile and she scowled.

"I'm fine, Jake. Except for this heat. Give me an hour and I'll be a pro at this."

And a pro at lying.

She wasn't fine at all. Her vision was wavering so much she had to close one eye just to focus—but damned if she'd say anything.

After a while, her fingers grew numb and the paddle felt like a lead weight. In a split second, it slipped from her hands and was sucked beneath the water.

"I've got it," TJ called out behind them.

When he passed her the wayward paddle, she gave Hawk and Jake a rueful look. "Sorry."

Hawk smiled. "No big deal. That's why they float."

"Take a break, Del," Jake insisted. "We can handle it for a while."

She wanted to argue with him, but he was right. Her muscles screamed for a break. Her legs were cramped and aching.

Grateful for the reprieve, she aimed a look over her shoulder in TJ's direction. Francesca glared back defiantly.

Del was shocked by the hostility in the woman's eyes.

She shuddered.

If looks could kill…

The Nahanni wrapped around each canoe like an invisible force, sucking them downriver, and Del trembled as the murky water formed larger boils and the current grew stronger.

"We're nearing Virginia Falls," Hawk shouted. "We have to put off shore. So we don't get caught in the current."

As they paddled closer to the left bank, Del heard the pounding crescendo of the falls. The sound intensified as they drew closer.

"We're not going over them, right?" Gary hollered nervously.

"Not unless you really want to," Hawk laughed. "Virginia Falls is twice as high as Niagara Falls. I'm pretty sure we wouldn't survive the drop. If you all check out that rock over there, that's Mason's Rock. It splits the falls into two. When we're on the other side, you'll see it in all its glory."

Mason's Rock.

The river circled the rock, the foamy water crashing down and swirling around its base. The monstrous, towering, jagged spire was enveloped in a strange, ghostly mist. Even stranger was the cluster of trees that sprouted from its tip.

Del forgot all about her pain, spellbound by the sight.

When the canoes safely reached the shore, she felt a weak humming wrack her body. She unfolded her stiff legs and stood shakily.

A wave of dizziness assaulted her.

"Crap!" she whispered.

There was no denying it. Her MS was definitely taking a turn for the worse.

While the others cleaned up after dinner, Del gathered Hawk and Jake around the journal.

She pointed to a short wiggly line. "Another river?"

Hawk pulled a folded map from his river bag. Laying the map beside Schroeder's journal, he traced the path of the Nahanni and compared it to the line drawing.

"It's not the Nahanni River. Sorry."

He folded the map, then leaned down to put it back in his bag.

Del nudged Jake, indicating a v-shaped object on the previous page. "I think we have to find this tree first."

"It looks more like a valley."

"My friend, Lisa, thinks it's a tree," she said sharply.

Jake shook his head. "The sides are steep, maybe covered in grass. It's a valley."

"It's a tree, Jake! This is the trunk and two branches, or maybe a split trunk."

Hawk raised his head abruptly. "She's right, Jake. It's a tree."

Del sent Jake a triumphant smile.

"It's off the main portage," Hawk added. "The one to the bottom of the river. Unless you veered off the path, you'd never know the tree existed. It's a bit of a hike in."

"Maybe we should leave the canoes here and check it out," Jake suggested. "It's only after seven."

To Del's surprise, Hawk agreed.

"Sure. There's over three hours of daylight left. If everyone packs extra food, matches and water in their day bags, we can carry some of the gear and camp there. We'll take two tents, one for the guys and one for the ladies."

Del left them to discuss the plans while she went to find her day bag. Opening it, she grabbed a plastic container. She emptied an assortment of pills into her palm, most of which she hadn't touched in over a year. A year of remission.

Of all the worst times to have an exacerbation.

She gritted her teeth.

Mind over matter. You've gotta get a grip on this, Del.

Francesca interrupted her thoughts.

"Here," the woman said, holding out a granola bar and a mug of water. "You didn't eat much."

Del was surprised. A peace offering?

She popped the handful of pills into her mouth and chased them down with a long drink of water, ignoring Francesca's curious stare.

The woman cleared her throat apprehensively. "I wanted to apologize. I know Jake and I are over but it's hard to see him with another woman."

Del was floored. "He's not *with* me!"

Francesca shuffled her feet restlessly. "Do you have any idea how it makes me feel to see him look at you the way he used to look at me? He really likes you. I can see it in his eyes. I feel…betrayed. But you probably wouldn't know what that's like."

Del thought about TJ. About finding him in her bed with her neighbor. A neighbor who was now pregnant with the baby that *she* had wanted to have with TJ.

"I know exactly how it feels, Francesca. But I can assure you, my focus is on finding my dad—not getting involved with Jake."

The woman let out a deep breath. "I wanted you to know…I'm not over him yet. He hasn't exactly been a saint since we broke up. Hell, Jake's not the loyal type. Just ask his wife."

Del's head shot up.

Jake was married? Why was he flirting with *her* then? And why wasn't he wearing a ring?

Francesca gnawed her lip. "Jake is only concerned about one thing,

Del. His research."

Del exhaled slowly when Francesca was gone.

She couldn't fault the woman for being jealous. She would be too if she thought someone was honing in on her man, her territory.

Which Jake isn't.

The man in question strode past her and she eyed him furtively.

Jake had a wife. Someone who was probably patiently waiting for his return. What was it about men and commitments? It was so easy for them. They could turn their emotions on and off again—like a switch. They could screw around on someone they supposedly loved, then toss them aside like a used wad of toilet paper.

"Heartless bastard!"

Sexy, heartless bastard, her mind argued.

She hastily wolfed down the granola bar, finished the water, then hurried off to find Hawk.

They were wasting valuable time.

She shuddered, recalling Arnold Schroeder's warning.

The little bastards have him, Delly. You have to destroy the cell.

"You ready?" Hawk said.

"Almost." She took a steadying breath. "Hawk, do you know anything about a secret river?"

"I've heard rumors. Why?"

"Do you know where it is?"

He shook his head. "They're only stories, legends."

"Schroeder told me we had to find a secret river. I think that's where the map leads to." *And that's where my dad is.*

"There are branches off the Nahanni, marked tributaries. But that's it, Del. If there was another river, people would've found it by now. It would be marked on my map."

Disappointed, she picked up her day bag and joined the others at the top of the path.

"We'll follow the trail halfway down," Hawk said. "After that we veer off."

Gary gave him a worried look. "Won't we get lost?"

"I've got GPS mapping on my satellite phone. And a compass. But as an extra precaution we'll tie ribbons around the tree branches to mark the way. Anyone want the job?"

When Peter volunteered, Hawk passed him the roll of ribbon and a small pair of scissors.

"We all ready?" Jake asked, moving to Del's side.

They set off down the winding trail, talking loudly, in hopes of scaring off bears or other predators. Between the trees, they glimpsed Mason's Rock and Virginia Falls. The roar of the cascading water intensified as they drew closer. Even the ground vibrated.

"Here's where we leave the path," Hawk said, removing a small compass from his pocket. "We head north. That's where the Gemini Tree is."

Del's eyes widened. "The Gemini Tree?"

He motioned for the journal and indicated the v-shaped drawing.

"We've called it that for years. It's an anomaly." He returned the book to her. "When you see it, you'll understand."

His vagueness sparked her curiosity.

What could be so unusual about a tree?

In the middle of a charred circle of land stood the only sign of life.

The Gemini tree.

At its base the trunk was thick and knotty, twisting and turning like a creature rising from the ashes. About three feet from the ground it split in two. Someone standing from afar might have thought it simply had a split trunk.

When Del approached the tree, she was startled to see that it was actually two different varieties. They had grown together, melded into one, wrapping sinuously around each other. Then they split away. One side was a needle-bearing evergreen. The other had jade-green leaves—balsam poplar.

Carefully, she knelt on the ground beneath the tree and brushed a hand against its rough bark. Then she reached out and caressed a shiny leaf.

"How come I've never heard of this tree before, Hawk?"

"We didn't want scientists coming in, taking samples or chopping it down."

"It's fascinating."

"The map starts here," Miki said. "2*M...N. T*wo meters north?"

Hawk took out his compass, headed six paces north—straight into a thick patch of trees. "It can't be two meters. There's nothing here."

Del compared their location to the map.

Hawk was right.

Nothing on Schroeder's map matched. So 2M had to mean…

She chuckled, immediately feeling very stupid.

"What?" Jake asked.

"Schroeder was old school. He didn't *do* metric. We have to go two *miles.*"

Heaving her bag over her shoulder, she followed Hawk through the woods. The trek was mostly uphill, and the ground uneven. Uprooted trees blocked their path and they had to climb over them, or around.

It didn't take long before she stumbled.

"Could I possibly be any clumsier?" she said with a self-conscious laugh.

Jake held out a thick tree branch. "Here."

She scowled. "A cane?"

"A walking stick," he said, snapping off a second branch.

Then he turned on his heel and walked away, digging his stick into the ground with each step.

Why is he so thoughtful…and so damned married?

As they wandered deeper into the shadows of the alpine forest, they remained constantly vigilant for signs of bears. It wasn't long before they found some. A cluster of birch trees had been gouged by long, sharp claws, the bark shredded like paper. Golden tree sap oozed from the open sores.

Like blood.

Del shivered.

Then they came across large prints in the muddy ground.

"Fresh grizzly tracks," Hawk said, worried. "Heading north."

They veered slightly east, then backtracked to stay on course.

An hour later, they stopped.

Hawk eyed the GPS map. "This is about two miles. What are we looking for, Del?"

"Something that looks like a lady's shoe."

Beside her, Miki considered the journal and gave a sudden laugh.

She hurried toward a patch of colorful bushes. Examining the foliage, she shook her head and strode through the tall grass, past Peter and Gary.

"Over here!"

The girl pointed to a bush with sunny yellow blossoms.

"*Cypripedium calceolus.*"

Seven pairs of eyes stared blankly in her direction.

"Yellow Lady's Slipper," she explained with a laugh.

Del's excitement mounted. They were on the right track.

"The map says head northeast from here," she said. "One mile."

Gary scratched a patch of angry mosquito bites on his arm. "Then what?"

With one finger, Del traced a wavy line on the page. "A short, narrow river, I think."

"Trust me," Hawk said, leaning against a tree. "There aren't any rivers around here."

"But what else could this be?"

"A creek," Miki blurted.

Hawk shook his head. "No creeks either."

"Maybe we should stop for the night," Peter said tentatively. "Set up camp here."

It was getting late, but Del didn't want to stop. It was difficult to quell her anticipation…and her fear. They were so close to finding the secret river. So close to finding her father.

Her stomach churned.

"Why don't we go for another hour?"

Everyone agreed and she was very grateful.

Ignoring the sinking feeling in the pit of his stomach, Hawk headed northeast.

Could the legends be true? Is there really a secret river?

He led them across beds of wildflowers, past a ridge of boulders and down a steep incline of scrub grass. At the bottom, he stopped, shocked.

An old, abandoned campfire lay nestled in the grass.

"People live around here?" Jake asked him.

"Not that I know of."

"So who made the fire? Schroeder?"

Hawk darted a nervous look toward the trees.

"I don't know, Jake."

Strange...very strange.

A harsh shout distracted him.

Hawk spun around and saw Gary Ingram standing a few yards away, flapping his arms up and down. The man's mouth gaped open as he pointed to something.

"Look!"

☥EN

Alerted by Gary's cry, Hawk rushed to his side.

"What's wrong?"

"Isn't that a river?" Gary asked.

Hawk's jaw dropped.

Between the leafy branches and looming shadows, the ground crumbled away and a ten-foot drop plummeted below. At the bottom, a constricted serpentine river slithered across the land. Polished smooth by sun, rain and wind, a winding graveyard of vanilla-white pebbles littered the floor of the river, like golf balls at a driving range.

The river was bone dry.

Perched on the pebbles, a lone raven with glossy black feathers created a stark contrast to the off-white gleam of the riverbed. It picked voraciously at the bloody corpse of a small, furry animal trapped between the rocks.

Suddenly, it lifted its head, glaring with small beady eyes.

"Raven was created as the leader among leaders," Hawk said.

He acknowledged the bird with a humble nod.

"More like a scavenger," Francesca snorted.

She lit a cigarette and blew a smoke ring into the air.

Hawk eyed her candidly. "The most powerful and clever of all peoples, its knowledge was sought by all. But thinking that it was nearly perfect, Raven insisted to be painted better than all the other birds."

"But it's ugly!"

"Because of its vanity and selfishness, it was painted black."

"Hey!" TJ said indignantly. "Black is beautiful!"

Hawk flicked a disparaging look at Francesca.

"All things of nature hold beauty."

Somewhere.

Jake turned to Del. "Is this the river on your map?"

"Yeah, but not the secret river."

When she tipped her head to look up at him, strands of short golden hair caught the rays of the fading sun, and the sight made Jake's heart race.

Delila Hawthorne was stunning.

"We'll find it, Del. What next?"

"We follow the riverbed until it ends."

Holding out the journal, she turned to Hawk.

"What's this circle thing look like to you?"

Jake peered over her shoulder, then sucked in a breath.

Wait! This is impossible!

"I don't know," Hawk said. "But, *that*…is a key. We'll head out first thing in the morning. Jake, you and Gary get a fire going. I'll rig the food cache and set up the tents. The women'll be in one and the five of us guys in the other. TJ and Peter, you get latrine duty."

Jake nudged Gary, grabbed an axe and headed toward the trees.

"I'm not very good outdoors," Gary apologized.

"Then we're even," Jake smiled. "I'm not good with computers."

He spotted Del standing near the riverbed. She was staring at it longingly. He could almost read her mind. *We're so close…*

"Think her father's still alive?" Gary murmured.

"She thinks so. And she may be right."

Del's father had taken Jake under his wing shortly after he joined Bio-Tec. Having earned a Bachelor's degree in Biomedical Engineering Technology and a Master's in Nanotechnology, Jake had been honored to be assigned as assistant to Dr. Lawrence Hawthorne, whose notable work included research into aging, cellular reconstruction and rampant disease annihilation. He had worked alongside Lawrence for five years, listening to unusual theories and progressive ideas.

Jake rubbed his tattoo self-consciously.

The DNA strand on his shoulder represented the essence of life. It was the same symbol that was inside the circle on the map, in Schroeder's journal. The same symbol used in the new logo of a cutting-edge bio-medical research corporation—*Bio-Tec Canada.*

But Schroeder's been gone seven years. How the hell did he know anything about the new logo? Not even Lawrence knew.

Jake thought about the last time he had seen Del's father. A few months before Lawrence's disappearance, his behavior had become increasingly odd. He was more secretive, displaying signs of paranoia, especially when Edward Moran was in the lab.

Had Lawrence and Schroeder stumbled upon something significant at Bio-Tec—something that had resulted in their supposed deaths? Or was it coincidental?

Jake shook his head. *I don't believe in coincidence.*

The next morning, after a restless sleep, Jake stood with the others at the top of the riverbed, while Hawk picked his way down the side of the embankment. The loose rock made the path treacherously slippery, and he stumbled a few times but managed to stay on his feet.

"Hasn't been a river here in decades," Hawk shouted.

A hand grabbed Jake's arm.

"For balance," Del said, blushing. "I get vertigo sometimes."

"What about me, Jake?"

Francesca stood three feet behind them, but before he could say a word, TJ slipped up beside her.

"I'll help you down," he said.

Francesca turned, taking TJ's arm and rewarding the tall black man with a tremulous smile. Then, with a backward scowl, she followed him down the embankment.

Jake rubbed his forehead, frustrated.

Francesca was obviously pissed, and that made him angry. They were over. Why couldn't Francesca get that? All he wanted from her was friendship and a pleasant working relationship—nothing more.

What do I want?

His head jerked, catching sight of a familiar face.

He wanted...Del.

Shocked by this revelation, he felt his face grow warm.

"You okay?" Del asked.

He nodded. "Take your time, the rocks are loose."

"I'll be fine as long as you stay right in front of me."

His eyes narrowed at the trace of humor in her tone.

She shrugged. "That way if I fall, I'll land on you."

"It wouldn't be the first time you've landed in my arms. I kind of like it. Maybe I'll trip you up on purpose."

His teasing flustered her and she looked away.

So Del wasn't immune to him after all. *Interesting...*

He turned and took a hesitant step forward, searching for the easiest route down. All of a sudden, something slammed into him. Hard. Arms flailing, he fought to keep his balance but his feet slid from under him. With a dull *thud*, he landed on his rear end.

"That's gonna leave a mark," he groaned.

Lifting his head, he spotted Del sprawled on top of Peter.

"It was the Domino effect," she said. "Peter slid into me, I slid..."

She burst into laughter, struggling to her feet.

The others moved toward him but Jake waved them away. The last thing he needed was an audience to complete his humiliation.

He shifted slightly, testing his joints. Nothing was broken.

"You gonna lay there all day, Kerrigan?" Del demanded.

He bit back a snide reply.

Taking her outstretched hand, he grimaced when he stood.

"Your jeans are ripped."

Del was right.

Below the left back pocket, a large tear exposed his black boxers. He reached back and tried to tuck in the flap of denim, but as soon as he moved, the flap drooped.

"How's your butt?" she asked.

"Bruised."

Like my ego.

The corner of her mouth lifted. "Well, if you're done making an ass of yourself—pun intended—let's get going."

"Jesus! Can't a guy get a little compassion here?"

"What do you expect, a pity party?"

He swiftly reached out and gripped her arms, just above the crook of her elbows. His eyes drifted over her soft, luscious lips, and resisting the impulse to kiss her, he leaned within inches of her mouth.

"I kissed your owie better when you cut your finger."

"So what, you expect me to…kiss your butt?"

He flashed a sly grin.

"Dream on, Kerrigan!"

"I will."

He pulled back slightly. "Can't you feel it, Del?"

"What?"

His eyes narrowed. "This…*spark*. Or whatever it is between us."

She slipped from his grasp. "There is nothing between us, Jake. You're here for one reason and one reason only. To help me find my dad. Got it?"

His reply was interrupted by TJ.

"You gonna live, dawg?"

Jake's head swiveled.

Six pairs of eyes were aimed at them.

"Yeah," he said wryly. "At least for another day."

Peter picked up Del's bag from the ground.

"Do we keep going, Jake?"

"Any reason not to?"

The young man shook his head and handed Del the bag.

As they followed the riverbed, a shiver of apprehension trickled down Jake's spine.

There's no turning back now.

A few yards ahead of everyone, Del hid a smirk.

Although she had a few bruises and sore spots, it was nothing, compared to how Jake probably felt. At least Peter had cushioned her fall. Poor Jake was hobbling like an old man.

Kiss his butt? Not bloody likely.

She was more apt to kick his butt. The man was an infuriating flirt, and she didn't have the patience for mindless head games—regardless of how handsome the rogue was.

Or how kissable.

She scowled.

When he had grabbed her, she had wanted him to kiss her. For a moment, she thought she would die if he didn't kiss her. There *was* something between—

What in God's name am I thinking?

Without warning, her balance shifted and a rush of dizziness swept over her. But she managed to recover before anyone noticed.

She wasn't surprised that her exacerbations were getting worse. Stress was her number one downfall. What she needed was a holiday, not some bloody trek through the wilderness.

Del stopped to rest for a moment, waiting for the others to catch up. She was dying for a drink. Her tongue felt as though it were glued to the roof of her mouth. She pulled a water bottle from her day bag, twisted the lid off and drank greedily.

Jake rushed toward her and ripped the bottle from her grasp.

"Jake! What do you think you're doing?"

"Probably saving your life, you idiot!"

She glared at him. "It's water, for crying out loud! It's not like—"

"Damn it, Del! Look at it!"

He held up the bottle and she stared at the water inside.

Cloudy, *unfiltered* river water.

She muffled a cry, her stomach churning in rebellion.

Hawk rushed toward them. "What's up?"

"She drank unfiltered water," Jake said grimly.

Del shivered.

How long would it take for the *Giardia lamblia* parasite to invade her body, for symptoms to show? A week? No, two. Then she'd have fever, cramps, nausea...

Oh God!

"Better check all the bottles," Hawk advised.

After every water bottle was examined, she felt a mix of relief and confusion. No one else had to worry about becoming sick. Because only one bottle contained unfiltered water.

Hers.

Miki pulled her aside. "Did you forget to filter it, Del. Or did someone give you the water?"

"It was resting on my bag. I just figured whoever filled the bottles left it there."

"Do you have any idea who?"

"None at all, Miki."

"Well, I think I know."

Del followed the girl's burning gaze.

Francesca?

Ever since she had apologized earlier, the woman had seemed more relaxed. Although she still complained about every little thing.

But if Francesca hadn't given her the water, then who had?

Del's eyes drifted from Francesca to TJ, Peter, Gary, Hawk, Miki...Jake.

None of them would do such a thing.

Would they?

"There's nothing here!" she shouted, kicking at the rocks at the end of the riverbed.

There was no sign of a key or a circle.

Defeated, she collapsed on the ground, not knowing what to do or where to go next. She was exhausted to the core, frustrated by Schroeder's hidden code.

TJ dropped down beside her.

"What exactly did Professor Schroeder say to you the last time you saw him?"

She tried to recall Schroeder's words.

"All I remember is something about a key. Find the key...leave no stone unturned...get Kerrigan."

Jake uttered something under his breath, then swiftly bounded to his feet. He strode to the center of the abandoned riverbed, and cocking his head to one side, he surveyed the ground.

"Check this out."

He pointed to an assortment of flat, multicolored stones. They were arranged in such a way that it was obvious that Mother Nature had nothing to do with it. The pile measured maybe six inches off the ground, which was why everyone had overlooked it.

Del recognized the formation immediately. "It's a cairn."

She held her breath as Jake reached down and scooped up the single mauve rock that topped the cairn. The stone fit neatly into his palm and he rolled it between his fingers, examining it carefully.

Then he passed it to her and she gaped at it, stunned.

The rock's smooth surface was etched with a symbol.

A corkscrew.

Instantly, she dropped to her knees. She pushed aside the stacked rocks and began to dig furiously, despite her bruised knuckles and ragged, bleeding fingernails. Part of her was terrified at what she might find beneath the cairn. The other part didn't give a crap—as long as she found something.

Anything.

On either side of her, Jake and TJ started digging, and Del murmured a soft thanks, brushing a grimy hand across her forehead.

TJ scooped up a handful of dirt and rocks. "What if there's no key here, Del?"

"It's got to be here!"

As soon as the words were out of her mouth, Jake said, "I've found something!"

Using a knife, he carefully uncovered a metal box, maybe three inches in diameter. It was buffed to a satin sheen.

"You'd think it would be rusted," Del murmured.

Jake passed her the box and she flicked open the clasp.

The only thing inside was a pendant suspended from a heavy silver box-link chain. No note, no explanation. Nothing.

She carefully removed the pendant and examined it.

It was a thick cross, maybe three inches long and an inch wide. One side was smooth and unmarked while the other was etched with the same corkscrew symbol as the stone. The top of the cross was looped.

"This is an *ankh* or an *ansate cross*. It's the ancient Greek symbol for life."

Jake took the necklace from her hand and slipped the chain over her head. He tucked the pendant inside her jacket, then leaned close and wiped a smudge of dirt from her face. His expression was grave.

"Del...I need to talk to you. Privately."

Following him away from the others, she took a steadying breath, but it didn't stop the trembling of her voice.

"W-what's wrong?"

"The symbol on the ankh and the stone isn't a corkscrew."

She gave him a blank stare.

He grabbed the collar of his shirt and pulled it low, exposing his left shoulder.

"It's a DNA strand, Del. Like the tattoo on my shoulder."

"So?"

His eyes captured hers.

"The DNA ankh is Bio-Tec's *new* logo."

ELEVEN

A numbing fear settled in the pit of Del's stomach.

Bio-Tec's new logo?

She rubbed her eyes. It was getting more difficult to focus. She was seeing two of everything, including Jake.

She eyed one of the Jakes.

"How come I haven't heard anything about a new logo?"

"As far as I know the design was being kept under wraps. Bio-Tec is set to launch it next year, along with an entire restructuring of the company."

"Well, someone's obviously given it the go-ahead."

Bio-Tec *was* involved in her father's disappearance and it all smelled like a cover-up to her. She wracked her brain, struggling to think of what the company could possibly be hiding and why Bio-Tec would kidnap her father, a man who already worked for them.

And why would they threaten to kill him?

Jake's voice brought her back to the present.

"Want me to carry you up the bank?"

Her smile was mocking. "I'm not the one who slid down the side on my ass and tore a hole in my pants. Anyway, I don't get vertigo going uphill."

Ironically, she was halfway to the top when her legs gave out.

Jake caught her around the waist. "Gotcha."

When they reached the grass above, she gave him an embarrassed grin and slumped to the ground, panting. Her legs vibrated with numbness and she rubbed them briskly, avoiding her throbbing, scraped knees.

Miki squatted beside her. "Are you all right?"

"Not really." *I have some explaining to do.*

She called everyone over.

"Some of you already know, but I think it's only fair that you *all* know. I have Multiple Sclerosis."

She was surprised to see acceptance on their faces. Quiet, calm acceptance. Most people didn't know where to look when she told them she had MS. If they did look at her, it was usually with pity—and pity was something she didn't want *or* need.

Peter eyed her, concerned. "Should we camp here for the night?"

"No, I just need a short break. And a drink."

TJ rummaged in his day bag and handed her his water bottle.

"Give me about ten minutes, okay? I'll take some pills and rest for a bit."

Reaching into the front pocket of her day bag, she froze.

The pill bottle wasn't there.

Alarmed, she emptied the contents on the ground and sifted through them.

No sign of her pills.

"Damn! They must be in my river bag."

"We're heading back then," Jake insisted. "Right now."

During the long hike back to where they had left the canoes and gear, Del was anxious. She had no idea what kind of danger she was leading everyone into. Finding the *key* solved one piece of the puzzle. But would they find the mysterious secret river…and her father?

We have to!

Del's stomach was tied in knots as she watched Jake make his way toward the canoes and gear.

A few minutes later, he returned, smiling.

"Everything's exactly as we left it."

Relieved, she grabbed her river bag and sat down to look for her pills. But she didn't get very far.

"I found something!"

Miki rushed toward her, waving the journal in the air, her face flushed with excitement. She opened the book and pointed to the page that had a drawing of the Nahanni. A small red X marked one side of the river. Two numbers were scribbled above it.

"They're coordinates!" Miki said, excited.

Del's eyes landed on the one person who could track them.

"We need your phone, Hawk."

He tossed it to her, but she shook her head and handed it back.

"I have no idea how to operate this thing. Miki thinks these numbers are coordinates. Can you check them?"

Hawk reached for the journal. "Sure, no problem."

While everyone waited in silence, Del stretched her legs in the grass and reached for the chain around her neck, thinking. If they couldn't figure out the map, they'd have no choice but to turn back.

"Miki's right," Hawk said. "These coordinates lead just past a bend in the river. Under normal circumstances, I'd lead you past it and down about a mile."

TJ's brow arched. "But this ain't normal. Is it, dawg?"

Hawk shook his head. "We'll be fighting the current after the bend. We have to stay right."

"What are we looking for?" Del asked.

"The only thing on that side is sheer rock, which means we're looking for a cave."

She shivered uncontrollably.

Another goddamn cave. Great!

"I think your secret river is underground," Hawk added. "Like Grotte Valerie."

She stroked the ankh pendant.

An underground river? Maybe her father was being held captive in some kind of underground cell. A cell she needed to destroy. Maybe that's what the key opened.

Jake turned to Hawk. "You mentioned Grotte...something."

"Grotte Valerie. It's the most famous cave system in the Nahanni region."

"Is that where we're going?"

"No, those caves have already been explored. And the coordinates don't match. We're going into the Fourth Canyon. It's class three water, then it evens out."

Del raised her head, swallowing hard. "Class three?"

"You'll do fine. For the most part, just let the river take you. But watch the boils and standing waves at the bend."

"How far downriver?" TJ asked.

Hawk checked his satellite phone. "Past the first bend a short ride. I'll leave first, with Peter and Miki. That way I can keep an eye on the GPS. We'll paddle in when we're close to the coordinates. Then we'll help bring in your canoes."

Del had an awful thought. "What if we go right by you?"

"When you get past the standing waves after the bend, hug the right wall. Oh, and watch out for the rock on the left, after the bend. Once you're past it, you'll see us. Aim for the right of us. If your canoe looks like it's going past us, we'll throw you a line. It shouldn't be too difficult."

"Yeah," she mused. "A piece of cake."

Hawk strolled toward the latrines, leaving Del to her thoughts.

What if one of them is trying to stop me?

She peeked under her lashes and swept a cautious look over the people she hoped were friends. TJ would never do anything to hurt her—not again anyway. And Hawk was responsible for them so he wouldn't do anything to put them at risk. But what about Gary and Jake? What did she really know about either of them?

Then there's Francesca—

"Hey!" Miki called breathlessly. "Can I see the book again?"

Del passed her the journal.

Miki read something, then her eyes widened. "Where's Hawk?"

"Latrine. What's up?"

"I need a phone."

"ET phone home," TJ mimicked, creeping up behind them.

Del swatted him. "Hawk has the only phone that works out here."

"Any phone will do," Miki insisted.

Del bit her lip.

Only one other person had a phone on them.

"Francesca?" she called hesitantly. "Can Miki borrow your cell?"

Francesca opened her day bag and retrieved the phone.

Passing it to Miki, she said, "It doesn't work. I already tried. Hawk said only satellite phones work out here."

Miki ignored her and walked away, mumbling in Japanese.

Francesca shrugged. "Fine, don't listen to me then."

Del eyed her suspiciously.

The woman wanted to go home. That was evident by her attitude, and she couldn't really be faulted. But would that push her over the edge, make her get rid of a canoe and contaminate Del's drinking water? Or was Francesca still jealous?

Even though there's no reason for her to be jealous.

Del raised her head and caught Jake's intense stare.

"Feel any better?"

"Actually, I do," she said. "But I didn't take my pills, in case you were going to ask. They make me too tired. Right now I need to be focused."

Her eyes drifted in TJ's direction.

He was leaning against a tree, arms crossed and eyes closed.

Jake followed her gaze. "Is he sleeping?"

"Like the dead. TJ can fall asleep anywhere. Once he fell asleep standing in line outside the stadium, waiting for the doors to open."

"Did someone wake him up?"

She grinned. "Yeah, after a few hundred people passed by him. By the time he made it through, all the best seats were gone."

Del heard a noise behind her, turned.

Miki strode straight for her, a huge smile on her face.

"I broke the code."

"You're amazing!"

The girl's cheeks reddened. "It'll take some time, but now I know it's based on the keypad of a telephone."

She passed Del the journal and quickly showed her a page.

"See? *ABC* is on the number two key. If you want the letter *A*, you use the key number then the letter's position. *A* would be *2-1* or *21*. If you need the *K*, it would be—"

"52."

Miki smiled. "That's why there were no zeros."

Del was relieved that Miki was making progress, and when they set off down the trail to the bottom of the falls, she couldn't wait to get back into the canoe…and back on the Nahanni River.

Hawk climbed into the canoe with Peter and Miki.

"Give us a ten minute head start. Then the next canoe should follow. Ten minutes later, the last one. Okay?"

As they pushed away from shore, Del chewed her fingernails.

Now that they were below Virginia Falls, the river's current moved more rapidly. It didn't take long for the canoe to pick up speed, vanish from sight.

Ten minutes later, Gary, TJ and Francesca set off downriver.

"Alone at last," Jake said, grinning wickedly.

Del felt a quiver run down her body, right down to her curled toes.

Time to nip this thing in the bud.

"Yeah, just me, you…and your *wife*."

He paused in midstride, cocked his head. "My *wife*?"

"Yes, your wife!"

She backed away but he slinked toward her, like a panther ready to spring.

"My *ex*-wife, Del. We've been divorced for two years."

She was about to respond but he touched his index finger to her mouth, silencing her. He gently traced her lips and she shivered from the unexpected contact.

"You know, there's only one reason why my having a wife—*ex* or otherwise—would bother you."

"W-what's that?"

His head dipped close to her ear. "You like me."

She was speechless. So the man had an ex. Who cared if he was single? That didn't mean *she* was interested in him. Getting involved with Jake Kerrigan was pointless. The timing was off. Wrong place, wrong time…

Probably wrong man.

"You like me," he repeated softly. "If you didn't, you wouldn't be pissed that I had a wife. Or ex-wife."

Gulping in a mouthful of air, she clenched her teeth and focused on a tree behind him. "Our ten minutes are up, Jake."

"You really like me," he teased in a singsong tone. "You wanna kiss me."

She flung him a death stare. "Get in the goddamn boat, Kerrigan!"

"Canoe," he corrected smugly.

She swore loudly, her palms itching to slap the silly smirk off his face. It was frustrating that he had such an affect on her. The man was maddening—not because he had the nerve to suggest that she liked him, but because, damn it, he was right.

Hawk scrunched his eyes, surveying the river. It had taken a bit of maneuvering to make it to the spot that the coordinates indicated, and they had almost missed the cave's entrance because the river was high from the last rain.

At least the canoe's not going anywhere.

The thick rope bowline was tied around a ridge of rock that protruded overhead. It was the only way he could think of to keep the canoe from veering downstream.

Miki gave him a worried look. "Is it going to hold?"

"Yeah, it's on good."

"Here they come!" Peter warned, waving his shirt.

TJ's canoe made a beeline toward them.

"Stick to the wall!" Hawk yelled. "Paddle hard on the left."

Within minutes, the canoe was securely tied next to them

Hawk breathed a sigh of relief.

One more to go.

"You think Del's strong enough to paddle?" Peter asked.

Del was an admirable woman with an unwavering spiritual energy, Hawk thought. Stronger in spirit than most of the others.

"She'll make it."

Fifteen minutes went by and TJ gave him a worried look.

"They're late, dawg. What's holding them up?"

The words were barely out of the man's mouth when Hawk noticed the third canoe veering around the bend. He released a slow breath, thankful to see that Del and Jake were close to the wall. As they drew closer, he threw them a line and reeled them in.

"The gang's all here," Del greeted him, visibly relieved. "Hey! Look at this!"

Hawk followed her gaze and his mouth dropped.

Above the entrance, a four-inch ankh was carved into the rock.

"This is definitely it," he said, staring at the cave opening.

The river level was high, he realized. And that would create a problem. There was very little clearance, so they wouldn't be able to paddle inside, not if they were in the canoes.

"The canoes'll be a tight fit," Jake said, reading his mind.

"We'll have to push them inside."

Francesca was outraged. "You mean *swim*?"

"They won't fit through the opening if we're in them. You'll need your wetsuits, so you don't get hypothermia. And don't forget your PFD's."

"Why the life jackets?" Gary asked. "There's no real current in the cave. Is there?"

"We've still got to get from here to the entrance. I don't want anyone to get swept downriver, especially without a PFD. Once we're inside, we'll look for a place to change. And hopefully get back in the canoes."

He secured a short rope to one side of each canoe, hoping for Del's sake that the swim would be short. He didn't know much about MS, but he did know one thing. She was much worse off than when he had first met her.

He took out his satellite phone.

"I'm gonna let McGee know where we're going. Someone should know."

In case we don't make it out.

From the somber expression on Del's face, he knew she was thinking the same thing.

Del zipped up the wetsuit, afraid to exhale. She couldn't believe she had actually gotten the damned thing on without toppling overboard. She slipped the life jacket on over top, wondering how the hell she was supposed to swim when her arms felt like they were stuffed into sausage wrappings.

"What next?" she asked.

Hawk pulled out a headlamp and held it high.

"You all have one of these in your river bag. Make sure it's on tight. You don't want it slipping off in the water."

Francesca frowned. "What is it?"

"It's a headlamp," Del replied. "For exploring caves."

Hawk tested a large flashlight.

"This one is waterproof, so I'll go first. The rest of you stay close to your canoe. If you're not a strong swimmer or if you get tired or cold, hold onto the side rope. That's what it's there for."

He paused, throwing Del a wary look. "Everyone ready?"

"As ready as I'll ever be," she muttered.

Her heart raced as Hawk slid over the side, grabbed the bowline and gave the thumbs up. Then he vanished inside the mouth of the cave, dragging the canoe behind him. Peter and Miki climbed into the water and swam after him.

For a fraction of a second Del saw a light flickering deep within the cave. Then the canoe blocked the entrance and the light disappeared. Peter shoved the canoe until it lurched through the opening. Then he and Miki slipped into the shadows.

Next, Gary and TJ quickly eased themselves into the water, followed by a hesitant Francesca.

"Jesus!" the woman hissed loudly. "The water is freezing!"

Jake sighed impatiently. "I warned you, Francesca. I told you this wasn't a damned holiday. You were the one who insisted on coming."

"Well, this isn't exactly what I bargained—"

A wave crashed over her head and she came up choking, her cool green eyes latching onto Del. "If I drown, it's your fault."

With a curt nod, she swam after the others.

Del watched as the black mouth of the cave devoured them all—devoured, swallowed...consumed.

The damned thing's alive!

Her entire body trembled at the thought.

"What's wrong?" Jake asked.

"I, uh, think I should warn you. I'm a bit claustrophobic. Especially when it comes to caves."

"I would think in your profession..."

"I know," she said self-consciously. "People think I'm fearless, a modern day Indiana Jones. But in all the digs I've been on, I've never been part of the recovery crew. I've always managed to stay above ground."

"You can do this, Del."

She shook her head. "I'm not sure I can."

"Listen," he said, gripping her arm. "I'll be right behind you. When you're in the cave, move to the far right and I'll push the canoe through. Once I'm in, I'll stay right by your side."

He paused. "We're wasting time, Del."

She drew in a deep breath, then lowered herself into the cold Nahanni. Jake slipped into the churning water beside her, and with a few strokes they reached the entrance to the underground river, tugging the canoe behind them.

He passed her the bowline. "Hey, even Indiana had a phobia. He was afraid of snakes, remember?"

Del winced. "That's my other phobia."

With a few hard kicks, she was swallowed by the gaping black maw of the cave.

☥WELVE

☥he underground river tunneled through the rock, reminding Del of a dank sewer. The waterway was about four feet across, widening a few yards inside. The cave walls were covered in calcified mineral and rock layers, with feathery ice crystals clinging to the ceiling and sides. Light from the headlamps and Hawk's flashlight flickered across them, the crystals glittering brightly.

Jake swam toward her. "It's breathtaking."

"Like a galaxy of miniature stars."

The glacier cold water numbed her body, even through the wetsuit. She swam faster to get her circulation going, the light from her headlamp bouncing off the crystals as she moved. She focused on her breathing and tried not to think of the looming cavern that seemed to be closing in on her.

Up ahead, Hawk's shadowy figure waved in the dim light.

"Over here! There's a ledge."

His voice echoed eerily in the cave, and as soon as she reached the slab of stone, he grasped her hands and pulled her up.

"How are you doing?"

"Just a bit cold."

The ledge was barely wide enough for the eight of them to stand on. They turned most of the headlamps off for privacy, and TJ, Jake and Hawk had to crouch so they could dry off with a towel and change into warm clothes without smacking their heads on the rock ceiling.

"Okay, turn your headlamps back on," Hawk warned as they climbed into the canoes. "We don't want any surprises."

Francesca's head jerked. "Like what?"

"There could be stalactites or stalagmites blocking the way."

"Or a cave-in," Del squeaked.

She shivered and peered over her shoulder.

The entrance to the Nahanni River—to fresh air and light—had vanished.

TJ spoke up. "I hope we don't get lost, dawg."

"We should have no problem navigating the river," Hawk replied. "I'll keep the GPS on. We'll be fine."

"As long as the GPS is working," Peter said.

Del had a sudden thought. "What if we lose another canoe, Hawk?"

"We'll have to be careful. Watch for shallows, narrow areas."

Jake tapped her with his paddle. "You okay?"

"It feels like my ribs are being crushed."

"Just take slow, deep breaths."

His voice was low, comforting.

As they ventured farther into the tunnel, their distorted shadows flickered on the walls. Some were thin and stretched up above their heads. Some were squat and fat.

It was like wandering through the *Hall of Mirrors* at the PNE.

Everyone grew deathly quiet.

The sound of water dripping from the ceiling reverberated down the long tunnel, and Del closed her eyes, inhaling hesitantly. The air in the cave was humid and musty. It reminded her of sweaty running shoes. Or wet dog.

In the canoe ahead of her, TJ groaned. "Aw, man. Who cut the cheese? Smells like something died in here."

His words made her gasp for breath.

"Uh, sorry Del. Wasn't thinking."

"No, you certainly weren't," Jake replied sharply.

"Hey, man—"

"Quit it!" Del snapped. "Both of you! TJ's right. It does smell like death in here."

But not Dad's!

Hawk cleared his throat. "Uh, folks? We've got a problem."

"Houston, we have a problem." TJ's voice echoed in the cave.

Ignoring him, Del aimed her headlamp in Hawk's direction and swore out loud. "I don't fricking believe it!"

Up ahead, the underground river split into three tunnels—each leading in different directions.

"Of course there'd be more than one route," she moaned. "Otherwise, it would've been too damned easy."

"Did it show anything in the journal?" Jake asked. "A direction, coordinates...anything?"

She shook her head, thinking of the book that was wrapped in two waterproof bags and stored in an airtight container in her day bag.

Peter cleared his throat. "We could split up."

"No way, dawg!" TJ said. "You know what happens when people

split up, don't you?"

When no one answered, he let out a belabored sigh.

"The black dude's always the first to get sliced and diced. Jeesh! Don't any of you watch movies?"

"No one's going to get sliced *or* diced," Jake said dryly.

"Maybe we could go down the first one for half an hour and see what we find," Gary suggested. "If we find nothing, we could come back, try the next tunnel."

"That would take too long," Jake said. "Del, try to remember what Schroeder told you."

"He said leave no stone unturned. We did that, Jake! That's how we found the key."

"What else?"

"He said to get *you*." *And you're here, aren't you?*

"He must have—"

"My people believe that most humans have stopped trusting in the unseen," Hawk cut in. "That's why we're destroying each other and our spiritual world."

Del cocked her head. "So you're saying…to have faith?"

"If we only hear a wolf's howl or a bird's cry but don't see them, are they really there?"

She smiled. "Like the tree falling in the forest analogy."

"Kind of. Just because we don't see something, Del, doesn't mean it doesn't exist. Often we can see through our mind's eye better than our human ones."

Jake shifted. "So, what are you suggesting, Hawk?"

"We need to welcome the dark."

Del gasped, darting a look at Jake.

It was difficult enough to fight her phobia of the cave. It would be even harder if she was plunged into pitch-blackness.

"I'll leave this flashlight on," Hawk said. "That way we can see where we're going."

One at a time, the flashlights and headlamps were extinguished, except for the one at the bow of Hawk's canoe. The lone light shimmered over the walls, casting ominous shadows amidst the crystals. Three canoes behind the light, Del could barely see her own hand when she raised it to her face. It was so black inside the cave…and so damned quiet. The only sounds were the water lapping at the canoes and the odd pinging droplet of condensation hitting the river's surface.

Without warning, the canoe scraped the jagged wall.

Del jumped, her nerves shifting into overdrive. The canoe swayed abruptly as Jake moved closer. His hand sought hers and she reached for it, impulsively, comforted by his touch.

But the comfort was short-lived.

The longer they sat there, the more she began to wonder how much fresh oxygen was in the cave. She was sure that they were inhaling every last drop.

Her chest grew tight and her breathing, labored.

Were they slowly being poisoned by carbon monoxide?

Jake squeezed her hand. "How are you doing, Del?"

"Not...too good."

A piece of rock broke away from the wall and dropped into the water with a loud splash.

"Oh God," she moaned. "The walls are caving in."

"No, they're not."

"I have to...get out of here, Jake. I can't...do this!"

I can't breathe.

Suddenly, all she could think of was escaping to fresh air and sunlight. She panicked, twisted in her seat, and then stood abruptly.

"Sit down, Del! Think about something else. A happy memory."

She forced out a bitter laugh. "I haven't had many of those lately."

Jake crawled forward, reached out and cradled the back of her neck. His hand rested there for a moment, then slowly he drew her close—so close that she couldn't pull away. *Even if she wanted to.*

"What are you doing?" she hissed.

Strong lips fiercely clamped down on hers, stifling anything else she might have said. His lips moved slowly and she was oblivious to everything except the scintillating fire that burned deep in her belly. His tongue sought out the very depths of her soul, begging her to surrender.

She gave in.

Completely...utterly.

He nuzzled her mouth, eliciting a response. His hands slid through her cropped curls. He finally came up for air, and she entwined her fingers through his hair and drew him back to her eager lips.

She wanted more. She wasn't finished with him...yet.

Suppressing a soft moan, she reminded herself that they were not alone. Somewhere in the dark six people were oblivious to the searing heat she felt as Jake's mouth clamped down on her lips, drawing out the fear and replacing it with desire.

Jake drew away, resting his forehead on hers.

"You have no idea how long I've wanted to do that."

"Do it again," she whispered.

When his fingers stroked her bare skin, she shuddered. Starving for a taste of him, she returned his kiss with a passion that surprised her. She rested both hands on his chest, just inside his jacket and was stunned to feel the rapid beating of his heart.

Damn.

Del had always suspected that having Jake around would be

dangerous. Now, as his mouth ravaged hers, she knew for sure. He had tempted her from the first day she had met him—the carefree, flirtatious banter, the smoldering expression when his eyes feasted on her. Hell, since they had left for the Nahanni he hadn't even bothered to hide his interest.

What was there about him that made her ache? She wanted to crawl inside his skin and stay there, safe and protected. It had been a long, long time since anyone had made her feel safe. Men usually stayed far away once they knew they were dealing with someone who would end up in a wheelchair.

Dead woman walking!

Abruptly she broke away. *"Wait!"*

He silenced her quivering lips with a kiss that robbed her of all rational thought. When it turned tender and sweet, an aching need slowly crept up her body, sweeping her away on a tidal wave of yearning.

She longed to strip naked, press skin against—

"Hey! What are you two doing back there?"

Her head shot up at the sound of TJ's voice.

"This ain't the Tunnel of Love," her ex-boyfriend hollered.

"Del was having a panic attack," Jake said smoothly, releasing her hand. "But she's fine now."

Her face burned with humiliation.

Is that the only reason why he kissed me?

Miki's shout made her push thoughts of Jake Kerrigan aside.

"Over there! There's something on the wall."

Del turned, held her breath.

"I don't see anything."

"There!" Miki said impatiently. "By the third tunnel.

Then Del saw it.

A glowing yellow heart.

Hawk moved the flashlight over it.

"It's some kind of phosphorescent paint."

She grinned slowly. "Schroeder said to follow my heart."

As the canoes drifted past the glowing heart, she didn't think about the fact that they were going deeper into the cave. No, this time she had other things to consider. Like, why *did* Jake kiss her?

Her stomach flip-flopped and she chewed her nails in the dark, trying to forget how she had kissed him back—but that was next to impossible. She needed a distraction.

She thought about his ex-wife. "Do you have kids, Jake?"

"Kids? No. What about you?"

There was an awkward moment before she answered.

"I can't have any. I had some complications a few years ago."

"I'm sorry."

He sounded like he wanted to say something more, but then he pressed a bottle into her hands.

"Water. Maybe you should take your pills now."

Del searched her bag in the dark, feeling for the familiar bottle.

"My pills are gone."

"Are you sure?"

"I know what the pill bottle feels like, Jake. They're not here."

"What about your day bag?"

"I checked it earlier. Maybe I dropped them."

"There's another split in the tunnel up ahead!" Hawk yelled.

Del shoved her river bag aside, determined to do without the medication. She focused on the crystal walls and this time it was easier to spot the yellow heart—now that they knew what they were looking for.

Paddling toward the left tunnel, they followed the river down a winding passageway, navigating around a tight, sharp corner with only Hawk's flashlight to guide them.

"Everyone, hold up!" he shouted. "Turn on your lamps!"

Del aimed her headlamp in Hawk's direction and gasped loudly.

Something solid blocked the underground river.

A metal door.

She stared at it, speechless.

The frame of the door was entirely embedded into all sides of the cave. From top to bottom, side to side. The door itself was twice as wide as a regular door and at least twelve feet high.

Hawk gave the door a shove.

Nothing happened.

"Push it up," Jake suggested.

Hawk shoved the door upwards, grunting from the effort.

It didn't budge an inch.

"Uh, Del?" Gary said hesitantly.

She ignored the man and let out a frustrated huff. "Can we swim under it, Hawk?"

"I think it goes straight to the bottom."

"Del!" Gary said forcefully. "You have a…key."

She stopped dead in her tracks. A smile crept across her face and she could have kissed the man.

"Gary, you're a genius!"

"We need you up here, Del," Hawk called. "Can you make it?"

"Damn right!"

With Jake's assistance, she climbed over the side and into TJ's canoe. Crouching low and half-sliding, she carefully made her way past Francesca and Gary. When she reached Hawk and Peter, they clutched her hands and helped her into the canoe.

Miki gave her a brief smile. "Glad you didn't go for a swim."

"Me too."

Hawk held onto the rocks beside the metal door to keep the canoe from drifting away. "Ready?"

"Just give me more light."

With all headlamps aimed on the door, Del carefully scoured every inch of the metal obstruction for a place to insert the key.

"Crap! I can't find the goddamn keyhole."

Hawk ran his hands over the door.

"Del's right. There's no keyhole."

Frustrated, Del glared at the wall.

That's when she saw it.

A smooth bare patch that didn't quite match the rest of the cave.

Her heart began to pound.

"I think I found it. We need to get closer."

A metal panel was embedded in the crystal to the left of the door, and she stretched out a hand. With her index finger, she traced the object that was painted so it would blend with the wall.

An ankh.

The middle of the loop held a smoky glass DNA symbol.

She held her breath, unzipped her jacket and reached for the ankh pendant. Removing the necklace from around her neck, she placed it against the ankh on the wall.

But the door remained locked.

Then she noticed that the horizontal line of the cross was slightly indented, scratched. She pressed the pendant into the line.

She waited.

Suddenly, a tremor raced along the metal door, into the pendant. Without warning, the groove in the ankh opened and yanked the pendant inside. It slid in about an inch, making muted clicking sounds.

"Jesus!"

A bright green light emanated from the DNA strand on both the panel and the pendant. In undulating waves, the light moved up and down the symbol, intensifying each time.

Suddenly, with a loud clanging sound, the door sprung free.

No one said a word.

Mouths gaping, they stared at the open door.

"Bizarre technology," Francesca mumbled.

Del had certainly never seen anything like it.

She stumbled back toward Jake, and if it wasn't for everyone's help she probably would have ended up in the water. Her legs felt wobbly, but this time it was from fear and excitement.

One by one, the canoes drifted through the doorway.

Then Jake let go of the door, and the heavy metal slab swung shut with finality, the sound echoing down the tunnel.

"There's no panel on this side," he said soberly.

She frowned. "So we won't be coming back *this* way."

Jake watched her with an intensity that made her uncomfortable, edgy. He opened his mouth, then snapped it shut firmly.

Something was bothering him.

"What?"

"I'm just thinking that whoever put that door there obviously doesn't want intruders. We could be walking into something very dangerous, Del. And you have nothing for protection."

"I have you."

It was the first thing that popped into her mind.

His eyes locked on hers. "Yes, you have me."

Up ahead, Hawk's flashlight began to flicker.

TJ groaned. "You need new batteries, dawg."

"I put in new batteries this morning..."

Hawk's voice trailed away as his flashlight *and* headlamp died.

Miki and Peter's headlamps went out next.

Del hissed in a strangled breath as, one by one, every light went out, hurtling them into absolute darkness.

"What just happened?"

Her voice was hoarse with fear.

"Must be some kind of electrical interference," Hawk called from the dark. "My GPS is out too."

Francesca whimpered. "We should turn back."

"I have to agree," Peter said. "Maybe we should turn—"

Miki interrupted him. "No. We can't go back that way, remember? We should keep go—"

Hawk made a sharp shushing sound.

"Listen!"

Del couldn't hear a thing—except silence. She strained, listening, holding her breath.

Then she heard it.

A faint droning sound.

"We're at least a mile into the mountains," Jake said. "What could possibly be down here?"

She shivered with anxiety. "Bees?"

"Sounds electrical."

The humming intensified as they floated past a large jutting rock. Ahead, a faint blue glow emanated from the bowels of the tunnel and Del could just make out the shapes of the people in front of her.

"Maybe it's a way out," Gary mumbled.

The canoes drifted on the current. A few yards further the walls closed in and the canoes began bumping and grinding against the rocks.

"We're not moving anymore," Francesca said nervously.

She was right. The canoes were lodged on a shallow underwater ledge.

Del's stomach lurched.

We aren't going anywhere.

Muffled sounds caught her attention.

A shadowy shape jumped from the first canoe. Someone with a long ponytail and sharp nose.

Hawk.

"Just bring your day bags," he said. "Leave the rest of the gear."

She turned to Jake's shadow. "Is it safe to walk in here?"

"I don't think we have a choice."

After making slow and careful progress through the winding tunnel, the blue light brightened.

And they stopped.

They had to. It was a dead end.

The tunnel ended in a cave, roughly the size of an average family room. The walls were solid rock, with no visible exit. On each side of the cave, two strips of large, sharp, sapphire-like crystals ran down the walls, from ceiling to floor. They gleamed, casting an eerie blue glow over everything and everyone.

She shuddered.

This can't be the end of the underground river.

"Very unusual," Hawk said, staring at the light.

Jake nodded. "I've never seen anything like it."

Del marched forward, determined to find a sign.

Jake's arm snaked out. "Wait!"

She raised a hand, warding him off, then strode toward the far wall. She made it halfway across the room when the air shifted around her. She stopped.

There has to be something! Schroeder wouldn't lead us here for nothing.

She stepped forward, between the two strips of crystal.

And something weird happened.

The blue light of the crystals flared…*alive.*

Jake pulled her back. "Don't go any closer, Del. It's not safe."

His blue eyes pleaded with her, but she shook her head, ignoring him. Her father needed her. She was his only hope. And there was no way on earth that she had come this far only to give up.

Out of the corner of her eye, she saw Peter heave a frustrated groan. He muttered something beneath his breath, then stumbled between the crystals.

"Peter!"

Frozen with fear, she gulped in a huge breath as two slender trails of metallic sapphire light crawled down the cave walls toward him. The tentacles of light slithered across the floor, colliding at his feet. Inch by inch, they wrapped around his legs, throbbing to the beat of the alarm. Within seconds, he was enveloped in a strange liquid mercury radiance.

"Oh my God," she whispered.

Peter's jaw dropped and his eyes widened, terrified. Bit by bit, his entire body disintegrated—each molecule separating, stretching grotesquely. He slowly became...*dust.*

In a flash, Peter Cavanaugh was gone.

Del knew that there were times when a decision must be made, and made fast—regardless of the possible outcome. A decision of fate. Or destiny.

Catching Jake's eye, she threw him a beaming smile. Before he could stop her, she stepped between the crystals, welcoming the sapphire light that skimmed icily up her body.

Jake's mouth opened in horror. "No, Del!"

She dissolved into an infinite number of particles...

PART THREE

UNDER WORLD

When you arrive at your future,
will you blame your past?
~ Robert Half

✟HIRTEEN

Hans VanBuren sat his spacious—although windowless—executive office, trying to find a way to creatively and secretly siphon more funds into his offshore account before he had to hand over his carefully adjusted financial report.

It was due in a week.

And damned if it wouldn't be ready before then.

He picked up a coffee mug and drained the last drop.

Where was Faith? She knew he liked a fresh pot at midnight.

His eyes fastened on the glaring warning that flashed on the bottom right-hand corner of the computer monitor.

Intruder Alert!

Suddenly, he heard footsteps pounding past his office door. His mouth twitched nervously, then he leaned back in the leather chair, forcing himself to relax. Clasping his hands behind his head, he stared at the ceiling…waiting.

He didn't have to wait long.

The door opened.

Faith, his lovely blond-haired receptionist with her barely-there breasts, poked her head inside.

"It's time, Mr. VanBuren."

He savored the sight of the silver ankh on her ID tag that marked her as his. He'd give anything to drown himself in her.

A sly smirk spread across his face. With a flick of his hand, he motioned her forward.

Faith hesitantly stepped into the room.

"Lock the door behind you."

Barely out of her teens, the young girl shifted uncomfortably, then did as he ordered. When her eyebrows rose in question, he shrugged and unzipped his pants. Standing tall and erect, he faced her.

"Faith," he chastised. "I always have time for you."

He could sense her awkwardness, but he didn't care.

He said nothing.

A heartbeat later, his silence was rewarded when she slowly began to remove her blouse and skirt, dropping each piece on the floor, just the way he liked it.

With eyes like pools of liquid jade, she released a trembling breath. "I'm ready, sir. You look wonderful."

On the wall across from him was a simple silver-framed mirror.

Hans smiled slowly, admiring his handsome face and muscular body. Faith was right. He did look wonderful.

In fact, he had never looked better.

Bending the girl over the desk, he held her down with one hand, and with a groan of anticipation, he plunged into her for the second time that day.

I always have time for a little faith.

A guard in his mid-twenties stood outside the entrance to the tunnel, weapon raised, vigilant. Blazing warning lights flashed overhead but the man remained frozen in place, unblinking.

Justin Blackwell, chief of security, strode toward the guard.

"Are they back?"

The guard shook his head slightly. "Not yet."

"Blackwell!"

Justin cursed under his breath, turned and hid a frown.

Hans VanBuren, with his long, sleek, white-blond hair, did not look happy. Judging from the angry, curled lip, Justin suspected that the man had been interrupted.

Probably torn away from one of his many dalliances.

As VanBuren approached, his mandarin-styled jacket gleamed softly, the silver satin fabric rippling under the flashing light. The man had expensive taste in everything from clothing to wine and seafood.

Justin gave him a quick nod.

He was about to compliment VanBuren on his jacket when the man raised a hand.

"I want to know one thing and one thing only."

"What's that?"

VanBuren's ice blue eyes were steel. "How did this happen?"

Justin knew damned well that anything he said would not be well received, so he settled for the truth.

"Honestly, I have no idea."

The glint in VanBuren's eyes made Justin shiver.

"Aren't you paid to know?"

There was a deadly threatening tone to his words.

"Paughter understood the risks—"

"Paughter's an idiot!" VanBuren hissed between clenched teeth. "The plan was to lead them *away*—sabotage their efforts so they'd have to turn back. Why in God's name did he go in the first place?"

"To keep an eye on Hawthorne's daughter—and because the Director ordered it."

VanBuren gave him a look that said *shut the hell up.*

"For Christ's sake, Blackwell! You're in charge of damage control. I want this mess taken care of. Do you understand me?"

As VanBuren spun on his heel and stormed away, Justin released a pent-up breath and ran his tongue nervously across his bottom lip. If the man wanted it taken care of, that only meant one thing. Heads would roll.

Thank God it wouldn't be his.

Hans strode purposefully past the receptionist cubicle.

When Faith started to say something, he glared and her mouth instantly closed.

"I'll be in my office," he barked. "I'm not to be disturbed."

"Yes, sir."

Her voice was muted and submissive.

The way it should be.

Alone in his office, he slumped on the couch.

The Director was not going to be happy. Not one bit.

Hans clicked off the lamp.

Sitting in the dark, he ran a quivering hand through his gelled hair, his facial muscles tightening with frustration as a barrage of thoughts plagued him.

Since Paughter's authorized *defection*, the Centre had become an efficiently oiled machine, running smoothly under his control. He only had one problem. The doctor. Hawthorne had grown increasingly difficult. It wasn't until the Director threatened to harm the man's daughter that Hawthorne had become more compliant.

Hans scowled. *But we still don't have the files!*

Hawthorne swore that they had everything—everything that Blackwell and his team had stolen from Bio-Tec's lab a few years back. They had cleaned out Bio-Tec's mainframe and obliterated all of Hawthorne's files after making copies of everything. They had even taken his laptop in hopes that the hidden file was somewhere on the hard drive.

Hans reached for a decanter and poured himself a drink.

"There's a hidden file. I know it!"

Somewhere, Hawthorne had concealed the DNA coding that they desperately needed to complete Project Ankh and make it flawless…eternal. Currently, the project had one drawback. A drawback that meant death—to everyone concerned. But Hawthorne would certainly be more productive after he discovered that his precious daughter was about to join them.

Hans rose abruptly, tossed his jacket carelessly over the back of the couch, then flipped on the lamp. Unable to resist, he stole a peek at the small chrome-faced refrigerator that was built into the oak wall cabinet across from his desk.

It called to him. *Hans…*

He strode over to it.

Opening the door, he reached in and grabbed a fresh syringe and a vial of pale yellow liquid. He inserted the syringe into the protective cap of the vial, then he drew it back, the liquid trickling into the belly of the syringe.

"Ah…nectar of the Gods."

He sat down at the desk and quickly pushed up his shirtsleeve. Tying a thin strip of amber hose around his upper arm, he used his teeth to pull it taut.

Then he glanced at the clock on the wall.

He had almost an hour before anyone would disturb him. That would be more than enough time.

Holding the syringe to the light, he flicked it. With a deep breath, he slid the sharp tip beneath the tender skin of his arm.

The familiar burn was overwhelming.

His eyes watered and glazed over. He gritted his teeth, struggling not to bite his tongue as he pulled off the tourniquet. As the serum rushed through his body, a thought flashed in his tortured mind.

Is it worth this excruciating pain?

He studied his reflection in the mirror. It wavered slightly, but he glimpsed the vibrantly healthy thirty-year-old staring back at him.

Damn right, it's worth it!

The room began to spin. His head lolled to one side and hit the desk, hard and fast. The last thing he saw before slipping into unconsciousness was the precious vial of serum.

Project Ankh…life in a bottle.

Del awoke with a jolt.

Where am I?

She swallowed and the coppery taste of blood lingered on her lips as an icy chill vibrated through her bruised body. Wherever she was, it wasn't the cave. The last thing she remembered was the glowing crystals and a blinding light, followed by a thunderous, sucking sound.

She sat up slowly, her eyes darting everywhere.

It took her a moment to realize that she was actually on the shore of the Nahanni River, sprawled on the ground, with both legs trailing into the cold water. But it wasn't part of the river she knew.

Nothing was familiar.

She stood shakily, crying out as a piercing pain shot through her left ankle. Hobbling in a slow circle, she cupped one hand to her eyes and surveyed the area.

"Jake!"

Her head ached and she rubbed it tenderly.

It felt like someone had clobbered her with a tire iron.

This is not good. Not good at all.

To calm her nerves, she breathed deeply and slowly limped along the shore. In the shadows, she caught sight of something lying near the water—a day bag.

Mine?

She scooped it up, unzipped the bag and let out a triumphant shout. It *was* hers. And inside it was the journal, the Nahanni guidebook, a flashlight, some snacks...

And a half-filled water bottle.

Relieved, she stumbled toward a piece of driftwood. Sitting on the weathered trunk, she took a sip of water, then flicked on the flashlight and shone it on the journal. Using Miki's theory, Del scribbled the translation of one of the first lines of numerical code.

233253 = 3132218142!

She gasped. "*CEL = DEATH!*"

Twisting around in desperation, she swatted at the tears that pooled in her eyes. Her throat burned as she tamped down the terror that crept into her thoughts.

This was not the time to break down.

She had to remain tough, stay strong. Jake and the others had to be nearby. They must have followed her.

Wait! Peter went through first. Where is he?

"Peter!"

There was no reply.

With the flashlight guiding her, she followed the river, calling loudly for the others. Resting on a rock at the river's shore, she removed her boots and socks, then gently eased her feet into the cool water, hissing in a loud breath. High above her, the moon peeked from the clouds while the river trickled by, innocent and inviting. Not far upriver, the Nahanni took a sharp bend between two towering rock walls. An odd slab of rock stood like a sentry, blocking her view of the river.

Where am I?

She pulled out the guidebook that Hawk had given each of them back at Rabbitkettle Lake. A third of the way in, she found what she was looking for.

A photograph of The Gate—a narrow, winding pass.

That's where she was!

She stared at a peculiar rock formation.

Pulpit Rock, according to the guide.

Carved by the elements and erosion, Pulpit Rock hovered menacingly above the Nahanni, guarding the entrance to The Gate. Below it, the river was shrouded in a thick, sinuous fog that twisted and rose into the air. The dreary landscape was almost surreal and there were no signs of wildlife, no birds calling in the night.

Just an unnatural silence.

Del shivered uncontrollably.

How the hell did I get here? And where is everyone?

"Jake! Where are you?"

Her voice sounded weird, hollow.

She strode to the edge of the river.

"Help me!" she screamed. "Somebody...please...help me!"

The only sound she heard was her own voice, echoing.

She peered into the night, abandoned, desolate.

Maybe they're still inside the cave.

Her vision blurred suddenly. Then a sharp knifelike pain sliced through her optical nerve. Determined to fight it, she clamped her eyes shut.

"Damnit! Not now!"

After the pain subsided, she limped toward the grass.

But she didn't make it.

Without warning, she collapsed, falling face-forward to the stony shore. A searing pain ripped through her as razor-thin rocks scraped across her face. A trickle of blood dripped onto her hand.

She stared at it.

Barely conscious, one final thought hit her before she slipped into oblivion.

MS is a nasty bitch!

FOURTEEN

Jake heard a dull roaring sound. He opened his mouth to call out but swallowed muddy water instead. Blinking in disbelief, he peered at the cold dark shadows surrounding him.

Then it hit him.

Jesus! I'm underwater!

Spurred into motion, he kicked hard, unsure of which way was up. His lungs strained for air and his body ached all over.

He was going to drown. He knew it.

All of a sudden, a soft glimmer caught his eye. Thrashing toward it, he broke the surface, gulping in a huge breath of air.

"What the hell?"

Somehow he had landed in the Nahanni River—in the middle of the night, with only the light from the full moon to guide him.

"Help!" a voice called.

Treading water, Jake searched the water's murky surface.

"Someone help me!"

It was Miki.

She was a few yards downriver, holding onto a rock, her chin bare inches from the river's surface.

"I'm coming, Miki! Hold on!"

His muscles strained against the current of the river as it attempted to drag him away. He kicked with all of his strength, cutting through the water with a clean breaststroke.

It seemed to take forever but he finally reached her.

He grabbed her arm. "I've got you. We have to head for shore."

Miki shook her head. "I can't. I'm stuck."

Reaching below the surface, he quickly discovered her problem.

The front strap of her life jacket was lodged between two rocks, pinning her tightly against them.

Miki floundered in the water helplessly.

"Hurry, Jake! The water's rising!"

She choked on a mouthful of water.

Jake knew he had to get her out—fast. The water was up to her bottom lip. If the river rose much higher, her head would be completely submerged.

"Hold still."

He stretched around her and tugged hard on the front of the life jacket. Frustrated, he grabbed her, bracing his feet against the rock.

She didn't budge.

"You'll have to slip out of it."

Her eyes swelled with fear. "It won't unzip all the way. And it's a tight squeeze."

He smiled. "Not for a little thing like you."

She stared at him. "I know what you're trying to do."

"What's that, Miki?"

"Get me to relax."

"Is it working?"

"If I take it off…" Her voice trailed away.

Jake knew exactly what Miki was thinking. If she took off her life jacket, she could be swept away. He was thinking the same thing, and it worried the hell out of him.

"I'll grab you," he promised. "Unzip it as far as you can, then slide out from under it. Grab onto me as soon as you come up for air."

She stared at him for a moment, then nodded.

Jake took in a shaky breath, holding onto the top of the life jacket.

"Ready?"

Inhaling deeply, Miki wriggled her shoulders and sank below the surface. He could barely make out her head in the shadowy water, but he could sense her below, kicking. A tired numbness inched over him. The water was freezing. The motion of the river lulled him and he was tempted to lie on his back.

"Come on, Miki."

His mind drifted…

They had been in the cave looking at some weird crystals. That much he remembered. The rest was cloudy.

How the hell did I end up in the river? Miki too.

Suddenly, he realized that Miki had been underwater an awfully long time.

He gave the jacket a hard shake.

Oh Jesus!

The life jacket was empty.

"Miki?"

Frantic, he dove beneath the surface of the water.

There was no sign of her.

His arms and legs grew weak from diving, over and over again.

If you don't get to dry land, Kerrigan, you're gonna die.

Reluctantly, he swam to shore, crawled out of the river and collapsed on the ground. Under the soft glow of the moon, he listened to the hammering of his heart, praying that he'd hear Miki call out once more.

Only silence greeted him.

He sat up, gazing across the water's surface.

"Miki!"

There was no sign of her—anywhere.

Miki Tanaka was gone.

The moon gleamed above, clear and bright, as Hawk shook his head and tried to clear the cobwebs of confusion from his mind.

Beside him, TJ mumbled something incoherent.

They were clinging to a piece of driftwood while the easy current of the Nahanni River pushed them toward the shore.

TJ nudged him. "Hey, man. I can touch the bottom."

As they waded through the water, Hawk stared up at the star-filled sky. Then he fixed his eyes on the steep slab of rock that rose from the depths of the water a few yards away.

He recognized his surroundings immediately.

The Gate!

A shiver of fear wracked his body.

"Jesus! How'd we end up here?"

Reaching the shore, he dropped to the rocks, exhausted.

TJ stretched out beside him, one arm over his eyes.

"What happened, dawg?"

"I have no idea. But something is…very wrong, TJ."

The Nahanni—*his* Nahanni—felt foreign to him. It had changed somehow. Even the lush landscape was different—muted and lifeless.

"How'd we end up in the river?" TJ asked.

Hawk's memory of what had happened the moment he stepped between the crystals was hazy too. What he did remember was the exploding light that had rendered him virtually senseless. The last thing he had felt was a rush of air. And then cold, icy water.

"Your guess is as good as mine."

TJ sat up suddenly. "Where's Del? And the others?"

"I don't know, but we need to build a fire."

"Jesus, Hawk! We can't think about getting warm right now. They're out there somewhere—"

"A fire is visible. They'll see it."

Hawk staggered to his feet and strode toward a stand of trees.

"But we don't have a lighter," TJ called after him.

Hawk stopped, turned.

Why do white men have so little faith?

"The earth provides all things, TJ. You gotta have faith."

TJ shook his head slowly. "Me and faith haven't been on the best of terms lately. I've screwed up too many things. Including my relationship with Del."

"She seemed all right with you. She invited you, didn't she?"

"I don't think she sees me as anything but an ex who screwed around on her. That was the stupidest thing I ever did."

"Yeah. It probably was."

TJ cringed. "Del and I used to be great friends."

"There are always ways to redeem yourself," Hawk said in a quiet voice. "You came here, didn't you? Not many friends would do even that. She'll recognize that."

"Maybe…I'll go get something to start the fire."

While TJ went off to scour the beach for kindling and moss, Hawk tested a few nearby tree branches. He needed dry wood that was easy to break. Thankfully, he found a small burn area. Many of the trees were coal black, but some of the wood was salvageable.

On the beach, he dug a small pit in the ground. When TJ returned with a clump of moss and small pieces of driftwood, they added it to the pit.

"So how do we get this thing going?" TJ asked.

"I'll show you."

Hawk picked up two rocks and whacked them together. They crumbled and he tossed them aside.

TJ passed him two more. "Try these."

When Hawk smacked the rocks against each other, they held, and he gave TJ the thumbs up. Lying on the ground, he rubbed the rocks together, close to the clump of moss.

At first nothing happened. No smoke, no spark. Nothing.

He rubbed the rocks harder, faster.

"Want me to try," TJ offered.

As soon as he spoke, a spark ignited the moss, then the kindling.

"Hey, dawg, you did it!"

Hawk smiled.

He had never doubted for a moment that the great spirits would let him down. That was the Dene way.

Ten minutes later, a roaring bonfire lit up the beach.

"We'll be okay now," TJ murmured.

Hawk eyed the looming forest behind them.

TJ had no idea the danger they were in. There was a lot to worry about. Bears, wolves…hypothermia. Not to mention they had no food or drinking water.

Damn you, McGee! If you had been with us you'd have talked me out of taking these people on a wild goose chase.

They spent the next hour hovered over the fire. They removed their jackets, shirts and jeans, and draped them over two branches, suspending them high above the flames.

"Yum...smoked shirt," TJ grinned. "You'll have to add this to your Nahanni cookbook."

Hawk chuckled, then his expression turned sober.

"We'll head out first thing in the morning to look for everyone."

"Hey, man! I'm not leaving Del out there by herself all night. After I dry off I'm going to find her."

Hawk understood TJ's concern. Del hadn't been looking too good the last day or so.

"Fine. I'll keep the fire burning. That way you'll—"

"Hawk! Is that you?"

Jake Kerrigan stumbled toward them, a wild look in his eyes.

"Miki's gone!"

TJ's brow furrowed. "What do you mean, gone?"

"Her life jacket got pinned between some rocks. I told her to take it off."

"What happened?" Hawk asked, although he already knew the answer.

Jake looked at them, guilt in his eyes. "The current swept her away. One second she was there, the next second she was...gone."

Hawk stared wordlessly at the river.

What was there to say? Miki could never have survived without a life jacket. And that meant one thing.

The Nahanni had claimed another life.

"I'm sure you did everything—"

Jake's jaw clenched. "Obviously not enough."

His gaze drifted over the beach. "Where's Del? And the others?"

"We don't know, dawg," TJ said quietly. "Hell, we don't even know what happened. Like, how did we get here?"

Hawk jerked his head in the direction of the fire. "Get dried off, Jake. In the morning, we'll hunt for Del and the others."

"When exactly *is* that?"

"I don't know. My watch isn't working. What about yours?"

TJ and Jake looked at their watches, then shook their heads.

"We've got maybe four hours until the sun rises," Hawk said, examining the sky.

"Maybe they'll find us first," TJ muttered.

"Maybe."

But I'm not holding my breath.

Hawk threw another log on the fire and thought about the others.

Del was in bad shape because of her MS. And Gary, the computer guy, would never survive for long on his own in the wild. Peter might, though. At least the kid was accustomed to roughing it. As for Francesca? Well, that woman would probably scare off any predators with a single glare.

"We'll have to monitor the fire in shifts."

"I'm going to walk by the river," Jake said. "I'll take the shift after you, if that's all right with TJ."

After he left, Hawk and TJ quickly donned their somewhat drier clothes and settled near the fire, talking in hushed tones, even though no one could hear them.

They watched Jake. They were both worried about him.

Hawk knew that Jake was thinking about Miki Tanaka, that he felt responsible for her death.

We're all responsible.

He closed his eyes and murmured a prayer in his native tongue.

TJ eyed him. "What are you doing?"

"Praying for a miracle."

The next morning, Jake eyed the sliver of sunlight as it made its appearance over the horizon. He sighed, disappointed that none of the others had stumbled across their fire.

All night long, he had tossed and turned as flashes of memory seeped into his dreams. The peculiar crystal formation in the cave. Peter disappearing before his eyes. Miki vanishing beneath the Nahanni River. Del…

Where was she?

God, he hoped that she was okay.

A movement caught his eye.

Hawk was standing on the rocks near the shore. He gripped something in his hands.

"I got it!"

Jake straightened. "Got what?"

Hawk held up his day bag. "My miracle."

"Miracle Whip?" TJ uttered, shooting upright.

Half asleep, he blinked a few times, groaning, stretching his legs.

"Do I look as bad as you, dawg?"

Jake grinned. "Worse."

Hawk unzipped the bag. "Keep your fingers crossed."

A full water bottle was the first thing Jake saw. Beside it was a large Ziploc bag filled with granola.

"Water and food," he said. "It's a start. If we're lucky, TJ, we'll find our bags too."

"We'll have to ration everything," Hawk said. "Now for the best news."

Jake held his breath.

The satellite phone.

"Yeah, baby!" TJ shouted.

Hawk grinned. "I'll call for a rescue team."

He thumbed the switch and a loud hiss of static erupted from the phone. He frowned, clicked off the phone, then turned it back on.

Dead air.

Cursing, he shook it and stared at it blankly.

Jake held out his hand. "May I?"

Cradling the phone, he removed the lithium ion battery, then popped it back in. But still nothing happened. He gave the satellite phone a shake, then rapped it against his palm. Again.

"Come on, you piece of shit!"

TJ moaned. "Don't say it, dawg."

"That means no GPS either," Hawk murmured.

Jake released a frustrated sigh.

Things weren't looking good for them. They had very little water and food. And God only knew where the others were.

"Jesus! What else can go wrong?"

"Don't ask," TJ said.

Jake shifted uneasily. "So what do we do now?"

Without warning, branches snapped behind them.

"You come with us."

Startled, Jake spun around.

A man with a blond crew cut stood between two stocky men. All three wore black army gear, and none of them were smiling. But it was what they held in their hands that made Jake cringe.

Three high-powered sniper rifles—aimed at their heads.

"I told you not to ask," TJ groaned.

FIFTEEN

Hans tapped his foot impatiently. "Well?"

"Blackwell should be back shortly, sir," a young guard reported briskly. "He radioed in about half an hour ago."

"And?"

The kid, fresh out of basic training, swallowed nervously.

"I, uh…sorry. What did you want to know?"

Hans wanted to strangle him.

"Did they find them?"

His voice was glacier cold.

"They found three, sir."

Three more to add to the ones they already found, Hans thought, peering down his nose at the guard.

"You're to page me as soon as they reach the Centre. I'll be in my office. Got that?"

The kid's head jerked in response.

Hans stalked away, anxious to get back to the lab.

It was time for another meeting with Hawthorne, and he wondered how the doctor would feel after he found out his precious daughter was in a locked room on the same level as the lab.

There were *two* new women at the Centre, and Hans grew hard thinking of the other one—the redhead in the room next to Delila Hawthorne's.

Francesca Baroni, his sources told him.

A feisty little thing!

He preferred his women with a bit of fight. Made the conquering all the more exciting. And Francesca was still young. That was important too. Young…and ripe for the picking. The throbbing bulge in his pants told him he'd have to pay her a visit. The sooner, the better.

But business first. There'll be plenty of time for pleasure later.

Ignoring the elevator to the upper level, he passed Delila's room, then

Francesca's. Then he detoured down a winding hall and stopped in front of two steel doors.

Project Ankh.

Reaching into his shirt, he plucked out an ankh-shaped passkey, inserted it into a slot and waited for the light to flash green. When the doors unlocked and slid open, he stepped inside the lab.

The Project Ankh lab was filled with top-of-the-line research equipment, most of it supplied by the Canadian and US government. It featured a voice activated environmental system that controlled everything from lights to temperature to the computer terminals.

To the right, a door led to the Bot Room, where countless workers constructed miniature nanomachines. Farther down the wall, another door led to the Specimen Lab, an immense warehouse-sized room that housed the most recent lab specimens used in highly classified, experimental testing. At the far end was the entrance to the morgue—the final destination for the *husks*.

Surprisingly, it was empty.

But not for long.

He made a beeline for Hawthorne's room.

It was approximately twelve by twelve feet. Originally designed as a storage closet off the main lab, it had been used to house valuable chemical agents. But seven years ago, the room had been cleared out to accommodate the lab's most prized addition.

Without knocking, Hans entered the room.

Lawrence Hawthorne lay on the bed at the far end, reading the latest medical journal.

"What do you want now?" he asked bitterly.

Hans couldn't resist a smug grin. "Your daughter."

"I've told you before, leave my daughter out of this. Del doesn't know anything."

"She knew enough to come looking for you."

Hawthorne leapt from the bed. "That's impossible!"

"She's here. With Paughter."

"Liar!"

Hans pulled out a gun, carefully aimed it at the doctor.

"Pardon me?"

The man backed away, flustered. "How the hell would she even find this place?"

"Come on, old man! Your friend told her."

Holding the door ajar, he jerked his head and waited for Hawthorne to stumble through the doorway. He could almost read the doctor's thoughts.

But Arnold is dead!

Hawthorne started for the main exit, but Hans shook his head.

"Uh-uh, doctor. Lab first. You need to run those diagnostics."

He turned on his heel, unlocked the doors and stepped through.

"I expect a full report before you go to sleep."

"I want to see my daughter."

"Your family reunion will have to wait until you've given me what I need."

"You'd better not hurt her."

"Hurt her? I have other plans for your daughter—and they don't include pain…unless she likes it rough."

The doors closed between them and Hans headed for his office.

Sitting at his desk, he thought about Hawthorne's daughter. He had first seen her when Blackwell's team had brought her in, unconscious and bloody.

Sometimes the crossing was hell.

He recalled *his* first time…the shooting pain, the sudden shock of being slammed into the icy cold Nahanni. Yeah, he remembered it like it was yesterday.

He leaned back, tempted to pay Delila Hawthorne a visit—just to spite her father.

His pager beeped and he jumped.

Blackwell was back.

He slowly pushed himself from the chair and poured himself three fingers of rye, straight up, no ice. Sipping it leisurely, he eyed the clock on the wall.

He'd give Justin Blackwell fifteen minutes.

Fifteen minutes proved to be too generous.

Twelve minutes later, Hans greeted the blond-haired chief of security and motioned him to sit in the armchair. A surreptitious inspection of Blackwell proved one thing.

The man looked ill.

Hans raised his glass. "Drink?"

"No, I'm still on duty."

"Oh, for Christ's sake, Blackwell! It's two in the goddamn morning. Once the kiddies have been put to bed, you have nothing else to do but pick your nose."

He threw Blackwell a look of disgust. "How many?"

"Three. All men."

"Excellent. I'm sure we'll find a use for them."

Blackwell cleared his throat uneasily. "The Specimen Lab?"

Taking a long swig, Hans locked eyes on him.

"I'll have a little chat with them first."

Something was wrong. Very wrong.

Del was floating on a cloud, disjointed.

Everything around her was hazy, out of focus. Her body felt cold and heavy, and there was a godawful taste in the back of her throat, earthy and pungent. It reminded her of Lisa's mystery tea.

A bright light came into focus.

She tried to close her eyes but nothing happened. She tried to speak but her lips wouldn't move. No sound came from her throat. There was just that peculiar, horrible taste.

Something moved above her.

Two shadows. They were...dancing.

She wanted to giggle.

Someone tipped the light away from her. When her vision came into focus, she would have gasped in horror—if her mouth was working.

She was lying flat on her back. Her head was strapped into an odd metal contraption. What terrified her most were the metal rods and clamps that forced open her eyes.

She tried to scream.

"She's semi-conscious, doctor," a woman's voice murmured.

"Give her twenty mils of Necrovan," came the clipped reply. "That ought to knock her out completely. She won't remember a thing."

Del panicked when she saw the glimmer of a syringe filled with a pale golden liquid. The sharp point moved closer to her left eye and she desperately wanted to lash out.

What were they doing to her?

No! Stop!

A familiar voice reached out to her. "Relax, Del. Don't fight it."

A vortex of nothingness claimed her...mercifully.

Lawrence Hawthorne gazed through the one-way glass as his daughter slept. Looking at her, he realized that he had never expected to see her again.

Delila.

Part of him was overjoyed. But the rational part of him knew that her presence could only lead to disaster. The Director would use her to get to the damned file.

He sighed heavily.

There was an aching in his heart, a desire for the familiar...the past.

But once something is in the past, it needs to stay in the past. Dead. Like Neil and Arnold.

He recalled VanBuren's words—that Arnold had told Del how to find him. But that was impossible. He had seen Arnold the day he had been shot. The day they had tried to escape. Before Vance had unleashed his henchmen.

It had all started with Vance Paughter.

The bastard!

A few days into their trip to the Nahanni River, Lawrence had discovered that Paughter wasn't quite what he seemed. The young man had acted so excited about being the new intern assigned to him at Bio-Tec. At least that's what Lawrence had thought. If he had guessed that Paughter was leading them into a trap, he would have turned back. But none of them—not even Arnold—had seen it coming. One minute Paughter was the happy-go-lucky research assistant—the next he turned cold. Lethal.

It was Paughter who callously and unemotionally led them into an ambush. Two men with sniper rifles and a machete had been waiting for them at the base of Virginia Falls. When Paughter grabbed the machete, Neil tried to run.

That had been a deadly mistake.

Lawrence cringed, remembering how Neil had pleaded with Paughter mere seconds before the machete came down. *Swoosh!* A fine mist of crimson death had sprayed everywhere, staining their clothes and skin. Neil's blood.

He could still taste it.

"How's she doing?"

Lawrence spun around, surprised to see Justin Blackwell.

For a long moment, the man stood beside him, a strange look on his face as he silently stared through the glass.

"I'll see if you can visit."

Lawrence gaped at the man, speechless.

Why does he care whether I visit Del or not?

Blackwell's eyes locked on his. "I have a daughter too."

There was actually a spark of humanity in the man.

Stunned, Lawrence watched Blackwell walk away and he realized that, for the first time in seven years, he had hope. And if he had hope, then there was hope for Del. And the others.

He pressed a hand against the glass, wishing fervently that he could have stopped her from searching for him. But it was too late. She was already at the Centre.

And so is Vance Paughter.

Jake's hands were tied behind his back.

He stood stock-still while one of the armed guards removed his blindfold. As light penetrated his eyes, his vision slowly cleared and he blinked uncomfortably. Swiveling his head, he took measure of his surroundings.

TJ and Hawk stood on his left. To his right…Peter.

The kid had made it! Thank God!
Finally, he examined his captors.

All three were standing on the opposite side of the room, weapons exposed. Crew Cut was pacing the floor. Beside him, a bald guy whispered frantically to a man with spiked black hair.

Jake let his eyes drift across the room.

It was a boardroom, modestly decorated with polished wood and chrome accents. A large conference table with fifteen chairs, seven down each side and one at the head, was the main centerpiece. It was the kind of room that one would expect to see in a huge corporation in downtown Vancouver—not in the middle of nowhere.

Crew Cut strolled toward them.

"Sit down, please."

Jake cocked his head. "Kind of hard to sit when our hands are tied."

The man jerked his head and his cohorts cut the ropes.

Jake sat down beside Peter. "Where the hell are we?"

The kid shook his head, looking utterly terrified.

"This doesn't make any sense!" Hawk whispered. "I've never seen this building anywhere on the Nahanni Reserve."

Baldy glared at them. "No talking!"

"Maybe we're underground," Jake murmured as soon as the guard was occupied.

Hawk shook his head slightly. "I'd have seen something."

"Unless the government is involved."

"Yeah, I guess. Still, it's...odd."

Jake had to agree. Hawk lived in the area and knew it thoroughly. It would have been next to impossible for him not to notice a complex or office building.

He looked at the guards.

Three men. *Correction!* Three *armed* men.

Crew Cut's cell phone buzzed and Jake strained to hear, but he only caught one word. *"Director."*

He snuck a peek at Hawk and TJ who sat on the opposite side of the table. Hawk's expression was one of suspicious observation. TJ's was just plain grim.

After Crew Cut finished his phone call, he tossed his rifle to Baldy and pulled out a handgun. He aimed it at Jake's head.

"Please remain seated."

"You three," Spike said, pointing to Peter, Hawk and TJ. "Follow us."

Spike and Baldy led them to the door.

Jake caught Hawk's eye.

He knew that the native man was thinking the same thing. If their captors had wanted them dead, they'd have been shot in the woods.

When the door closed behind them, Jake was alone.

With Crew Cut.

"The Director is not happy with you, Dr. Kerrigan."

Jake's brow winged.

"We know everything," the man said, reading his mind.

"Then why don't you fill me in."

"All in good time."

A knock sounded at the door.

A man dressed in a white lab coat stepped into the room. As he headed toward Crew Cut, Jake caught his eye and gasped loudly.

He recognized Del's father immediately.

Dr. Lawrence Hawthorne looked the same as Jake remembered. The same as in the photograph Del had shown them…the photo that had been taken *seven* years ago. Other than appearing as though he hadn't slept in days, Lawrence was in perfect shape. His high forehead was smooth, unlined, and his thick brown hair was touched with golden lights.

Jake frowned, perplexed.

For a man whose hair had been thinning and partially gray, and who always wore prescription bifocals, Del's father was doing exceptionally well.

Without a word, the doctor took the chair directly across from Jake. He leaned forward, about to say something, but an imposing man entered the room.

"Hans," Crew Cut said tensely. "I—"

Hans raised a hand, silencing the guard immediately. Then he unfastened the button of his silver jacket and took a seat at the head of the table.

Jake eyed him suspiciously.

The man had a Nordic—almost albino—appearance, with long, straight white-blond hair, a proud nose and effeminate, full lips. His ice blue eyes glinted, the pupils enlarged, dilated.

He was high on something.

Jake raised a scornful brow. *The Director?*

When the man spoke, his voice was smooth and educated.

"My name is Hans VanBuren. And this is the chief of security. Welcome to the Centre for Enlightened Living."

Jake stared at him in disbelief. "The Centre for Enlightened Living? A place that kidnaps people by gunpoint. What is this—a cult?"

VanBuren pursed his lips. "We do what we have to do."

"What have you done with my friends?"

"They're being taken care of."

Jake didn't like the man's sly tone.

He leaned forward and Crew Cut's rifle snapped up.

"Stand down, Blackwell," VanBuren told the chief of security in a clipped tone. "Everything is under control. Right, Dr. Kerrigan?"

Jake cursed under his breath and eased himself back into the chair, sending Del's father an angry look.

Do something!

"I'm so sorry, Jake," Lawrence whispered sadly. "If I had known that Del would come here, I would've stopped—"

VanBuren cut in. "What shall we do with you all? What do *you* think, doctor?"

Lawrence glanced nervously at the man. "I could use some help in the lab."

"The Specimen Lab, perhaps."

Jake saw the shudder that passed over Lawrence.

"No, with me. I need help with the cell sorter. And we can always use more technicians."

VanBuren's eyes narrowed, but he said nothing.

"Jake can assist me," Lawrence insisted. "And his friends can be trained. They can help with the bots."

Bots?

Jake's curiosity was piqued.

He turned to VanBuren. "How many of my friends are here?"

"All of them."

Jake's throat tightened.

All of them…except Miki. I couldn't save her.

Blackwell strode over to VanBuren. They consulted privately for a moment, then VanBuren shook his head firmly and whispered something in the guard's ear.

Blackwell nudged Jake with the gun. "Stand up."

Rubbing his bruised wrists, Jake stood slowly.

He was led into the hallway, followed by Blackwell, VanBuren and Lawrence. After they crowded into a large elevator, VanBuren flashed an expensive diamond ring and pressed his thumb against a panel. He punched in a code and the elevator began its descent.

"We've set up a cot for you," he said.

"A cot?" Jake said dryly. "I don't really plan on staying."

VanBuren's gaze was sharp as steel. "You don't have a choice, Dr. Kerrigan."

Jake clenched his fists, then relaxed them.

The man was right. At least for now. But damned if he'd sit on his ass and do nothing. Once he found Del and the others, they'd figure out a way to escape.

He glanced at Del's father.

Lawrence's eyes were filled with sorrow and for a moment, he almost looked his age. Almost.

What are you thinking, Lawrence?

SIXTEEN

It's too damned late!

That's what Lawrence was thinking.

He'd have to explain to Del and Jake—and their friends—the mess they had gotten themselves into. They didn't have a clue where they were. He recalled his own naivety, years ago. And the shock of finding out that he wasn't where he thought he was.

When the elevator stopped and the doors opened, he nudged Jake, keeping his voice low. "Tunnel to the left."

They followed VanBuren to the lab.

Once they were inside, the man gave Jake a hard look.

"Your accommodations are a bit cramped, but I'm sure you'll make do."

"How long do you expect to keep us here?" Jake demanded.

VanBuren forced out a laugh. "Well, that depends on the good doctor. Once he gives us the file he's been hiding, you'll all be free to go. Until then…welcome to the future."

The doors closed firmly, sealing off any possibility of escape.

"Welcome to the future?" Jake grunted. "What the hell's that supposed to mean?"

Lawrence placed a finger to his lips. "Let's get you settled."

He motioned Jake to follow.

Entering his living quarters, he immediately noticed that the space had been made even smaller by the addition of an extra cot.

"I guess you're sleeping in here with me, my boy."

He did a quick but thorough search of the room while Jake watched on, confused.

"They haven't gotten around to bugging the place yet. Nothing to hear since Arnold escaped…except maybe my mindless ramblings."

Jake's eyes flashed dangerously. "The lab is bugged?"

"Maybe you should sit down. What I have to tell you is a bit…uh, mind-blowing."

Lawrence strolled toward a counter furnished with a microwave and coffeemaker.

"I'll get us something to drink."

While Jake sat down in a chair, he poured two mugs of coffee and added lots of cream and sugar—just the way he remembered his assistant had liked it.

He handed Jake a mug. "How many people came with you?"

"Eight. Including me and Del."

"Damn! Who are they?"

"Well, there's my assistant, Francesca Baroni. You never met her. She started at Bio-Tec after you...left. Then there's TJ Jackson, Del's ex and Hawk Hawkins, our Nahanni River guide—although I think VanBuren has taken over that role."

Jake took a sip of coffee.

"And the others?" Lawrence asked.

"Gary Ingram, a computer programmer. Peter Cavanaugh, one of Del's students and..." His voice trailed away.

"Who else?"

"Miki, Peter's friend. She...didn't make it."

Lawrence heard the hitch in Jake's voice when he mentioned Miki. The Nahanni River had claimed far too many lives.

Of course, the Director was responsible for most of them.

Watching the man who had been his trusted assistant for five years, Lawrence didn't know what to say. He wasn't usually at his wit's end. But now...where to begin?

"Jake, this is the future."

"Yeah, right."

From the grin on Jake's face, Lawrence knew it wasn't going to be easy.

"You're in the future," he repeated.

Jake stared at him for a long moment.

"You can't be serious!"

Setting the mug on the table, Lawrence stood and paced the floor.

"I'm dead serious, Jake."

"Jesus!"

"When you stepped between the crystals in the cave, it transported you to the future. The crystals are an energized...portal. That's why they phosphoresce. When you crossed between them, your DNA molecules were fragmented and reassembled on the other side."

"What other side?"

"This side. Twenty-six years into the future. It's 2031, Jake."

"But how's that possible?"

"I haven't a clue. All I know is that the crystals aren't man-made."

"So the cave is a natural...time machine?"

"You could say that," Lawrence said, sitting on the bed. "How in the world did you find the cave in the first place?"

"Your friend. Arnold Schroeder."

So Arnold *was* still alive. And back in 2005.

"He's dying," Jake murmured.

That didn't surprise Lawrence one bit.

"Arnold crossed back. VanBuren would've had Blackwell put the bots on self-destruct."

Jake's brow lifted.

"It's a long story, Jake. Where do I begin?"

"How about at the beginning?"

Lawrence cracked a grin.

Jake had always had a great sense of humor. He missed that. Hell, he missed having someone around he liked. *Or trusted.*

Refreshing their coffee, he took a steadying breath.

"Back in 1998, we were on the brink of discovering how to use nanobots to repair human cells. That's what our research was all about at Bio-Tec. We knew that cells could recognize, disassemble, rebuild and reassemble. But now the technology has advanced beyond our wildest dreams. Or nightmares."

"So who's responsible?"

"In the early 1900's, a man named Vance Paughter went in search of gold with the McLeod brothers."

Lawrence looked up. "Have you heard the story?"

"Yeah, the brothers were murdered in their sleep."

"They were found headless. That's the legend, but the real story is that Vance Paughter stole their gold and headed off downriver with it. That's when he stumbled across the cave. He went inside to hide the gold. And you can guess the rest."

"He was transported to the future."

"Not only that, but once he had been on this side for a few years, he noticed that he wasn't aging. When the molecules are reassembled for the first time, it alters the body's entire biophysical composition. Aging is virtually halted."

Lawrence paused, waiting for his comments to sink in.

"So you're saying that we won't age because we were transported here?" Jake asked, stunned. "That's why you look so young! But you said it would only halt aging, not reverse it."

"Paughter was greedy. After over a decade of living in the future without aging, he wanted more money. So he searched old documents to find out where to invest, then crossed back to the past to get more gold."

"And invested it in companies that would eventually become successful," Jake guessed.

"Right. But once he returned to the future he discovered that he began aging again—although much slower than normal."

"What's the rate of aging if you cross to the future twice?"

"It takes about five years for the body to show one year's worth of aging after a second crossing."

"Not bad. Some people would kill for that."

"Paughter and VanBuren certainly have."

There was a moment of silence and Lawrence had to give Jake credit. For a man who had just been told he had been thrown into the future, his composure was impressive.

"You'd think Paughter would've been happy," Jake said. "With an extended life, I mean."

"You'd think. But he wanted to stay young. That's why he brought me here—to head Project Ankh. He heard I'd made some major discoveries. It's all in a file that I would've made public in 2003. The file he needs to make the serum permanent and painless."

Jake flicked an uneasy look at his surroundings. "And you won't give it to him because…"

"Because if I did, the Director, VanBuren and everyone else involved would literally try to take over the world. And they would succeed." Lawrence gave a quick shrug. "Of course they'd also kill me as soon as they got their dirty hands on it."

"But if you had the key to the cure in the past, why didn't Paughter just sift through your research from 2003? Why go through all the trouble to bring you here?"

"That's easy, Jake. I died in 2002."

"What?"

"In 2002, there was an explosion in Bio-Tec's lab. Thirteen people were killed. Myself included. All of my research went up in smoke."

"But there was no explosion at Bio-Tec in 2002!"

"Because I wasn't there to inadvertently cause it. Paughter thought that if he got to me before the explosion, he could get his hands on the file. It's ironic, really."

"What is?"

Lawrence clenched his teeth. "Paughter saved my life."

The thought still choked him.

"Christ!" Jake groaned. "I can't wrap my brain around this whole time travel concept."

Lawrence felt sorry for him. It was a lot to absorb and he still had more to tell him.

"Decades ago, Paughter built the first Centre in the mountains. Beyond the Nahanni River, farther north. Back then it was called FOY Enterprises. Not many people knew it existed, and no one knew its true purpose. Leading scientists were brought in from all over the world to find a serum to duplicate the crystals' initial effect. To stop aging."

Jake raised a brow. "Project Ankh?"

"That's right. When I arrived, everyone who crossed here for the first time was tested extensively. Once we located the molecular anomalies in each cell, we were able to reproduce them and develop a nano-delivered serum. The technology is that much more advanced here. But, as it stands, there are three problems with Project Ankh."

"What are they?"

Lawrence shifted uneasily. "The serum must be administered weekly to those who have crossed twice to the future—otherwise aging resumes. The nanobots are injected along with the serum to rapidly distribute it to each molecule of the body within half an hour. But this makes the injection excruciatingly painful."

"Obviously you've been injected."

Lawrence nodded. "Arnold and I were both injected, numerous times. Which is why I look younger. Paughter wouldn't trust the serum until we tested it first. We were our own lab mice."

"What's the third problem?"

"Over the years, it's become more and more difficult to manufacture because of the base we use. We can't keep up with the demand for the serum. Especially for the ones who've doubled the dose in order to dramatically reverse their age—like Paughter and VanBuren."

"What's the base?"

"Active brain stem cells."

"But that means…" Jake's voice trailed away, horrified.

Lawrence eyed him warily. "We suspected for decades that live brain tissue was a possible solution but we didn't understand how to use it. Now we know that the nanobots can use stem cells to repair damaged cells. Otherwise, waiting for total reconstruction by the nanobots would take too long."

"How'd you know to use brain tissue?"

"Paughter was actually the first to stumble across that link. He went back after the McLeod brothers, a few months after stealing their gold. He sliced off their heads and brought them back here. I don't know if he took them as trophies or if he suspected the crossing might rejuvenate the cells."

"Did it?"

"Temporarily," Lawrence said. "When his scientists studied the brain stem cells, they discovered that they could use them to regenerate other cells. And they realized they needed more brain cells. Of course…you know what that means."

"But that's mass murder!"

"Paughter's been using the past as a hunting ground for stem cells. That's why so many people have gone missing or been found headless along the Nahanni River. That's why they brought Neil's head back."

Neil Parnitski had been a good man. And a decent boss. Lawrence had admired his dedication to the search for the extermination of all disease. It was sadly ironic that a man who devoted his life to finding a cure for diseases like cancer would become a *cure* himself.

Lawrence was suddenly exhausted. "Perhaps we should leave the rest for another day."

"No! I want to know what these assholes have planned for us."

Lawrence knew exactly what the Director wanted. The men would become nothing more than bodiless heads, their brains kept alive in the Specimen Lab by artificial means. And the women?

He swallowed hard. "You and the other men are scheduled to be…specimens. They'll slice off your heads. Paughter uses the women in the Centre as breeding mules, impregnating them. We use the babies' brain cells for the serum."

"But the babies would—"

"Die." Lawrence eyed him, unblinking.

"That's obscene!"

"It's easier than hunting down people along the Nahanni. In this year, no one comes here anymore—unless they're brought here by the Director. The women, including the nurses, are prime real estate. And VanBuren and Paughter have first dibs. Their property is marked by a silver or gold ankh symbol stamped on the women's ID tags."

"Del and Francesca?" Jake whispered.

Lawrence shook out his clenched fists.

The thought of either of those men laying their hands on his daughter made him want to lash out.

"Paughter and VanBuren will rape them. Repeatedly. Unless you all escape."

Jake jumped to his feet. "Where's Del?"

"In one of the recovery rooms on this level."

"She's okay?"

Lawrence heard the concern in his voice and he smiled.

Jake and Del?

"She's fine."

Jake rubbed a hand over his pale face. "Lawrence, why haven't you tried to escape?"

"The Director has unlimited funds. He's the chief investor and he developed a safeguard—just in case anyone tried to steal the serum, or escape to the past with it. Everyone who's been administered the serum has been also injected with a rogue nanobot. It can be set to self-destruct."

Jake threw him a questioning look.

"It'll attack every cell, plus the other bots, Jake. The rogue bot mimes a Progeria-like effect. You'll die a painful death."

"Like your friend."

Lawrence nodded. "Arnold's body is shutting down, cell by cell, and there is nothing that anyone can do for him."

"How did he escape?"

"We stole a passkey, knocked out one of the guards and made it down the tunnel. Arnold crossed first, after Blackwell's men shot at us."

Lawrence paused. "Only one person can cross at a time, Jake. Otherwise, the two sets of DNA will scramble. And you don't want to see what that creates."

"So why didn't you go through, after Schroeder?"

"It takes five minutes for the crystals to recharge on this side. That's how the bastards caught me. I was still waiting."

"What happened then?"

"VanBuren took me down with a bullet to the shoulder. The bots in me rejected the bullet and reconstructed the damaged cells within ten minutes. By then, the bastard had me in handcuffs. If he had hit me in the head...I'd be dead. It's the only way to shut down the bots permanently."

Lawrence stood up suddenly and paced the room.

He felt like a caged animal, ready to lunge at those responsible for imprisoning him. He wanted to rip open their throats.

Especially Paughter's and VanBuren's.

"What's VanBuren's role?" Jake asked.

"He's Paughter's right-hand man. When Paughter reached this side, they hooked up for mutual gain. He needed VanBuren's business connections, VanBuren needed money."

"But he must get more than money out of this."

Lawrence stopped, gritted his teeth. *"Eternal life.* Hans VanBuren is over one hundred and forty years old—same as Paughter. And neither of them looks a day over thirty. Pretty damned good deal, huh?"

He saw the shocked expression on Jake's face.

"It's a lot to take in. I know."

"So Paughter has seniority?" Jake asked after a while.

"Only the Director ranks higher. But no one seems to know who he is, except Paughter and VanBuren."

"You've never met him?"

"Not that I know of. For a long time, I thought the Director was VanBuren."

"Could it be Paughter?"

"Could be. But I haven't seen him in almost a year."

Jake cocked his head. "How'd he know you'd be on the river?"

The answer to that question still filled Lawrence with rage. It was difficult to admit how deceived he had been, how clueless...how trusting.

"There was an intern at Bio-Tec. The one who talked me into coming to the Nahanni River."

"He was connected to the Centre?" Jake asked.

Cold fury rose from the pit of Lawrence's stomach.

"The intern was Vance Paughter."

Del heard her father's voice in the dark.

"Honey, wake up!"

I'm having a nightmare, she told herself. A cruel nightmare. Her father was dead. Dead and buried, her mother had said.

"Come on, Delila! It's time to open those eyes."

But she didn't want to. She knew what she would see if she did. Not her father, but his corpse. Lying in a coffin. The one that she and her mother had picked out. The one they had buried in the ground.

But it had been empty, her mind reasoned.

Yes, but the investigators had said that there was no way her father could've survived without medical care. Because of all the blood he had lost. And where would he have found medical care on the Nahanni River?

Nowhere…

Her father was dead. The voice she heard calling to her was nothing but a trick.

Maybe the Giardia Lamblia had finally struck. After all, she had drunk the water. The dirty parasitic Nahanni River water. Someone had filled her water bottle with it.

My friends wouldn't do that!

But someone had given her the infected water.

And now she was sick…delirious.

That's what's wrong! I'm hallucinating because those damned parasites are in me.

Jesus Christ!

I can feel them invading my body. They're crawling all over me. They're under my skin…burning me.

I'm on fire.

Oh my God!

Get them the hell out of me!

Pleeeeease!

SEVENTEEN

Del opened her eyes cautiously, blinked.

She twisted her head, letting out a relieved breath when she saw peach-colored walls. The room was immaculately clean, barely used. State-of-the-art medical equipment surrounded her. An IV was inserted into her left hand, feeding a clear liquid into her veins.

A strong chemical smell filled the room.

She was in a hospital.

She wrestled with her memories, but the last thing she remembered was passing out on the shore of the Nahanni River. Search and Rescue must have airlifted her out.

The door opened.

A young, redheaded nurse entered the room, her stomach bulging, swollen. She was about six months pregnant and still in her teens.

A child having a child...

Del bit back the surge of jealousy.

"Where am I?"

"Glad to see you're finally awake, Miss Hawthorne."

Actually, it's *Professor*, Del wanted to say. But she didn't.

As the nurse checked the heart monitor, Del noticed an ID tag clipped to the left pocket of her aqua-colored jacket.

Kate O'Leary.

Beneath the name was a silver ankh symbol.

"Where am I?" Del repeated impatiently.

The nurse leaned over, adjusting the IV before speaking. "You're at the Centre. You need to rest for another thirty minutes to promote healing. The doctor is taking very good care of you."

She moved toward the door.

Del frowned. "And which doctor is that?"

The young girl paused and gave her a startled look, the freckles across her nose twitching slightly.

"Why, you're father, of course."

As the door closed behind the nurse, Del swallowed hard.

Her father *was* alive!

To her dismay, her eyelids fluttered. Every inch of her body vibrated with exhaustion. All she wanted to do was sleep.

Give in, Del. Surrender...sleep.

Before she fell into the deep cocoon of oblivion, Jake's face flickered before her.

Where are you, Jake?

Jake sat at Lawrence's computer in the main lab. He stared at the monitor, fascinated by the files and 3-dimensional illustrations that were displayed on the screen. He studied the doctor's work, trying to make sense of it all.

Lawrence sat a few feet away, chugging back a beer.

"One of the perks," he said. "VanBuren wants to keep me mostly happy. Although I suppose the order comes from Paughter or the Director himself."

Jake raised his eyes. "I can't believe we were so close."

So bloody close!

"In 2008, nanotechnology will be in the forefront of all medical findings," Lawrence said. "That's when it becomes a legal, viable option. But anti-aging won't be its mission for a few more years. First it starts with disease annihilation. And that itself will take over a year before it's successful."

He tossed Jake a medical journal dated *January 2009.*

Leafing through it, Jake stopped abruptly at a familiar name.

His!

He read the passage aloud.

"Dr. Jacob Kerrigan, who formerly studied under the esteemed Dr. Lawrence Hawthorne, finds an answer to molecular reconstruction of human cells with the use of nanomachines—microscopic computers..."

Jake was stunned. "Our nanobot project."

"*Your* project," Lawrence said. "Your findings lead to more efficient nanomachines, and that leads to the slow eradication of common diseases, culminating in a final cure for AIDS and cancer."

"My findings? How can that be if I'm here?"

"When I looked back over the archives, I found references to your work. But now...I'm not sure, Jake. By coming here you've changed things. Maybe even the future. I wasn't even sure if that article would still appear in the journal. I simply don't understand how it all works. No one does, not even Paughter."

Jake thought for a moment. "So he wants you to find a way to halt his aging, without having to resort to the painful serum injections. So that he can stay young forever."

"And so he can go back to the past whenever he wants and change things in his favor."

The door to the lab buzzed.

"We have company," Lawrence said.

Escorted by Blackwell's men, TJ, Hawk and Gary stepped into the room. Gary's face was withdrawn and his glasses were mangled.

Spike and Baldy disappeared without a word.

Hawk rubbed his arm. "Good to see you're still here, Jake."

Jake smiled wryly. "Where would I go?"

"Jesus!" TJ blurted. "What's going down, man? Those bastards gave us some kind of shot. Said it was vitamins, but the damned thing hurt so bad it knocked us out."

Jake knew that it was only a matter of time before they came for him. Before he had a deadly nanobot injected into *his* bloodstream.

He motioned the men inside the small room and closed the door.

"This is the only safe place to talk. For now."

TJ's eyebrow arched in shock. "It's bugged out there?"

Jake nodded.

"Do you know what they gave us?" Hawk asked.

"You need to sit down. All of you."

Once introductions were made, Jake told them about the Centre and Paughter. Then he told them about the anti-aging effect of the portal.

Hawk shook his head. "But this is impossible."

"Actually it's not," Jake said. "Each of us has undergone a cellular and molecular metamorphosis."

TJ frowned. "What's that mean, dawg?"

"It means your bodies have stopped aging," Lawrence replied. "When you crossed, your cells were put on hold."

"And the shot?" Gary asked.

"A cellular rejuvenation serum filled with microscopic nanomachines. If you try to cross back, they'll set one of the nanobots to self-destruct. Like they did to my good friend Arnold Schroeder."

Jake saw Gary flinch.

The man pulled up his sleeve and stared in horror at the small bruise on his arm. "Nanobots?"

"Project Ankh," Lawrence said sourly. "Ankh means *life*. With each injection, the serum slows the aging process. Within the next few hours, you'll start to notice tiny changes. Gray hair will regain its color."

Gary frowned. "I don't have much hair."

"It'll start to grow back. Your muscle tissue will become more firm. Wrinkles will start to fade. Hearing and eyesight will improve. And your age will eventually be suspended."

"I don't wanna be young," TJ groaned. "I just wanna go home."

"When we find a way to eliminate the rogue bots, you'll be able to go home."

"And if we can't stop the bots?" Jake asked.

TJ let out a grunt. "We'll get old real fast and die."

"This place must cost billions to keep operational," Hawk said in awe. "How do they afford it?"

"In this year, most of the Canadian government, the military and the wealthy have paid for the serum," Lawrence replied bitterly. "An 'extreme makeover' for the rich, powerful and famous."

"Yeah," Jake muttered. "They get to watch while their family and friends wither away from old age."

"What do they want with all of us?" TJ asked quietly.

The answer to that question terrified Jake.

"Your brains," Lawrence whispered. "All of you, except the women and Jake are expendable. We're low on brain stem cells. We have five expectant mothers who are almost to term, but we only have enough serum for the rest of the month and—"

"How do we get out of here?" Jake cut in.

"I don't know. I don't think there is a way out."

"Then we'll have to find one," Gary said firmly.

Jake noticed the sudden spark in the man's eyes. The promise of a challenge, perhaps, because suddenly the introverted computer programmer from Ottawa looked as though someone had lit a fire under him.

"What are you thinking?" he asked.

Gary bit his lip. "When I first met you all, I told you I was a programmer. Well, that's not entirely true."

"Who the hell are you?"

"I'm a force to be reckoned with."

Shit! Could Gary Ingram possibly be one of Paughter's men?

"Actually, I'm the best programmer and hacker in Canada."

Jake's head snapped up. "You're a hacker?"

"That's a spy, right?" TJ asked.

Gary flashed a wide grin. "You could say so. I subcontract out to the Canadian government and the military. There isn't a program I haven't been able to crack. I've even hacked into Homeland Security."

"What the hell are you doing here?" Jake asked, his eyes narrowing.

"This trip was my once a year vacation. The only time I get to unwind."

"Well, it's just turned into a working vacation, Gary. What do you have in mind?"

"First thing I need to do is get into the Centre's security system and see if we can just walk out the doors. Of course, the guards will present a challenge. I'll check the video surveillance system. Once I figure out how to jam it or loop it, I'll look for building plans. Floor plans, maintenance, air, heating and exhaust vents."

"Don't forget, the lab's bugged," Lawrence warned them. "Everything you do out there will be on surveillance and audio."

"Whisper mode," Gary winked.

The man was certainly in his element around computers, Jake noted. Especially once they left Lawrence's room and ventured out into the main lab.

"Jake," Lawrence said loudly, for benefit of the audio surveillance. "I'll find Hawk and TJ something to do. Then I'll show you the AQUA-1250. It's the newest cell sorter. We're having some problems installing the software so it's not online yet."

Gary sat down at one of the computers. "I'll look at it—if you can show me how to operate this thing."

The monitor was sleek and compact, and currently disabled. The only other object on the desk was a thin slab of metal. No sign of a keyboard.

"Tap the screen in the center," Lawrence said. "Two times."

Gary did as he was instructed and the monitor lit up, along with the metal slab.

"It's a touch keyboard," Lawrence said, leaning down to demonstrate. "See? Rest your wrists on the front edge and the keys light up. Just type like you normally would. To stop it from recording keystrokes, just take your hands away and the keyboard shuts down. The monitor is also a touch screen. It's voice activated too."

The programmer's eyes widened.

Gary was in heaven, and Jake only hoped the man remembered where they were.

"Work fast, Gary. We don't have much time."

Lawrence showed TJ and Hawk to a long stainless steel counter where he instructed them to use an eyedropper to place a small amount of serum onto several slides for testing. After a few minutes he returned to Jake's side, then led him over to a sleek piece of equipment.

The future cell sorter.

"The technology's unbelievable!" Jake said, awed.

The AQUA-1250 had multiple compartments and functions, accomplishing ten times the job in a quarter of the time it took the machines back in 2005. It even recognized cancerous cells.

"Camera to your right," Lawrence whispered.

Jake studied the security camera perched high on the wall near the door.

"Dr. Hawthorne," Gary said suddenly. "I think I see the problem with the cell sorter."

"Can you fix it?"

"I think so but it'll take me about a couple of hours."

Lawrence hesitated as if he were thinking about it.

Finally he nodded. "Okay, go ahead."

Jake released a pent-up breath.

Hopefully their plan would work and Gary would have enough time to get into the Centre's system before security started wondering what he was doing.

"We have to find your other friends," Lawrence murmured, rubbing his strained eyes. "Peter and Francine, was it?"

"Francesca."

Jake hoped that she was all right. Lawrence had no news of the woman. No one seemed to know where she was. Yet, according to VanBuren she was in the Centre...somewhere.

Francesca was a hellcat, he mused. He pitied the men who came up against her. Blackwell and his armed guards would be no threat to her and her fiery Italian temper.

Peter, on the other hand, was just a kid. A smart, young, resourceful kid who would be better put to use than killed. The boy certainly wouldn't be a threat to Paughter or his men. If they were smart they'd try to recruit him. Peter was young enough to be scared and naïve enough to think he had no other choice.

Jake thought of Del.

Thank God she was safe.

His feelings for Lawrence's daughter surprised him, but he wouldn't deny them. Not any longer. He ached to see her, to be reassured that she was all right.

I'm going to get you out of here, Del.

He wished to God that he had never laid eyes on the future.

It's no place for any of us. It's just an accident...waiting to happen.

And according to Lawrence, it had already happened.

EIGHTEEN

Restless and annoyed, Del stabbed the button beside her bed for the fifth time. Someone had better start answering her questions. The pregnant nurse had been no help at all. Other than telling her that her father was somewhere nearby.

Why haven't you come to see me, Dad?

She heard a sharp, metallic click.

The door opened and Kate's anxious young face peered inside.

"Need something?"

Del scowled. "I want to see my dad."

The girl threw a furtive look over her shoulder, then darted into the room and closed the door.

"I'll let him know. I'm sure he'll visit you when he's able. Why don't you have a nap or read a magazine?"

Del straightened, walking toward the redheaded nurse whose belly seemed even larger than earlier.

"Can you tell me why my door is kept locked?"

Kate stiffened. "We don't want you wandering the halls. You might hurt yourself."

Del's eyes drifted to the girl's stomach.

What was it like to feel life growing inside, to be a creator of another living, breathing soul?

Too bad she'd never know.

"When are you due?"

"Next month."

Kate was farther along than Del had realized.

"Your husband must be very excited."

The girl flinched and fingered her ID tag.

Del's brow lifted. "Boyfriend, then."

Kate's demeanor underwent a rapid transformation. She drew herself up to her full height, a bare five feet, and examined Del with cool eyes.

Turning toward the door, she wrenched it open and tossed an angry look over her shoulder.

"I was chosen by a great man. And it's an honor."

With that, Kate slipped from the room.

Del was baffled. *What the hell is going on?*

A sharp rap on the door signaled the arrival of someone new, and she held her breath, praying that it was her father.

It wasn't.

A pale-faced man entered the room, his shoulder-length blond hair tied back in a ponytail. He wore a silver jacket over sleek, black dress pants. He had the air of money and power.

Del disliked him immediately.

"Are my friends here?" she demanded.

When the man smiled, it was the kind of smile that attempted to be genuine, but failed. It didn't quite thaw his unfriendly, glacier blue eyes.

"They're being taken care of."

She glared at him. "I want to see my dad. Now."

"All in due time, my dear."

The man's voice was vaguely familiar.

"How are you feeling, Delila?"

"I feel great. Ready to get out of here, Mr...uh..."

The man's eyes narrowed. "Call me Hans."

"Hans," she said, ignoring the sudden bad taste in her mouth. "I expect to see my dad today. After that we'll be on our way."

Hans perched on the edge of her bed.

"That could be arranged. But first your father has to give us some information."

"What kind of information?"

The man sighed heavily. "It seems he's misplaced a file somewhere. One that is vital to our research here at the Centre. If he gives it to us, we'll let you go. All of you."

"Including my dad?"

Hans rose slowly, moving toward the door.

"Here's the deal, Delila. You convince your father to give us the file and I'll let him go...home."

"How do I know I can trust you?"

The man's shoulders twitched slightly. "I'll give you something as a sign of good faith. What do you want? Other than your father, of course."

Del gulped in a breath.

What did she want? That was simple. She wanted the one thing that made her feel safe.

"I want Jake Kerrigan, here in my room...for one night."

The words were barely out of her mouth before she realized how they sounded.

Apparently Hans had the same thought.

"Now what would you two be doing all night long?"

Revolted by the man's lewd insinuation, she crossed her arms and thought of Jake. She had asked for him because he was the one person who might be able to figure a way out of this mess. The one person she and her father both trusted. She had no intention of doing anything with him. Certainly not what Hans was thinking.

But, hell! Let the asshole think what he wants.

"Just bring him here. Then I'll talk to my dad."

With a nod, Hans turned and walked out of the room.

She flopped into a chair.

Bored and lethargic, she flipped through the magazines stacked on the table beside her. She had never even heard of them before. Oddly, the pages were filled with advertisements for beauty products, yet there were no wellness articles, no health tips.

None of the normal *How to Get Rid of Acne* or *PMS in Teens*.

Frowning, she dropped the copy of *Beauty & Brains* on the table.

The magazine opened automatically to a photo of a man in a white lab coat. According to the article, he was working on an experimental drug called *Project Ankh*.

Examining the photo, she let out a startled gasp.

The man in the lab coat was someone she knew.

Her father.

Without warning, the door to her room swung open.

Jake stumbled inside and the sight of him made her eyes water. As soon as the door slammed and the lock clicked into place, she flung herself into his arms.

"I thought you were dead, Jake."

"So did I."

"Where are we? What is this place?"

He took her hand and led her to the chair. Then he began pacing the floor, a grim expression on his face.

"Del, there's no easy way to tell you this. It's 2031."

2031?

"You mean…the year?"

Gingerly, she picked up the magazine.

Her mouth opened and a strangled sound rose from the back of her throat as she read the date on the far left corner of the cover.

February 2031.

She listened in stunned silence while he told her about the crystals in the cave. When he reached the part about Vance Paughter, Hans VanBuren and the mysterious Director of the Centre, her eyes narrowed.

"I've met VanBuren. He's an arrogant prick. What about this Director fellow?"

Jake shook his head. "Not even your father knows who he is. It's not VanBuren, because he mentioned the Director."

"So it could be this Paughter guy. Have you met him?"

"No. And your father hasn't seen him in a year, which is peculiar considering Paughter is a bigwig in the Centre."

"I thought I was in a hospital," she murmured.

He gave her a look that said he wished to God she *was*.

"This is the Centre for Enlightened Living," he said dryly.

She froze. "CEL!"

"What?"

She told him about Schroeder's code, about his strange message.

"CEL = DEATH!" she said. "But what's it mean?"

Jake raked a hand through his hair. "They're producing a Fountain of Youth serum. And selling it on the black-market to the highest bidders—including politicians and world leaders."

Del hissed in a breath.

The article in the magazine!

"Project Ankh," she said softly.

"They injected me before they brought me here to your room, Del. It's agony. They think your father has the formula for perfecting the serum. For making it painless, permanent. That's one of the reasons why they kept you separate from us. They want to use you to get to the file. Your father told me you were injected too, while you were unconscious."

She shivered, vaguely recalling something…eyes.

"So I have a self-destruct bot running loose in my blood?"

When he nodded, her gaze shifted to her arm, half-expecting to see something move beneath the skin.

"Where's everyone else, Jake?"

"The guys are back in the lab with your father." His eyes darted around the room and he lowered his voice. "There's a camera on the wall above the door. Maybe audio too."

Del's gaze shifted slightly and she saw the tiny flickering red light on a small silver eye.

Standing, she moved toward the bed.

"Scoot over and lie on your side, Jake. Away from the door."

His brow arched slightly and a half-smile formed on his lips.

"Just do it," she sighed.

Climbing onto the bed, she stretched beside him, facing him so that their mouths were almost touching.

Whoever was spying on them would assume they were kissing.

"My, my," Jake whispered. "Aren't you crafty?"

She rolled her eyes at him, trying hard not to laugh.

"Ok, Kerrigan. Give me an update."

His arm curled over her, pulling her closer.

"Don't want the camera to see your lips moving," he said with a grin. "Unless they're moving on mine."

"Shut up, Jake!"

She snuggled closer, just in case.

It didn't take long before she knew everything, including the fact that Gary turned out to be a government hacker. She was relieved to hear that the other men were safe, but she was upset that no one had a clue where Francesca was. When he told her that Miki had drowned, her mouth quivered and she gripped his hand tightly.

Jake's gaze was intense. "Del, we have to get out of here!"

"I know."

"We might not make it…the security is pretty tight."

She touched a finger to his lips, shushing him.

She didn't want to talk anymore. She was exhausted and scared. She was drained from living with a disease that wanted to kill her. Based on how awful she had felt the last few days, her remission was over. She wanted, *needed*, to feel alive.

She leaned close and pressed her lips against his.

She wanted to lose herself. Forget how damned afraid she was. Forget VanBuren, Paughter, the Director—everything.

Her lips coaxed his.

"Del, wait a minute."

She kissed him harder, flipping him over on his back and climbing on top. Briefly taking her lips off his, she quickly peeled off her shirt. Then, unhooking her bra, she tossed it on the floor.

"Del—"

She silenced him again with her mouth.

When would Jake learn to shut up?

Jake tried to push her away, but she clung to him and she slid out of her jeans before she could change her mind.

He opened his mouth. "Uh, you—"

"Could you please stop talking?"

Wearing only a sheer pair of panties, she straddled him, smiling triumphantly.

"One of us is wearing too many clothes. And it isn't me."

"Wait!"

She was tired of waiting.

She bent down, bit his lower lip. Then she devoured him.

His hot hands slid along her ribs and she gasped at the contact.

"I thought you wanted me," she moaned when his head jerked away. "What the hell is your problem?"

"The camera!"

She stiffened.

Crap! She had forgotten about the damned camera.

He gave her a wicked smile. "You're giving them quite a show. Not that they mind, I'm sure. But I'd prefer to keep this between you and me."

Keeping her back to the camera, she slid to one side.

It was humiliating to be baring it all in front of VanBuren and his security hounds. The thought made her sick.

Jake sat up and inched off the bed.

In one swift movement, he tore off his shirt and flung it toward the camera. He gave a loud grunt when it settled over the lens. Then he stalked toward the bed, his blue eyes blazing with desire, and before she could blink, she was pinned under him.

"Jesus, Jake!"

His mouth came down, hard, impatient. His hands moved over her body possessively, sliding sensuously to her breasts. He caressed them until they throbbed with pleasure. Her body was on fire. Every inch of her craved for his kiss, his touch.

"Jake…"

His mouth greedily tasted her, grazing her throat, her jaw…lower. He returned to her lips and his touch softened, deepened. It became honey sweet.

She was lost.

This might be their only chance.

That single thought spurred her on and made her almost manic with desire. She felt insanely euphoric, drugged. She didn't usually throw herself at a man.

But Jake wasn't just any man. He was fate.

And if this was their only time together she wanted it to be something to remember—hospital room and security cameras aside.

He sighed in her ear. "This is crazy."

"I'm crazy," she said, locking her gaze on him. "About you."

"I've been crazy about *you* since day one."

"I know."

She fisted his hair as he kissed a trail, lower.

"One night, Jake. This may be all we've got."

His mouth found her breast and she gasped.

"So you'd better make it good."

NINETEEN

Hans was edgy. Even an early morning romp with an overeager clerk in the mailroom hadn't relieved the pressure he felt building up inside.

He thought about his partner.

Vance Paughter had been away awhile. Now he wanted a complete status report. That meant a face-to-face meeting.

And that made Hans nervous.

Last time they saw each other, they had both looked about forty.

Hans anxiously paced across the hardwood floor, his shoes clicking as he moved. Then he stopped in front of the mirror and flexed his arms.

"Now you look thirty. He's not going to like this one bit."

He suspected that Vance kept his age roughly around forty, so that Del and the others would trust him. The man was cunning and resourceful. A year ago, he had insisted on doing the job himself.

Whatever it took to get the doctor to give up the file, he had said.

Hans flicked a glance at the clock.

In five minutes, he'd head to Vance's three-room suite. It was almost as large as the main floor of an average home. Sixteen hundred square feet of luxury. Situated directly above the entrance to the cave, it had a magnificent view of the Nahanni River.

He frowned, miffed.

Perhaps it was time to ask the Director for a bigger office, maybe his own suite. After all, he deserved it. Especially after everything he had done for the Centre in Vance's absence.

He strode into the hallway, locking the door securely behind him.

Faith peeked up, but he ignored her and turned down the main corridor toward Vance's suite.

Taking a deep breath, he knocked hesitantly on the door.

"Enter!"

When he stepped inside, Hans was greeted by what appeared to be an empty room—empty except for a few pieces of expensive mahogany furniture. A few feet away, a large round table and eight unoccupied high-backed chairs blocked his way.

He swiftly closed the door and weaved past the chairs, coming to an abrupt stop in the middle of the room.

He frowned. *Where's Vance, for Christ's sake?*

Then he saw him.

At the far end of the room, Vance Paughter sat in a leather chair, the top of his head barely visible. He faced the floor-to-ceiling window that stretched across the entire back wall. Above him, an atomic mushroom cloud of cigarette smoke hung suspended—a cloud of doom.

"I see the place is still in one piece, Hans," Vance said without turning.

"Everything is as it should be."

"Sit down and give me a verbal report."

Hans pulled out a chair and when it squeaked, he cringed. Then he sat quickly and opened the laptop that was sitting on the table in front of him.

"Specimen report first."

A smoke ring lifted into the air.

Hans glared at the back of Vance's head.

The man's arrogant demeanor ticked him off. After all, they were partners. Hans deserved some measure of respect. Unquestionably, speaking to the back of Vance's head wasn't his idea of a face-to-face. But he wasn't about to say anything. Vance would find out in due time just how exceptional he had performed.

Hans hid a scowl and tapped the screen, bringing up the latest report. "Specimens are down to three."

"Three? Why the hell so few?"

"W-well, uh…a couple didn't make it. We had to terminate early."

"What about the reserves?"

"The demand has increased the past three months because of our government friends. President Robertson just came on board—with his entire family."

"Goddamn Americans!"

"The good news is that Robertson paid enough to order five more nanomachine assemblers and three cell sorters," Hans said proudly. "But we need more specimens. We're down to two adults and they're already three-quarters depleted."

A detailed report flashed on the monitor and he listed off the statistics. Then he revealed his personal pride and joy.

"Pregnancies total eighteen, with five near their due dates. Four are mine. We have three babies—"

"Young specimens!"

Smoke erupted above Vance's head.

"Yes, young specimens," Hans corrected, grinding his teeth. "They're being processed. Two husks are in the morgue."

Husks. Another one of Vance's fancy terms.

"Good. Bot report?"

Hans wiped his sweaty palms on his thighs. "We had a minor issue with the new nanobots. Some of them malfunctioned and set off the rogue bots. We lost a man in accounting and three lab workers. We're still waiting on an assembler and two cell sorters, compliments of our military."

"And Colonel Mandrusiak?"

"He's been patient—so far. But he'd like to start implementing the rogue bots over in Pakistan. He still plans to use them to infiltrate the water system, wipe out Pakistan completely."

Vance grew silent.

Hans impatiently drummed his fingers on the table.

"What are your plans for our guests? I'd like first dibs on Francesca Baroni."

No answer.

"Vance?"

"Francesca and Del, we can use. And Jake Kerrigan. But the rest? You know what to do with them."

Hans frowned. "I'm not sure it's wise to have them all together. What if they try to escape?"

A snicker erupted from behind the chair.

"If they try, I'll know about it. Won't I?"

Vance rose abruptly from the shadows and turned slowly.

Speechless, Hans stifled a gasp with a quivering hand.

"How do I look?"

Vance wore a ripped Edmonton Oilers t-shirt and jeans that had seen better days. He was younger than Hans—maybe twenty. His smooth face was glowing, youthful. His blue eyes twinkled with mischief, as if he were privy to some private joke.

"You look…young," Hans said, stunned.

He had to give his partner credit.

Vance Paughter was brilliant. He had infiltrated Del's group in the guise of a kid, barely a man. One with an innocence that would never be suspect.

"Meet *Peter Cavanaugh*," Vance said.

Hans couldn't resist a smile. "Nice to meet you…*Peter*."

"Ah, it's great to be home!"

Vance—aka *Peter*—flopped in the chair across from Hans.

Clasping his hands behind his head, he stared up at the ceiling, reminiscing.

"I was Del's protégé for the past year. Even faked a crush to get close to her. And of course I was one of the first to volunteer to help her look for *Daddy*."

"I thought you were going to stop her from coming here."

Vance shrugged. "I tried to sabotage things in the beginning. I got rid of a canoe, stole Del's pills, gave her unfiltered water. But then the Director made me change my mind."

"Why?"

"Two reasons, I suppose. The Director realized Del would be more useful here. And we'd get Jake Kerrigan."

Hans gave him a blank look.

"You read the article we found, Hans. Jake is very close to completing Lawrence's research. If we can't get Lawrence to tell us where the file is, at least we'll have Jake."

"You were right, Vance. You said Schroeder would head straight for his daughter."

Vance let out a dissatisfied sigh. "Yeah, but I wasn't expecting him to barge in while she was tutoring me. For a second I thought he recognized me. Thank God he only had eyes for Del."

"And now we have something to hold over Hawthorne's head."

"Exactly. How is he, anyway?"

Vance took a moment to study Hans while he waited for the man to answer. What he saw made him furious. It was obvious where their supply had gone.

"The doctor is still his stubborn, old—"

"*Hans?*" Vance murmured, his voice deadly quiet. "You've been dipping into the sauce."

Speechless, the pasty-faced man across from him flinched.

"You know the limit, Hans. It's there for a reason."

"I apologize, Vance. I-I'll cut back. I promise. It's just that—"

Vance eyed him sharply. "No excuses! I don't envy you. You'll have to deal with the Director."

He hid a smug smile when he saw Hans flinch.

"Meanwhile," he continued. "*Peter* will join his friends. Del and the others haven't seen me for a while. Eventually, they'll wonder why I was separated from them and they'll become suspicious. Then again, they haven't seen Francesca either."

"Why even bother keeping up the charade?"

"If they're plotting anything, they'll share it with me. If Hawthorne's told them where the file is, they'll share that as well. We'll plan a reunion in an hour."

Hans licked his lips nervously. "And the Director…"

"Will see both of us in the morning," Vance finished.

He allowed his thoughts to drift while he gazed toward the window. He was finally home, and the Nahanni had never looked better. 2005 had been so far out of his element—a rat race of stress and chaos.

He let out a relieved sigh.

Thank God! No more studying or boring classes.

Sure, he had a knack for anthropology, but the homework was a killer. It had totally cramped his style.

He stole a peek at Hans.

The Director would not be pleased.

It was mid-morning, and Jake's stomach was making a racket—probably more from nerves than from hunger. He wondered what the others were going to say when he returned to the lab. What would Lawrence say?

How does he feel, knowing that I spent the night with Del?

An image of naked limbs and hot, soft skin flickered before him.

Pushing the scintillating memory from his mind, he followed Blackwell to the lab. The man stepped aside and waved him in. Then the door slid shut between them.

Lawrence, TJ and Hawk stood around Gary, watching something on the monitor.

"Good morning," Jake said self-consciously.

Lawrence gave him a curt nod, then disappeared into his room.

"They moved us in," Hawk said, pointing to the three extra cots in the far corner.

Jake nodded, relieved.

It would be much easier to escape if they were already together.

"Hey, man!" TJ said with a grin. "Pulled an all-nighter, huh?"

Jake didn't want to discuss his night with Del—especially with her ex-boyfriend.

He glanced over his shoulder. "How's Lawrence?"

"Ah, he's fine, dawg. Just doesn't want you to hurt his little girl."

Jake sighed. "I'd never hurt her."

"I know, man."

There was an awkward silence.

"Ever see the movie The Notebook?" TJ asked hesitantly.

Jake raised a mocking brow, but said nothing.

"Hey! I'm a movie buff, Jake. What can I say?"

"Yeah, but...*chick flicks?*"

"They're even better if you bring the *chick*," TJ grinned. "Anyway, the two main characters in The Notebook are destined to be together, but they've got to go through all sorts of shit first."

Jake cocked his head, amused. "So, you're saying that Del and I are destined to go through shit?"

Before TJ could answer, the door behind them creaked open and Lawrence reappeared, throwing Jake a bothered look.

"Yeah, dawg," TJ whispered. "Unless *he* kills ya first."

Jake swore under his breath, then headed straight for Lawrence.

"We've got to talk."

"So, you saw Del," Lawrence said calmly, one eye pressed to a microscope. "How is she?"

Jake kept his voice low. "She's fine, Lawrence. Just like you said. I filled her in on everything. Lawrence, I...uh...think you should know that I—"

"I don't need details, Jake. Just tell me, do you really care about her? And do you plan on sticking around?"

"Of course I do. On both counts...providing we get out of here."

"Del's had enough people disappear in her life, Jake. Not many dealt with her MS in a positive way—including her mother. Del needs stability, not a careless fling."

Jake's jaw flinched. "You know me better than that. I don't care about the MS. We'll deal with that as it comes. But I do care about Del, and I honestly don't have a clue what's going to happen when we get back. *If* we get back."

Lawrence's expression lightened. "I'm sure things will work out the way they're meant to. Now that we've got that settled, Jake, perhaps you should go see what Gary's working on."

He walked away.

Confused, Jake eyed him suspiciously.

Lawrence hadn't socked him in the eye, and to tell the truth that scared the hell out of Jake. Shit, if it had been *his* daughter...

He strolled toward the wall lined with heavy equipment where TJ and Hawk stood fiddling with the cell sorter. Neither had a clue what they were doing.

But Gary certainly did.

He sat at the main computer, tapping furiously at the keyboard.

Jake grinned. "Isn't this where I left you last night?"

"Getting the cell sorter online took longer than I expected. I'm rechecking the, uh...settings."

"Getting anywhere?"

"Keep your voice really low, Jake. I haven't been able to jam the audio. If I do, they'll suspect something."

"Mind if I observe?"

"Not at all."

Jake sat down and eyed the monitor. It flickered, then cleared and he hissed in a breath.

Gary had tapped into the security camera in the lab.

Without warning, the camera zoomed in and Jake discovered that he was staring at his own back.

"Blackwell's trying to see what we're doing!" he hissed.

Gary nodded. "Here's the camera for the hallway."

He brought up a split screen so they could monitor four areas of the Centre. The elevator, the hallway, the lab and a room with pale peach walls.

Jake knew that room.

"Don't worry," Gary smirked. "Your shirt hid everything."

Jake felt an awkward blush heat his face as he stared at the lower right screen…at Del. Curled up in a chair, she nibbled on a sandwich while reading a magazine, as though she didn't have a care in the world. He studied the curve of her face, noting the tired shadows under her eyes.

He smiled, remembering the night before.

Neither of them had slept much.

"Someone's coming!" Gary warned.

Jake eyed the upper left screen.

VanBuren stepped out of the elevator. Someone was standing behind him, just out of view of the camera.

"If we had audio, we'd be able to hear."

The person in the elevator stepped out into the hall.

Peter Cavanaugh.

Jake stifled a curse. "Where are they taking him?"

"They aren't taking him anywhere. Look at his hands."

Peter was walking beside VanBuren, looking as comfortable as if he had been invited to dinner. He walked freely, talking casually. No handcuffs, no armed guards.

Gary gnawed his lower lip. "They seem pretty chummy, Jake."

Like old buddies.

On the monitor, Jake saw a young pregnant girl pass the men in the hall. Peter grinned at her lecherously and VanBuren muttered something in his ear. They were joined by the chief of security. When Peter said something to both men, Blackwell shook his head emphatically.

Jake tried to make sense of Peter's appearance, but what he saw seemed impossible. Contemptible. The kid's behavior pointed to something much more insidious. Peter was involved with the Centre, with Paughter and VanBuren …*with murder.*

"Hey, are you two done yet?" Lawrence called, moving closer.

"We've run into a snag," Jake answered calmly.

"What's the problem?"

Lawrence leaned toward the screen just as VanBuren drew back his fist and slammed it into Peter's face. The kid stumbled against the wall, then he grinned.

"That's Peter Cavanaugh," Gary said in a low voice. "Del's

anthropology student."

"He's also part of the Centre," Jake added.

Lawrence shook his head sharply. "Your friend isn't *part* of the Centre. He *is* the Centre."

"What?"

Lawrence stared at them. "Peter Cavanaugh is an anagram."

"An anagram for what?" Jake asked.

"For *Vance A. Paughter.*

"They're coming," Gary said.

He shut down the computer while Jake struggled to absorb the fact that Peter was a traitor. A traitor who had been close to Del for a year. Someone who had known all along that her father was still alive.

Bastard!

The lab doors opened.

VanBuren stepped inside, calmly removed a pistol from his jacket pocket and flicked it at Lawrence.

"Doctor Hawthorne, I'll take you to see your daughter now."

Jake exchanged a knowing look with Lawrence. Peter/Paughter couldn't have the doctor around for their reunion. Because Lawrence would recognize him.

Immediately after they left, Jake led everyone to Lawrence's room.

"What's going down?" TJ asked as soon as the door closed.

"Peter's not who we thought," Jake said briskly.

Hawk raised a brow. "What are you talking about?"

"The kid we knew as Peter Cavanaugh…is really Vance Paughter."

"What the f—" TJ bit back the curse with an angry grunt.

When Jake told them what he had seen on the security camera, they were shocked. TJ paced the room, clenching and unclenching his fists, while Hawk stared mutely at the floor. Gary slumped on the bed, depressed.

"Del's the one he wants," Jake said, gritting his teeth. "He can use her to get to her father's file. And if Lawrence gives it to them…"

"Then the future is doomed," Hawk said quietly.

Gary nodded. "And we're all dead."

"The little bastard!" TJ fumed. "When I first heard he had a crush on Del, I wanted to kick his puny little ass. Now I want to—"

"Easy does it," Jake cut in. "We need to buy Gary some time. If Paughter finds out we know, he'll have us separated. We have to put on a front and welcome *Peter* back into the fold. Got it?"

"That ain't gonna be easy. I'm not sure I can, Jake."

"You have to, TJ. You have to greet him like he's still one of us. And whatever you do, don't tell him anything about Gary being a hacker. If he knew, he'd see to it that Gary's brains were used in the next batch of serum."

Beside him, Gary flinched.

Jake led them toward the door. "We'd better go back out or someone'll wonder what we're doing in here. And remember, don't let on that you know who he is. He's just *Peter*."

Half an hour later, Peter entered the lab.

Paughter, Jake reminded himself.

Escorted by Blackwell, the kid dropped into a chair, groaning loudly. His face was swollen and an angry welt had erupted under his right eye where VanBuren's ring had caught him. Blackwell moved beside him and Peter jerked his head away, as if he were terrified of the man.

"Peter!" Jake said in mock concern. "Thank God you're okay."

I'll rip you a new asshole later.

"I thought I'd never see you guys again," the kid moaned. "They kept me locked in a room."

"What happened to your face, dawg?" TJ asked.

Paughter tossed Blackwell a scornful look. "I wasn't walking fast enough."

Jake pressed a cold, wet cloth against the kid's face.

"Christ! What's on this, Jake?"

"Just some alcohol. Wouldn't want that to get infected."

Paughter tossed the cloth aside. "They gave me some kind of injection. Said it would make me heal faster."

Suddenly, a red light flashed outside in the hallway and a loud piercing alarm cut through the air.

Everyone jumped—including Paughter.

Blackwell grabbed the kid's arm. "That's enough visiting for one day. We can use you someplace else."

Jake caught the anxious look that Paughter flicked Blackwell as he was dragged from the room. At least the kid had the sense to make it look good. Kicking and screaming, he fought with Blackwell, even managing to get in a few good punches.

Jake gritted his teeth.

"Maybe they'll beat the hell out of each other. Save me the trouble," he muttered to TJ.

"What's happening?" Hawk hissed.

"I don't know. But we'd better find out."

Gary moved quickly, and within seconds he had hacked back into the Centre's security program. Searching the different cameras in the Centre, he quickly discovered the problem.

"It's Francesca."

Jake's eyes were immediately glued to the monitor.

On it, Francesca was stumbling down a hallway in her bra and panties. VanBuren stormed after her, struggling to fasten his pants.

Hawk gasped. "Oh, shit! He's trying to…"

"Rape her," Jake finished. "The bastard's got her trapped."

They saw Francesca stop dead in her tracks. Twisting, she lunged at VanBuren and clawed at his face. Within minutes, he had her backed into a corner. She was screaming…begging.

Jake's eyes widened as VanBuren grabbed Francesca's arm. In a flash, the man violently ripped off her bra and backhanded her across the face. Her head snapped sharply to the side. Then she collapsed on the floor.

She didn't move.

VanBuren hovered over her, his back to the camera. He swiftly dropped his pants and for a long moment he simply stared at her. It was impossible to tell if he was speaking…or waiting. Then his body twitched and his head arched.

"What's he doing?" Jake whispered.

TJ scowled. "The five knuckle shuffle."

They watched in horror as VanBuren moved toward Francesca.

Jake jumped to his feet, swearing loudly.

"Shut it off!"

He stalked into Lawrence's room and slammed the door.

♀WENTY

Del was ecstatic when her father entered her room. She couldn't believe how vibrant he looked, how young and handsome. In truth, he looked ten years younger than the last time she had seen him.

Jake was right.

Project Ankh *was* a success.

She wrapped both arms around her father, comforted by his familiar embrace. He kissed the top of her head, then hugged her so hard she couldn't breathe.

"Ok, you can let go now, Dad. Before you smother me."

Sending her a rueful look, her father stepped back and ran a restless hand through his hair. Deliberately, he flipped his middle finger at the surveillance camera.

"They're watching us, Del."

"Yeah, probably listening too," she said. "*Bastards!*"

"I'll second that."

He hugged her again.

"When are we getting out of here, Dad?" she whispered.

"You won't be here long—neither will your friends. Thanks for coming after me, honey. Your heart's in the right place. Remember that.*"

"They think I have the cure but I don't," he said in a normal voice. "This secret file they're after is a figment of the Director's imagination."

Del gave him a startled look.

Is there really no file, Dad, or are you saying this for show?

He released her and gave her a wink.

"So, Del. How are things in 2005?"

"Grab a chair," she said. "We've got a lot to talk about."

Desperate to quell her fear and unable to talk about escape plans, she filled her father in on the last seven years. She told him about the investigation into his disappearance. Afterward, she described his empty-casket funeral and the celebration of life that his old poker buddies had thrown in his honor.

"How's your MS, Del?"

She stared at the wall.

Should she lie?

"I was in remission for over a year."

"When did it start again?"

She shifted uncomfortably. "The last few days. But I'm on a new medication."

She paused. "Or I would be if I hadn't lost my pills. I'll have to go on injections when I get back. *If* I get back."

"Have faith," he said, squeezing her hand. "How's your mom?"

"Remarried." *To an asshole.*

He smiled. "Probably less than a year after I was presumed dead."

Her lip curled in disdain. "Four months actually."

"So she's happy?"

"They divorced a year later. Now she's married to Ken."

"Is he a good guy?"

"Yeah, good and drunk most days. He's a lecherous pig."

Her father's expression was sad. "Your mother deserves better."

Del gazed at him for a long moment. "She *had* better."

"And Jake, how'd you find him?"

"Through Arnold's journal."

"That journal," her father chuckled. "Arnold would write in that thing practically every day, making notes of our formulas and keeping track of events."

Leaning forward, he dropped his voice even lower. "How the heck did you decode it?"

"Miki Tanaka," she replied. "The girl who drowned. She was a classmate of Peter's, my—"

She caught sight of her father's face. "What?"

"Del…"

His expression turned deadly serious as he rose and summoned her to the small sink. Under the guise of washing the dishes from her lunch, he ran the water.

She gave him a questioning glance.

He kissed her cheek.

"They can't hear us if we make some noise, Del."

"What's going on?"

He handed her a glass to dry. "I, uh, don't know how to tell you this, but…*Peter* is not who you think he is."

She gawked at him. "He's one of my students, Dad. Just a sweet, shy kid."

"His name isn't Peter Cavanaugh. It's Vance A. Paughter. We haven't seen him here much over the past year, but every couple of months he returns. I always wondered where he went."

"Why didn't Jake tell me last night?"

"He just found out, today."

She thought about Peter, with his awkward glances and timid smile. She recalled the times he had been away for a week or two. Looking after his sick grandmother, he had said. It was difficult to accept that he had actually flown back to the Nahanni River and stepped through a time portal into 2031. Or that Peter had fooled everyone at the university—especially her.

Suddenly, everything began to make sense.

Francesca hadn't been the one responsible for sending the canoe down the river. *Peter* had! And he must have been the one who gave her the unfiltered water. He had tried to sabotage their trip.

He probably took my pills too.

Her father gripped her shoulders. "The man you knew as Peter was sent by the Director to spy on you, to see if you know anything about the file."

"So it *does* exist!"

"Shh!" he cautioned, eyeing the camera behind him. "Not here."

She was about to argue when a deafening siren went off. Muffled angry shouts filtered through the door and heavy footsteps thundered down the hall.

Her father frowned, one ear pressed to the door. "Damn!"

She grabbed his arm. "What's wrong?"

"Someone's loose, trying to escape."

A security guard came and silently spirited her father away, leaving Del alone, terrified. She felt a shiver of dread race up her spine and settle between her shoulder blades. It wasn't easy being separated from the others, not knowing…waiting.

The alarm abruptly shut off, signaling the end of the chase.

Del pressed her ear against the door, but the hallway was silent.

I hope they make it out of here…whoever it is.

Hans carried a barely conscious Francesca into the nearest room—an empty operating room used by surgical teams to decapitate live adult specimens. A metal table with a thin plastic covering lay unoccupied in one corner. Beside it, a small draped cart held an assortment of surgical saws, scalpels and IV supplies. Unused monitors and other equipment bordered the walls of the room—abandoned. For now.

Reaching the table, he dropped her on it, his eyes skimming over her body. He brushed his lips against her ear.

"Don't you know who you're dealing with? Here, I'm God! I can give life…or take it."

He bit down hard on the soft cartilage.

Francesca cried out and the sound made him hard again.

"Vance may be back," he said, stroking her silky-smooth skin. "But I'm the one who brought in over twenty million dollars this year. I'm the one who ensured that the stem cells are created, and I'm the *only* one who deserves you."

He reached between her legs and spread them slightly.

He'd remove her panties in a moment. For now, he wanted to take in the sight of her.

Slowly, he moved to the head of the table. Bending over her, he licked along the line of her jaw, tasting her fear. He stroked her face, one finger trailing over the bruised lip.

"We can create dozens of cells, you and me. And if you cooperate, I'll give you your youth, Francesca."

The words were barely out of his mouth when he was head-butted into the wall. Ignoring the searing pain, he spun toward the bed.

The stupid bitch is conscious!

Frenzied green eyes locked on his, and they were brimming with revulsion. Francesca jumped off the table and stood near the door, her breasts heaving with each ragged breath.

In one hand, she held a razor-sharp scalpel.

His mouth stretched into a tight smile. "So that's how you want to play, is it?"

"I'm not playing, asshole! Come near me and I'll slice you."

His heart beat faster with anticipation. The woman had guts—he'd give her that. But she didn't have a clue who she was messing with.

Once she submits to me, I will truly be God.

"I love it rough, my dear Francesca."

His voice was deceptively calm.

"And I'll guarantee you a visit at least three times a day to prove that to you."

He laughed when her hand shook. The sharp blade glinted in the light, but he wasn't afraid.

A millisecond of hesitation. That was all he needed.

And as soon as he got it, he lunged at her.

The scalpel slashed at him, cutting into his shirt and nicking his forearm. Annoyed, he whipped around, kicked her with one foot and sent her crashing into the wall. Francesca quickly straightened and threw herself at him. But he ducked and gave a swift elbow jab to her ribs. The scalpel clattered to the floor and she grunted and dropped to her knees. Then she grabbed the blade handle and scurried as far from him as she could.

"You can do better than that," he sneered.

Her eyes flashed contemptuously as she waved the scalpel in the air. With a bloodcurdling shriek, she flew at him again. This time she wrapped her legs around his waist. She sliced the air inches from his neck but he warded off the blade, his fingers digging into her arm, squeezing, bending it back. Her other arm gripped him around the neck, and for a moment he couldn't breathe.

The bitch was trying to strangle him!

He reached up with his free hand and shoved the side of her face.

Forced to let go of him, she fell to the ground but her foot lashed out, hooking the back of his leg. With a quick jerk, she pulled him down on top of her and a loud, stunned gasp escaped from her mouth.

Hans smirked when he heard the soft crunch of her ribs.

"I'll make you scream with pleasure."

Francesca's eyes greeted him, wide and terrified. Her lashes fluttered softly against her cheek. Her mouth gaped open and she whispered something breathlessly.

"What's that?" he snapped. "God can't hear you!"

She's like a fish out of water. A goddamn wet fish!

He felt a flash of heat in his chest. Frowning, he reached between his stomach and Francesca's chest. When he pulled his hand away, it was covered in warm sticky blood.

"You bitch! You stabbed me!"

Panicking, he peeled himself away, ripped open the front of his shirt and searched for a wound.

But there wasn't a scratch on him.

He let out a gleeful laugh. He was invincible.

Standing over Francesca, he leered down at her.

Then he scowled.

She wasn't moving!

That's when he noticed the spreading pool of blood and the glaring blade lodged deep in her chest. The blood bloomed outward, like a rose slowly opening its petals.

His smile twisted into a glower of rage and he clenched his fists, gazing into her fading green eyes.

"You haven't had the serum yet! You'll die!"

He watched in disbelief as her lips curved into a smile. Her mouth opened and she struggled to speak, but all he heard was a gurgling rasp coming from the back of her throat.

"What?"

She tried to speak again and he pressed an ear against her lips.

What was she saying?

A strangled gasp erupted from Francesca's lungs. With a dying breath, she uttered three words that made him tremble with fear.

"You're...no...God!"

Jake slumped on the bed and stared off into space.

I'm partly to blame for all of this.

Forcing his mind off Francesca and VanBuren, he thought about the Ankh serum. His research at Bio-Tec Canada had led to the discovery of the serum and that didn't sit too well. He and Francesca had been working on one of Lawrence's original projects for the past six months. They had hoped to solve one of the major barriers that nanotechnology faced. The emission of excess heat.

Because it took hours for the nanobots to repair a single cell, a few molecular machines produced enough heat to virtually roast a small lab mouse from the inside out. Jake had discovered this firsthand, after he walked into the lab one morning and found five of their test subjects roasted alive.

They were back to square one.

Until three months ago, when he had remembered something that Lawrence had said years earlier. Something about AQP-5. It was so obvious that he could have kicked himself.

That morning, Jake had arrived at the lab after a long jog around the park. His face was flushed and he was sweating heavily. The first thing he reached for was a cloth to wipe his brow.

That's when the connection hit him.

Working on mice, he had overlooked the AQP-5 factor. If overheated due to exercise, humans sweated and body heat was released as the sweat evaporated. The water channel aquaporin-5 found in human sweat glands had long been thought to be crucial to thermoregulatory sweat secretion. If the amount of AQP-5 expression could be safely stimulated and increased, it stood to reason that more sweat would be created.

Consequently, most of the excess heat the machines produced would be eliminated through the sweat. That would give the bots enough time to repair the damaged cells.

That was their project's fundamental core.

According to the 2009 article, he was obviously heading in the right direction. If he could find out more, dig into some of the Centre's records, he would know exactly what they needed to do.

If he ever got back to Bio-Tec.

The door opened.

Lawrence hesitantly walked in, eyes drawn.

"TJ told me what happened to Francesca. I'm sorry."

"I should never have brought her here. But she insisted on coming, damnit! She came here because of me."

Jake saw the doctor's curious expression and he sighed.

"I broke it off with Francesca months ago, when I realized that she deserved more from me."

He moved to the table and sat down across from Lawrence.

"And now?"

"We're friends, Lawrence. And co-workers. Nothing more. It kills me that I couldn't stop him from raping her. Jesus! He was savage!"

"VanBuren is an addict."

"To the serum?"

"Yes…and to youth. He's been injecting himself for years, all for a chance at youth and longevity. One hundred and forty years of it."

"Who the hell wants to live that long? I couldn't stand watching all my family and friends grow old and die while I stay…young."

"Some people will do anything, Jake. Go to any extent to look younger, feel younger. Others will go to any extent to be healthy, not suffer from pain or dis—"

"Not me! Who do we think we are—God?"

"This technology," Lawrence said softly. "It's powerful. The serum and the bots combined have the possibility of reconstructing every cell, almost from scratch. If someone was to examine Hans' cells right now, they'd see the cells of a perfectly healthy, young man."

"A psychotic man!" Jake said bitterly.

"Doing everything within his power to stay young, to stave off death. And what's worse, people in power all over the world will be able to bid on a taste of youth. Paughter will sell the serum to the highest bidder. Imagine if some of the world's most violent men had been given the serum years ago, like Stalin or Hitler."

"Paughter and VanBuren are no better."

Lawrence fixed his gaze on him. "Whoever holds the key to life…holds the world in the palm of his hands."

"Then their hands had better be clean," Jake said crisply.

Lawrence stood, then walked to the door.

"It's a responsibility of the highest order, Jake. Not to be taken lightly…or misused."

He stepped through the doorway, closing the door behind him.

Jake massaged his aching head as Lawrence's words came back to haunt him.

Whoever holds the key to life…holds the world in the palm of his hands.

The serum was the key to life, but was 2005 ready for it?

Jake didn't think so.

He gazed around the room.

His eyes rested on the doctor's laptop—the only computer in the lab that wasn't connected to the Centre's mainframe. Eyeing the door, he reached for it. Scrolling through the numerous folders, he found one labeled *NB* and brought it up on the monitor. A variety of subfolders on

nanotechnology appeared. He searched them until he found one titled
AQP. He clicked on it.

A dozen files materialized, but only one made him bite his lip.

The one marked...*Kerrigan*.

He opened it.

There it was! Right in front of him. Years of sweat and blood, his *own*
research. It was all on Hawthorne's laptop. The solution to the AQP-5
problem and much more.

Reading through it, he discovered where his theory had taken a slight
detour. He snatched a memory stick from a plastic storage box and
inserted it. His finger hesitated over the *save* key, but he took a breath
and hit it. Once the files were saved, he pocketed the stick.

He'd deal with his guilt later.

With a backward glance, he continued scrolling through the files.

There were word processing programs he had never heard of, articles
on biotechnology and nanotechnology, a nanobot synthesizer, a science
journal, a games folder and more.

Curious, he opened the games folder and let out a loud chuckle.

2031 hadn't evolved much when it came to basic computer games.
There was still the common list of FreeCell, Hearts, Pinball, Solitaire,
Spades...and then a list of variations of each.

The door creaked and Lawrence poked his head inside.

"We're taking a tour around the other areas of the lab, Jake, if you
want to come along. There's a new specimen I have to prepare. It's not
pleasant work, but—"

He stopped abruptly, moving closer to the open laptop.

"Sorry," Jake said, red-faced. "I hope you don't mind."

"This isn't the time for games."

"I thought it might help me get my mind off Francesca and Del. It's
hell waiting for Gary to find a way out of here."

Lawrence's eyes met his. "You know, Del and I used to play
computer games all the time. It's one of my favorite memories."

"Which games?"

"Baldur's Gate, Quake...Unreal Tournament."

"Del likes shooter games?"

"Yeah, and she's damned good at it too. When we played, she'd hide
somewhere with a sniper rifle and the next thing I knew...'*head shot*'!
She'd cream me every time."

Jake grinned, struck by an image of Del hovering over the keyboard,
hunting down her father. He could almost hear her gleeful shout as she
wasted her father's computer-generated character.

"I would have thought she'd be more into the friendly games, like
poker or some adventure game."

Lawrence chuckled. "Not my Del. However, she was partial to a couple of card games—hearts in particular. Usually Arnold and her mother played with us. I used to tease Del because she never changed her strategy."

"In what way?"

"She was too predictable. She always led with hearts. I used to tease her about that all the time."

Jake cocked his head, recalling something. "Del told me that when Arnold Schroeder visited her on campus, he said something to her. Something about hearts."

"She always leads with her heart," Lawrence nodded. "I told Arnold that if he ever reached Del before me, to say that to her. That way she'd know who sent him. I always knew that she may not recognize him…or me, if the bots self-destructed. But I was sure she'd understand the heart reference."

Jake's eyes widened. "The hearts on the cave wall! But that means…"

"I've crossed back once. I was accompanied by Blackwell and some of his men. We broke into Bio-Tec to recover my computer data and my laptop. Before we left the Centre, I stole a phosphorescent wax pencil and when Blackwell and his men weren't looking, I scribbled the hearts on the wall."

"We wouldn't have found the cave without them, Lawrence."

Lawrence was silent for a moment.

Then he gave Jake a questioning look.

"How'd you know to turn off the lights?"

"Hawk."

"Wise man."

Jake nodded.

A wise dead man—unless we find a way out.

TWENTY-ONE

Hans bumped into Vance, literally.

The man who resembled a kid was waiting for him outside the Director's office. With arms and ankles crossed, he leaned against the wall near the door, a sly smile on his face.

"I take it the Director wasn't pleased. I heard they found a vial of serum in your fridge."

Hans' eyes narrowed. "I knew you'd eventually stab me in the back. Maybe I have a slight…problem. With the serum and with my urges. But you—"

"I *what?* Did my job, informed the Director of your gross misconduct?" Vance grabbed his arm. "Jesus Christ, Hans! You killed one of them. We needed her."

"It was an accident!"

Vance was really starting to piss him off. Who the hell did he think he was? If it hadn't been for Hans' investment in the very beginning there would be no Centre, no Project Ankh…no serum.

"We can use the others, Vance."

The kid gave him an incredulous look. "You know how limited our supplies are? It'll take weeks before a new batch is ready."

"We have a new addition," Hans said with a shrug. "I've already notified the lab. What about you? Are you going to cut back? It must have taken a few doses to get you looking like that."

"You think I want to look like a fricking kid? I don't think so. But at least *my* reversal was approved."

Hans flicked a resentful look at the Director's door. "Yeah, I noticed that you two have become quite buddy-buddy since you returned. Just remember one thing, Vance."

"What's that?"

"The Director may control the Centre and you may control Project Ankh, but *I* control the investors. Without me, the Centre for Enlightened

Living would self-destruct."

Pivoting on one heel, Hans strode down the hallway, praying fervently that Vance hadn't seen the slight shaking of his hand. If he had played his cards right, the man would lay off him for a while. He needed some time to think. With Vance back and in the Director's good graces, he'd be ignored—again.

I can't have that. Not after everything I've done.

He needed a fix.

With a sinful smile, he hurried to his office. Once inside, he locked the door, opened the freezer section of the small fridge and pulled out the ice bin. Digging beneath the cubes, he groaned with relief, lifting out two full vials of Ankh serum.

Thank God, Blackwell hadn't discovered his secret stash.

With a backward glance, he hid one of the vials beneath the ice cubes and closed the freezer door. Admiring the other vial, he was seized by a terrible yearning, a voice that said *'Do it!'*

Soon, he was lying on the couch, watching an eternity of liquid life flow into his veins. Life was so very painful, agonizing.

He bit back a scream, clamping his teeth on a strip of rubber.

Before he floated away in a bittersweet fog of stinging pain, he had one last thought.

I'll go see Hawthorne's daughter—before Vance does.

Del was shocked when Justin Blackwell entered her room half an hour after the alarm shut off. He pulled out a gun but kept it lowered at his side. They both knew it was there.

"Follow me, please."

She let out a nervous laugh. "Where are we going?"

"To see your friends."

Her head jerked. "Why?"

The man shrugged. "The Director hoped you would reciprocate, maybe help us convince your father to give us some information."

"You mean find out where he hid the so-called missing file," she said dryly. "Don't you get it? There *is* no file!"

Blackwell's eyes fastened on hers. "If you're smart, you'll cooperate with them."

"You mean VanBuren?"

She scowled, thinking of the man's pale face and leering eyes.

"Why would I cooperate with the devil?"

"Because it's the only way you'll get to live. All of you."

He flicked the gun toward the door.

Del followed Blackwell down a hallway. They turned a corner and walked past the elevator, heading for a set of doors. Blackwell slipped an ankh key into a security panel and the doors opened.

The first person she saw was Jake.

He strode toward her, pulling her into his arms.

"The lab is bugged. Careful what you say."

She let her lips graze over his before hugging Hawk, Gary and TJ.

Relieved to finally be in the same room with all of them, she grinned. "I hope you all haven't driven my dad crazy."

She gave her father a peck on the cheek.

"They've been great company," he said.

She threw a backward glance in the direction of the armed man.

"Blackwell," her father said gruffly. "Why is my daughter here?"

Blackwell's eyes met hers. "The Director wanted you all in a safe place."

"You mean, in a safe prison," she snickered.

She caught her father's eye, then closed her mouth.

Frustrated, she gazed at Jake.

He was drinking her in and she blushed self-consciously. Her mouth opened to say something and a thought hit her. Everyone knew that he had spent the night with her. TJ, Hawk, Gary…

Even my father.

Mortified, she looked at Blackwell. "So, I'm staying here, then?"

"You have tonight. After that…"

Blackwell eyed her father, then shrugged.

After he was gone, Jake spun on one heel and faced Lawrence.

"What's that mean? *After that.*"

"It means that after tonight you're all dead." Lawrence dropped his voice. "Unless I give them the file."

Del shook her head. "You can't do that, Dad. As soon as they have the file, they'll kill us all anyway."

Gary tapped his mouth with a finger. "I may have a solution. But I'll need another hour."

Del watched him make a beeline for the computer.

"What's he going to do?"

"Get us out of here," TJ whispered.

"For now, it's business as usual," her father said. "If you look like you're being useful, they won't lock you up somewhere else. Like Francesca."

"How is she?" Del asked. "Does anyone know?"

Jake gave her a hard look. "She's—"

"She's alive," her father interjected. "Just like the rest of us. We'll get Gary to find out what room she's in."

Del bit her bottom lip.

Something was going on. She could see it in their faces. But for some reason, she didn't push it. Sometimes it was better to be left in the dark.

"I have a specimen to process," her father said quietly. "You can stay here and run samples, or come with me. Maybe it's time you had a tour of the lab of the future."

Leaving Gary behind at the computer, she followed her father, Jake, TJ and Hawk through the sliding doors that led to the Specimen Lab.

"What's this?" she asked as they entered a small white-walled hallway.

"It's a UV microbial disinfection chamber," her father explained. "It kills bacteria, germs...micro-organisms. We have to keep the environment sterile."

A gentle hiss of air escaped as the doors closed tightly behind them, and Del couldn't help but roll her eyes after a computer-generated sexless voice instructed them to relax.

"Relax?" she muttered. "Who the hell are they kidding?"

TJ shifted restlessly when a red light began to flash on the opposite door. "Gives me the creeps, dawg."

Her father gave them all an uneasy look. "Don't worry, it's safe. But I have to warn you—you won't like what's inside."

Del shivered at the tone of his voice.

Maybe she should've stayed behind with Gary.

"Be prepared," her father mumbled as the flashing light turned a steady green. "It's quite dark at first, until your eyes adjust."

Stepping through the doorway into the dimly lit Specimen Lab, she blinked and shook her head. As the warehouse-sized room came into focus, her chin dropped and she felt the blood drain from her face.

"Holy shit!"

"There's nothing holy about this place," her father said bitterly.

The Specimen Lab was long and narrow, stretching before them like a highway to nowhere. It was divided into four lanes, each monitored by a main computer station staffed by two uniformed technicians.

Above them, the high ceiling was spotted with electric-blue recessed lights. In the shadows, dozens of small glass boxes were suspended by chains. Approximately two feet wide by three feet tall, the boxes contained an opaque, milky liquid. An assortment of hoses and tubing were attached to the sides, trailing down to the bulky monitors below.

Del took a few steps forward, awed and terrified.

"The glass cages house the specimens," her father said. "They're kept in a viscous solution of saline and synthetic cerebro-spinal fluid. This allows the cells to function normally. In essence, they're tricked into believing that they're still alive. But unfortunately, it's a short-lived process. If we don't extract the stem cells within three weeks, we lose the batch."

"You got to be kidding, dawg," TJ blurted. "Are you saying there's human brains in there?"

"There are three severed heads—adult specimens. Two are nearly useless and will be disposed of tomorrow. The other is new. Paughter must have gone hunting again. It's probably some poor unfortunate fool who thought a trip to the Nahanni River would be an exciting vacation."

Del heard the self-contempt in his voice.

"What about the other cages?" Jake asked.

"We just processed three young specimens yesterday. The rest of the cages are empty. Apparently VanBuren expects to fill them all. Soon."

"This is an atrocity to nature," Hawk murmured.

Del agreed wholeheartedly. Sure as hell, murder could never be excused, regardless of the potential advantages of the serum.

"So what do you do now, Dad?"

"I have to physically hook up the new specimen, connect the wires for monitoring and oversee the initial preparation."

"Sounds gross," TJ scowled.

"It is. You don't have to come with me. None of you do."

Jake raised his chin. "I do. I want to understand *everything* about this place."

"Fine then. Follow me. But I'll warn you, you'll be looking at a severed head."

Del inhaled deeply. "I'm going too."

Her father moved toward the main monitoring station and she saw one of the techs peer at them nervously. The man cocked his head at a security guard standing near the side doors.

"You'll need an escort, doctor," the tech said.

"They're nervous because you're all with me," her father scoffed. "But, hell, no one said you couldn't come in here."

A beefy looking man with two pistols strapped to his waist followed a few feet behind them.

Del could feel his eyes burning into the back of her head.

"You can travel freely between the lab rooms?" Jake asked her father.

"Only the technicians can leave through the side doors. They have ankh keys, like the pendant Schroeder buried for you. And as you can see, the doors are well guarded."

Del blocked out the sound of their voices and thought about the severed head. The *adult specimen*, as her father had called it. Over the years, especially while studying anthropological cases from Africa and South America, she had studied some horrific occurrences.

In North Africa, bones from children who were believed to have been sacrificed to the god Ba'al Hammon were discovered in the Carthage center. In South Africa, a mass sacrifice pit piled high with dozens of emaciated corpses infected the drinking water. Outside of Peru, a dig revealed half-frozen mummified bodies, some with no obvious cause of death. Many of them were children. Authorities suspected that they had been smothered with tightly bound cloths—asphyxiated.

A severed head couldn't be any worse. Could it?

She stole a peek at Jake.

He was a doctor. He must have seen some appalling things in his time. Especially in his research on Progeria. Then again, severed heads weren't common in a nanobot lab—Progeria or no Progeria.

Her father motioned them toward the first station on the far right side, then laid a hand on a neon blue screen.

All of a sudden, a light flickered inside the glass cage above them.

The cage quivered. With a soft whining sound, it began to move lower until it stopped on a platform in front of them.

"This is one of the young specimens," her father murmured, touching the screen's upper left corner until the control panel glowed. "A few years ago, we had to create this viscous fluid. The technicians had a problem with seeing their own work. In a few minutes, the fluid will start to clear."

Somewhere beneath the floor, a pump groaned.

Del held her breath, waiting.

When the light inside the cage stopped flashing, she stared in horror as the shape of a newborn came into view. The baby's body floated in the liquid, one tube attached to its umbilical cord and one to the back of its head. Its sightless eyes were closed, its tiny hands clenched into fists and its perfect cupid lips were lifeless. Breathless.

She swallowed hard and fought the urge to cry. "Is it alive?"

Her father shook his head. "As soon as we hook it up to collect the stem cells, it is legally brain dead. It can't feel a thing, Del."

She caught TJ's eye.

He was in shock, probably thinking of Julie—and their unborn child.

"The newborns are delivered via C-section," her father said. "Then they're brought here. Shortly after I was brought to the Centre, I convinced the Director to allow us to sedate them, before attaching the tubes."

She struggled to conceal her fury. "Whose babies are they?"

"Sometimes the Director's guards get the honor of impregnating the women who are brought here. But these three..."

Her father scowled, as if he had eaten something rotten.

"They're VanBuren's progeny. He impregnates any woman he can get his hands on. Tells them it's their God-given duty."

The last three words erupted from him.

Del thought of Kate O'Leary, the young, pregnant nurse.

That's why the girl was so defensive about the father of her baby. VanBuren had Kate brainwashed to believe she was having a baby for the salvation of the world. Then again, the girl didn't have a choice. The only other alternative was rape.

Or death.

"This one is ready," her father said, hovering over the monitor. "The next step is extraction of the cells. They travel through the cord attached to the back of the baby's head and into a retrieval unit. Then the cells are sorted and processed. After that, the serum is mixed and the nanobots are added. Then the rogue bot is added…as a safety precaution."

He placed his palm down on the screen and the clear liquid slowly turned murky again, then he swallowed hard and strode past the next two cages.

The other babies, Del guessed.

When he reached the fourth one, he pointed. "This one and the next are the adults. Their usefulness is at an end, which is why the Director insists on using young specimens. They last longer."

He led them to another cage and placed his hand on the screen.

"This is the newest addition. It's been wired to preserve the head, but the extraction tubing hasn't been inserted yet."

The lights flashed as the cage dropped slowly.

"With this one, half of the fluid will be pumped out until I'm finished. Once I attach the final tubing, the extraction will begin immediately. Three weeks from now, the head will be incinerated."

A nervous tremor raced through Del's body.

Disassociate. Treat the head like an inorganic, inanimate object.

She stared at the cage, unable to turn away as the level of the fluid dropped, exposing the top of a bald human head.

Slowly, the murky liquid began to clear.

"I can see the nose," TJ grimaced.

"In a minute you'll see it clearly," her father warned.

One minute later, Del screamed.

Jake reached for her but she pushed him away, oblivious to the anxious stares of the technicians. Even the security guard was unsure of what to do. Nervous, the man moved closer.

Her father stepped in front of him. "Leave her alone!"

Out of the corner of one eye, she saw Hawk stalk away, cursing beneath his breath. Behind her, she heard TJ dry heaving, apologizing between gasps.

She swiveled back to the glass cage, struggling to regain her composure. Sickened, she stared in horror at the severed head lying half-submerged in cerebro-spinal fluid.

The head with the face they all recognized.

"Oh my God," she whispered.

TWENTY-TWO

Francesca Baroni's pale green eyes stared at Del…lifeless.

The fiery auburn hair that had matched her quick temper was gone. Her mouth drooped open grotesquely and, beneath it, the skin flaps of her neck were riveted to the bottom of the cage to keep her head in place. Her skin was flaccid, colorless.

Del's stomach heaved as a wormlike trail of fresh blood snaked behind the glass, suspended in the liquid bath. She backed away from the cage.

Francesca's eyes seemed to follow her, accusingly.

"What did they do?"

"The son of a bitch killed Francesca!" Jake snarled.

A tremor of fear shivered through her. "W-who killed her?"

"VanBuren," Hawk and TJ said in unison.

Her father's brow furrowed in confusion.

"I-I'm so sorry. If I had known…"

He punched in a code and the cage started to fill.

"It's not your fault," Jake said firmly.

"But this doesn't make sense. They don't kill women! They're too valuable—they can have children."

Del flinched.

Her father's comment cut her to the bone, but now wasn't the time to tell him that she could never make him a grandfather. All in due time.

"Francesca was on the pill," she mumbled, sweeping an edgy glance at Jake. "I saw them in her bag."

"But she could still get pregnant," her father argued. "She wasn't taking any contraceptives here. And with the serum in her, she'd be able to bear children within a week—if it wasn't for VanBuren."

Del recalled their nervous behavior earlier when she had mentioned Francesca's name.

"What really happened?"

The men exchanged nervous glances.

Trembling, she folded her arms protectively across her chest. She wanted to shake them and yell *'spit it out!'* She wasn't going anywhere. Not until they told her the truth.

"VanBuren raped her," Jake said. "Or at least he tried to. We saw them on the monitor after Gary brought up the Centre's surveillance."

"We turned it off, Del," Hawk added. "After VanBuren knocked her down."

"But why kill her?" Jake muttered.

Del's chin lifted. "Because she fought back."

She spun on her heel and hurried to the air chamber.

"Hey, Jake! I may have a solution to the problem."

Jake strolled to Gary's side, trying not to rush.

"Have any company while we were gone, Gary?"

"Nope, none."

Jake wasn't really surprised. No one had bothered to check on Gary because he was a programmer. Since the sorter was essential for the creation of the serum, the Director wouldn't run the risk of interfering. Not if the machine could be fixed.

Gary bit his lip. "I think I've figured out a way out, Jake."

On the monitor, Jake saw a multi-dimensional image and transparent layout of the Centre. He immediately noticed a narrow passageway marked by two red splotches. Throughout the maze that was the Centre, more splotches appeared. Some moved slowly.

"Is that what I think?"

Gary nodded. "Body heat, from infrared heat sensors. This cluster here is on the upper level. They must be having a party."

"Probably a welcome home party for Paughter."

And Jake would bet that VanBuren, the Director and all the other assholes that ran the place were there too.

"I'd like to crash *that* party."

"No, you don't."

Jake lifted one brow, perplexed. "And why not?"

"They're busy," Gary said slyly. "Maybe too busy to notice a few extra people or heat blips in the hall."

"Won't security miss us?"

"When we're ready to go, I'll run some dummy blips. I've already created a video loop of the hallway to the tunnel. What I need now is some footage from the lab. Footage of you all sleeping."

Jake clenched his teeth. "Done."

Gary turned slightly in his chair and his gaze drifted to the Specimen Lab door.

"I saw Del's face, Jake. She looked sick."

"Francesca's dead. VanBuren killed her."

He saw a glimmer of fear in Gary's eyes.

"Just get us out of here. Tonight! Or we're all dead."

The lab doors opened and a large cart rolled in, pushed by the security guard with the spiked hair.

"Dinner is served," Spike said in a bored voice.

When no one moved, he shoved the cart into the wall.

"It must be awful," Jake said sharply.

The guard scowled. "What?"

"Not to have a conscience."

Spike threw him a smug *you're dead* kind of grin, then vanished.

Jake's eyes searched the room.

Two men were mixing samples while a woman monitored the equipment. TJ hovered over her, offering her a hand as she stood. The woman thanked him. When she turned, Jake saw that she was at least seven months pregnant.

VanBuren strikes again.

He glanced at the clock.

Almost seven. Time for the techs to leave for the night.

Five minutes later, they were gone.

He headed toward Del.

"Gary needs some footage of us sleeping. We all need to take a nap. Let TJ know, and I'll tell Hawk and your father."

TJ and Hawk crawled onto the first two cots, their feet hanging comically over the ends. Del curled up on the last one.

"Move over," Jake said, lying down beside her.

"What are you doing?" she hissed.

"Sleeping."

"Oh."

He wrapped one arm around her and breathed in the scent of her, the fragrance of her hair. Her heart hammered in her chest, and he wanted to say something, *anything*, to comfort her.

But what could he say? They all had reason to be scared.

Hell, even *he* was scared.

Lawrence dimmed the lights in the lab, then stole a quick peek in Del and Jake's direction. For a long moment, he watched them.

They looked good together…as if they were meant to be.

Satisfied, he casually wandered over to the double-door refrigerator that housed the serum samples. On the top shelf lay a dozen labeled syringes. Most contained the pale yellow Ankh serum, a few contained placebo serums, and some were samples of blood taken from some of the residents of the Centre.

Hidden amongst them…were *Thanatos* and *Hypnos*.

Thanatos was the Greek god of death. He was the son of Nyx, the goddess of night, and the twin of Hypnos, the god of sleep.

Lawrence's *Thanatos* offered a higher concentration of nanobots—particularly rogue bots. And he thought it was fitting that a syringe filled with instant death be named for a creature of darkness.

He smiled grimly and slipped the capped syringe in his right shirt pocket. Then he grabbed the two syringes labeled *Hypnos* and dropped them in the left pocket.

"Want some help, Gary?" he hollered, meandering back to the computer station.

"No, I'm fine. I'll keep working. You should have a rest too."

Lawrence gave a brief nod, then disappeared into his room—as per Jake's suggestion. He needed to stay out of sight, to give Gary enough time to create a video feed.

His eyes landed on his laptop—the laptop that held a secret.

The solution to Project Ankh.

He snickered, thinking of how many hotshots from the Centre had tried to find the file on it. Eventually they had given up, convincing themselves that he had kept it on Bio-Tec's mainframe.

Idiots!

Thank God for his old Armed Forces buddy, Rufus.

Rufus Digby was an encryption expert. Before Lawrence's trip to the Nahanni River, Rufus had safely hidden the file where no one would look, making it only accessible with the correct password.

Lawrence flipped the computer open, inserted a memory stick and downloaded an assortment of what looked like miscellaneous files—useless files. He dropped the stick into a waterproof case, then tucked it in the pocket with the syringes filled with *Hypnos*. Then he wiped the laptop's memory clean and popped out the hard drive.

His eyes drifted across the room.

He needed a hammer, but VanBuren hadn't allowed him anything that could be used as a weapon.

The heavy bed at the far end caught his attention.

Palming the hard drive, he strode over to the bed, knelt down and slipped the metal plate under the foot. Then heaving up the bed he dropped it. The leg crashed down with a muffled *thud*.

He did it again. And again.

Bits of metal scattered across the floor. He swept the fragments into a dustpan, pouring half into the kitchen garbage can and the rest into the small recycling bin.

Then he sat on the edge of the bed.

"I'll do whatever it takes to make things right. Whatever it takes!"

He recalled the beautiful, perfect babies who had been sacrificed—all for an obsession with youth and eternal life. Babies who had been conceived and born within *six* months instead of nine—all because of a serum filled with industrious microscopic nanobots whose only objective was to create life, repair damaged cells and accelerate embryonic growth.

He remembered the hundreds of innocent people who had been slaughtered by a crazed lunatic's order—by a Director whom most people had never seen. A man whom some suspected could be the Prime Minister of Canada. Or the President of the United States.

Regardless, the Director had gone too far. The Centre for Enlightened Living was nothing more than a breeding ground for murderers. Murderers who thought they were God.

"They won't win. Not while I'm still breathing."

Hans smiled, raising his champagne in the air.

"To using the past as collateral."

A faint cheer trickled through the crowded room, a room filled with important, wealthy business executives. Some were already heavily invested in Project Ankh, while others were potential clients, waiting for a glimpse of eternal life.

He spotted Blackwell standing off to one side, listening to Boris Mironov, the Prime Minister of the Russian Elite Federation. Nearby, President Robertson and his family huddled close together…talking to Vance.

Hans scowled angrily.

His gaze drifted across the room, but in his mind he contemplated a hundred ways to kill off Vance—all of them very painful.

He examined the cool bubbly in the fluted crystal glass.

If someone were to add enough Necrovan…

He glanced up guiltily.

A young server walked by and he beckoned her over. He placed his empty glass on the tray, grabbed two full flutes and headed for Mironov and Blackwell.

"Justin," he smiled tightly. "Sorry I couldn't bring one for you too."

Hans offered a glass of champagne to the short, burly man standing beside the chief of security. "Boris. Good to see you again."

Mironov's dark eyes narrowed as he took the glass.

"I don't drink champagne," he said in a thick Russian accent. "Nor do I tolerate rudeness."

Hans gaped in disbelief as Mironov passed the glass to Blackwell.

His smile dropped. "Rudeness?"

The Russian gave him an icy look. "You have yet to introduce me to your Director. And I have been here one hour."

"I am so sorry, Prime Minister. The Director is not well and will not be attending tonight. I promise that at our next meeting, you'll finally meet. Until then, may I offer you a sample of the serum you'll be receiving next month?"

Mironov shrugged. "I'm in no hurry for serum. But next time, I meet Director. Let's enjoy party, my friend."

He gave Hans a vigorous pat on the back, then left in search of a tumbler of vodka.

"You've certainly brought in the orders," Blackwell said. "The Director must be pleased."

Hans flinched. "You could say that."

He recalled the Director's harsh words earlier and the restrictions that had been put on his serum usage. He needed to speed up production. If he did, then no one would care whether a few vials disappeared.

"How are our guests, Justin?"

"They're napping. I'll check on them shortly. That Ingram fellow is still trying to fix the cell sorter."

"When the hell are the new sorters getting here?"

Hans was ticked off.

The AQUA-1250 had broken down mid-production and they couldn't produce the serum without it.

"End of next week," Blackwell said. "The military is waiting for them to be shipped from the manufacturer. Then they'll send them here. By the way, the Specimen Lab had a few visitors today."

Hans jerked his head. "Who?"

"Our guests in the lab—everyone except Ingram."

"Did Hawthorne show them the specimens?"

"Yeah. And they saw your newest contribution too."

A man tapped Blackwell's shoulder and whispered in his ear.

"Something wrong, Justin?" Hans asked nervously.

"A phone call. But before I go, I have one question. Why'd you do it—why kill the Baroni woman?"

Hans shrugged. "She didn't believe in God."

Adrenaline pumped through Del's veins and her heart fluttered as Gary gathered them around.

They *had* to escape…undetected.

"Okay, here's the plan," Gary said. "I'm still working on breaking the code to unlock the doors—"

"I got that covered, dawg," TJ said in a low voice.

Del's eyes widened. "What does that mean?"

TJ slipped his hand into a pocket and pulled out an ankh key.

"How'd you get that?"

"I know how," Jake grinned. "The pregnant lab technician."

TJ nodded. "It was in her pocket. I swiped it when I helped her up. I knew she'd follow the two guys out."

Del hugged him tightly. "Smart move."

"We have to hurry," Gary warned. "I created a loop of lab footage. Basically everyone's sleeping and Dr. Hawthorne's in his room. I've already programmed it. That's what they're seeing now. I've also looped the feed for the hallway, from here to the tunnel."

"And the audio?" she asked.

"We can yell if we want to. They're listening to a recording of TJ snoring and me typing."

Del peered anxiously over her shoulder, watching the red light on the camera.

God, she hoped he was right.

"Trust me," Gary said, catching her eye. "They can't hear us or see us. But there is one problem."

A tremor of fear raced up her spine.

"In forty minutes, there'll be a guard change at the tunnel door. We have to get through it before then. That's when the video loop is set to go back to real footage. Otherwise, Blackwell will know something's up."

"Because he won't see the new guard arriving," she guessed.

"Exactly. And if we wait until *after* the guard change, the party might be over. And we could run into some trouble."

"Trouble as in VanBuren or Paughter," Hawk said.

Gary nodded. "Now, before the guard change, there's one man to deal with." He pointed to the red heat sensor. "The guard on duty."

"So we have to take out the guard," TJ said.

"There's a weapon room between here and the tunnel," Gary said. "No surveillance inside the room, no guards."

He paused, eyeing Del pointedly.

"What are you saying?" she asked.

"I think we should help ourselves to some guns."

Del was stunned.

"You mean kill the guard?"

Gary lifted his shoulders. "If it's the only way past him. We might need the weapons in the tunnel too. I can't tell if anyone's inside. Heat sources may not register through the cave walls. I don't know."

She sighed heavily. "Whatever it takes then."

"Yeah, dawg," TJ agreed. "If I gotta take a few down so we can get back, then that's what I'll do."

Gary traced a path on the Centre's map.

"We have to hit the weapon room first, then head straight for the tunnel entrance. Once we're inside, we have to move fast. It'll take forty-two minutes to get us all through the transporter. That's allowing for the five minutes of crystal recharging in between."

"Won't they just follow us through the portal?" Del asked.

"I have a feeling they're gonna be too busy on this side. I've programmed a virus to infect their system. Bit by bit, it'll infiltrate their entire network, obliterating everything—including Project Ankh. That should keep them busy for days."

Del was stunned.

If he could accomplish that, then Gary Ingram could bring the future to its knees.

"What about the rogue bots?" TJ asked, worried.

"That's the only problem I haven't solved," Gary admitted. "I'm into the program, but I can't figure out how to shut the rogue bots down."

Lawrence hastily shook his head. "They can't *be* shut down. If you try, you'll set them off. We'd better pray that we're all on the other side before someone activates them. If we're caught on this side, we'll be dead within five minutes of each other."

"Five?" Jake asked, swiveling his head sharply. "Schroeder lived longer than that."

Del flinched at the use of past tense.

"We updated the rogue bot program last month," her father said regretfully. "We had to, because of Arnold's escape. The only good news is that the Director can't activate all the rogue bots at once. The program will go through a random selection, killing us off, one by one. The only thing you could do is shut it off if they activate it."

Gary drew in a deep breath. "I'll stay behind then, until the last minute. I can make it to the tunnel just before the guard change. Most of you should be through the portal by then."

"No!" Del argued. "We all go together."

Gary raised his head, his soft eyes locking on hers. "If any of us are gonna escape, I need to stay here. When it's time, I'll run."

She swallowed hard, kissing Gary on the cheek.

"When we first met, you said you wanted an adventure."

He nodded. "I guess I got it, didn't I"

Tears pooled in her eyes.

"You'd better run, Gary. And run fast."

♀WENTY-THREE

♀J inserted the ankh key and the lab door hissed open.

"Walk fast," Jake said. "But don't draw attention."

Del flicked a look at the four men wearing white lab coats—her father's idea. The men walked out into the hallway first, but she hesitated in the doorway. Once she stepped outside the lab, there was no turning back. She'd be hunted down. Probably killed.

It's now or never.

She peered over her shoulder at Gary.

His round face lifted and he tossed his glasses aside. Then he raised a hand in a silent salute and smiled.

She swiped at her damp face, praying he'd be all right.

Jake nudged her gently. "We have to go, Del."

With a nod, she followed the four men down the hall. At the end, they turned right, moving quickly down a winding path of white walls and silver-flecked tiled floor. Nervous, she kept checking over her shoulder for VanBuren.

Del was just starting to relax when her father stopped.

"Someone's coming!"

She heard it too. The clacking of hard-soled shoes.

Juggling a messy pile of manila folders, a young girl in an aqua jacket rounded the corner. She seemed surprised to see them, but not overly concerned.

As the girl drew closer, Del flattened her perspiring palms against her thighs, wiping them on her jeans.

Please don't be Kate.

It wasn't.

Del had never felt so relieved.

However, her relief didn't last for long.

The next corner brought them face-to-face with two boisterous—and somewhat drunk—young men. They staggered unsteadily down the hall, supporting each other physically.

"They'll be perfectly sober in thirty minutes," her father whispered. "The nanobots don't like alcohol."

One of the men spotted her. "Hey, beautiful! Ya headin' for the party?"

Jake stepped protectively in front of her, but she sidestepped around him. Facing the young man, she smiled.

"We have some work to do first. See you later?"

The man winked boldly. "I sure hope so."

His friend nudged him and grinned. Then they waved and staggered off, singing at the top of their lungs.

"Nicely done," her father said.

Del peered over her shoulder. "Being out in the open is nerve-wracking, Dad. I feel like a sitting duck."

"Then let's not give them any target practice."

They hurried down the hall.

"We don't have much time before the guard change," Jake warned. "And we still have to get to the weapons."

They rounded another corner and released a collective sigh as they met an empty hallway.

Her father headed straight for a steel door.

"Let's hope Gary was right about no guards inside," he said, slipping the ankh key into the control panel.

The light turned green and the door swung open into a narrow room that was lined with benches. It made Del think of a men's locker room. Except there were no lockers. The walls were constructed from a satin-polished metal, similar to the ankh key, and near the door, on both sides, two computer screens were positioned in the wall. Other than the screens, the walls were bare.

Del let out a moan. "Where are the weapons?"

Closing the door behind them, she noticed a tiny peephole—the only blemish in the door's austere design. She couldn't resist looking through it.

A slightly distorted view of the hallway emerged.

A motor droned behind her.

She twisted her head and what she saw made her mouth drop.

The entire left wall had opened, revealing racks of weapons that disappeared deep into crevices that were maybe ten feet in. There were handguns, rifles, machine guns and technologically advanced military hardware. Hundreds of them. The far end held shelves stacked with boxes of ammunition and some kind of plastic explosive that looked like twisted strips of black licorice.

While the men grabbed an assortment of weapons, her attention was captured by a row of dome-topped black metal objects that reminded her of the touch-lights she had installed recently on her back deck.

She picked one up, examined it and turned it over.

A number was stamped on the bottom. *10.*

She put it back, picked up another. It had a *5* stamped on it.

Five what—bullets?

She shook it, but couldn't hear anything. She was about to twist off the top to see what was inside when TJ snatched it from her hands.

"Jesus Christ, Del! Are you trying to get us killed?"

"I just wanted to see—"

"It's a bomb. If you had twisted the top, it would've gone off in however many minutes it's set to."

"Five," she whispered, shaking.

TJ pocketed the bomb. "Sorry I yelled."

She smiled bleakly. "No problem. I'll be lookout."

The celebration had been the Director's idea, and at first Hans had been excited. Military and government representatives from around the globe were all gathered under one roof. But within an hour, the party had become dull, boring.

Especially with Vance hogging all the limelight.

"You should've drowned in the river, you little shit!"

"Pardon, sir?"

Hans was in such a funk that he hadn't even noticed the girl in the hallway. She was carrying a stack of folders pressed haphazardly against her chest. She was one of the new interns, a sweet thing he had hoped to bed.

However, one look at her ID tag made him clench his teeth.

It was stamped with a gold ankh. Vance had beaten him to her.

Fuming, Hans waved her off and stalked toward the lab.

Delila Hawthorne was going to help him release the pressure that was building, threatening to explode.

He pictured her perfect mouth, those lips that were made for pleasuring. By the time he was through with her, she would be begging for more.

But first, he had to get her out of the lab.

He spotted the weapon room a few feet ahead.

Perhaps he should grab a replacement, something more powerful. Her friends weren't going to allow him to take Delila without a fight.

Especially good ole Dad!

He stopped in front of the weapon room door. Removing a sleek pistol from his pocket, he stroked it, admiring it. An SX2 Omega semiautomatic was more than enough to show them he meant business.

And he had plenty of bullets to go around.

He had taken three steps down the hall when a muted sound rumbled from inside the weapon room. Puzzled, he listened, then moved to the door and pressed one eye against the spy-hole. Then he cursed under his breath, throwing a self-conscious look over his shoulder.

"Idiot!" he muttered. "You can see out, not in!"

He reminded himself of his rendezvous with Hawthorne's daughter. He had to get to her before Vance did.

As for the noises he had heard...?

He shrugged. *Probably some guard getting lucky.*

Spinning on his heel, he strode quickly down the hall.

The effects of the champagne had worn off. Now he was pumped, ready to go...ready to get lucky.

He smirked.

Delila Hawthorne, here I come!

"Everyone quiet!" Del hissed. "Someone's coming!"

Through the peephole, she saw a man rush down the hallway. He wore a white jacket and white pants. A technician? He moved closer, and the satin shimmer of the fabric sent a shiver through her.

She had seen only one person who wore clothes like that.

The man came to a sudden stop in front of the door and he pulled out a gun. As his head lifted, she glimpsed his face.

It *was* VanBuren!

She whipped around, pressed her back to the door, hands splayed in fear. Her heart hammered mercilessly and she was positive that the man on the other side could hear it.

"VanBuren's outside!" she whispered, petrified.

Jake and TJ each aimed a gun at the door.

Unable to resist, Del bent her head and spied on VanBuren again.

As he moved away from the door, something clattered to the floor behind her. She spun around, glaring at her father as he reached for the gun he had dropped.

She pressed her eye to the peephole.

"He left. Wait! I can't see anything! It's pitch bla—"

Suddenly, the blackness moved, shifting into gray.

VanBuren's bloodshot eye backed away from the peephole.

"Jesus Christ!"

She twisted toward the others, tapped a finger to her lips and felt her stomach lurch.

Everyone froze.

Stone statues.

Del finally gathered her courage and stole another peek.

Oh crap! This is not good.
VanBuren was making his way down the hall…toward the lab.
"We have to go!" she hissed. "Now!"

Hans paused outside the Project Ankh lab.
As the doors parted, he pulled out his pistol, then stepped inside the dimly lit room where menacing shadows greeted him. The darkness sent a shiver up his spine.
There must have been a power surge.
"Lights on fifty percent," he ordered.
Nothing happened.
He edged into the center of the room and stumbled clumsily into a chair. He looked for a beacon, something to guide him.
In the corner occupied by the cell sorter, tiny multi-colored lights flickered on and off, like miniature Christmas tree lights. The machine made soft clicking sounds, and it gave Hans the creeps. In fact, the whole lab gave him the creeps.
Everyone's sleeping. Good, I'll catch them off guard.
Suddenly, a glowing screen caught his eye.
One of the computers was on.
Jerking his head, he peered into the shadows of the lab.
Something moved to his right.
"Come on out!" he ordered.
A short stocky form took a few tentative steps forward.
"I have a gun," Hans warned. "So don't do anything stupid."
"I wouldn't dream of it."
"What are you doing?"
Gary Ingram stepped into the glow of the monitor.
"I was working on repairing the cell sorter files. But I fell asleep at the computer. Your serum may have improved my eyesight but I still need to sleep."
Hans lowered the pistol…just a bit.
Ingram wasn't a threat. The man worked in an office, filing papers and probably dreaming up annoying business programs that crashed every month.
He snorted at the thought.
"Where are the others?"
"S-sleeping," Ingram stammered.
The emergency backup lights kicked in, and Hans saw Ingram reach for something on the desk. He grabbed the man's arm and pulled him toward Hawthorne's room. Then he unlocked it, looking over his shoulder to say something to Ingram.
That's when he spotted the empty cots in the corner of the lab.

"What the f—?"

He darted a suspicious look from the cots to Ingram.

"How can they be sleeping in there if the cots are still out here?"

Hans whipped around as the door opened.

The room was empty.

Dragging in a panicked breath, he pressed the pistol against Ingram's temple. "Where…are they?"

"I don't know, Hans. But you have more important things to worry about."

"Like what?"

"Like the fact that your entire system is gonna crash in less than an hour," Ingram said boldly. "I've infected it with a virus."

"You're bluffing."

Ingram gave him a smug smile—the kind that Hans wanted to smack right off.

Maybe the man wasn't bluffing.

"What kind of virus?"

"The kind that'll make you lose everything—including the formula for the serum and your complete database. Not to mention that the Specimen Lab will be shut down, completely useless. The babies…*Francesca*…all of them! You're about to join the real world, Hans. And start dying like the rest of us!"

Enraged, Hans jammed the gun hard into the side of the man's head. "Mr. Ingram. It seems you have a problem."

Ingram flinched. "Don't you mean *we*?"

Hans pulled the trigger.

"No, asshole!" he growled, wiping the blood spray and brain tissue from his face. "I mean *you*!"

"The entrance to the tunnel is just ahead," her father said.

Del hurried as fast as she could, careful not to make too much noise. TJ and Hawk were a few feet in front, while Jake remained at her side, his hand firmly gripping her arm.

She heard her father greet the guard.

"We're running some tests."

The guard straightened.

"Shit!" Jake said.

"What's wrong?" TJ demanded, turning his head.

"That's Spike, or whatever his name is. He'll recognize us!"

Del's heart pounded as she stole a peek at the guard.

Spike's eyes drooped in an alcoholic stupor. Beer cans lay on the ground, surrounding him like a metal fairy ring. Only there was nothing magical or fairy-ish about the man. Particularly when he stumbled and reached into a pocket that wasn't there.

It's too late to turn back.

"There's only one solution," her father said quietly.

He shot the guard.

Shocked, Del hung back as TJ and Hawk promptly grabbed the unconscious man's arms and hauled him into a storage closet. Out of sight, out of mind. Then Hawk wiped up the blood trail with his lab coat.

Jake squeezed her arm. "The guard won't die, Del. Because of the nanobots in him. They'll force the bullet out and reconstruct the cells. A bullet to the brain or slicing his head off is the only way to kill him." He caught her eye. "Us too."

She shivered, envisioning a gleaming machete hacking off her head. "I think I'd prefer to keep my head right where it is."

Jake grinned. "Yeah, you've got a good head on your shoulders."

She rolled her eyes at him, unable to resist a smile.

Even in the darkest moments, he managed to shed a little light.

And we can certainly use some extra light here.

They passed through the unguarded doorway to the tunnel.

The tunnel to the transporter was manmade—excavated by explosives. Probably the same kind she had seen in the weapon room. The walls and ceiling were polished smooth by machinery and lit by a string of small clear bulbs. Sloping downward, the floor of the tunnel was tiled with raw slate in various natural shades. Every thirty feet or so, a set of steps would appear, dropping them to the next level. Then the giant wormhole burrowed lower, spiraling deep into the ground.

Del ignored the stitch in her side and hurried around a corner.

And came face-to-face with Justin Blackwell.

He held a sleek, black sniper rifle with an infrared scope. The tiny red dot was trained on Del—right smack in the middle of her eyes.

She stopped breathing.

"What are you doing down here?" Blackwell asked calmly.

"What the hell do you think?" she rasped.

His eyes drifted over each of them. "You're escaping."

When Blackwell gradually lowered his rifle, she was stunned.

Why didn't he just shoot them all on the spot?

An icy shiver crept up her spine.

Because they need us. Our brains.

"Yes," her father repeated. "We're escaping."

He motioned for the others to put away their weapons.

"You won't need them."

That's when it hit her. He was letting them go.

She didn't know what to say. Part of her wanted to thank him. And part of her wanted to run for the portal, in case he changed his mind.

She bit her lip. "Why are you letting us go?"

Blackwell let out a pent up breath. "I've had enough. I can't do this anymore. I got involved with the Centre because VanBuren and Paughter said they had a cure for my daughter. Amy had leukemia. But this has gotten out of hand. I've seen too many things. *Done* too many things."

He stared at the rifle as if it were the first time he had seen it.

"What now?" she asked.

"It seems you're the only one without some protection, Miss Hawthorne. Just flick this lever, aim and pull the trigger. Take it—you might need it. Especially on the other side. They'll send someone after you."

He handed her the rifle.

"But they won't send…you."

"No," he said, clenching his teeth. "I'm done here. VanBuren has let youth go to his head and he'll kill anyone for it. Paughter is obsessed with power and greed. And the Director…?"

"Who *is* the Director?" Jake demanded softly.

"I don't know. I've never met him. My orders came from Paughter or VanBuren." Blackwell's voice dipped low. "Sometimes I think the Director…is a ghost."

Jake leveled his gun at him. "How do we know this isn't some kind of trick? Maybe you've got another weapon."

Blackwell lifted his chin. "Dr. Hawthorne knows what it's like to be a father. I'd have done anything to protect my daughter. But Amy doesn't need protecting anymore. And what she really needed was a father she could be proud of."

Tucking the rifle into her right arm, Del reached out, gripped his arm with her free hand.

"Your daughter would be proud of you…for this."

Blackwell's jaw flinched. "I don't know how this time travel stuff works, but if you ever meet up with my past self, do me a favor? Tell me—no, *make me* take my daughter in to see a doctor. *Before* she turns four. She might have had a chance if we had caught it earlier."

"You—your other self won't believe me," she murmured.

"Give him these, then. *Please!*"

Blackwell pressed a photograph and something cold into her hands.

An ankh key.

In a heartbeat, he was gone.

"Won't he tell someone?" Hawk asked.

Del stared at the photograph of Blackwell and a sweet young girl.

"No, he won't say anything," she said. "His daughter is dead. The Centre for Enlightened Living never saved her. Why would he save it?"

"We gotta go," TJ warned.

She had no idea how much time they had before someone sounded the alarm. But it probably wasn't much. She hoped to God that they were all safely through—*before* the rogue bots turned them into withered old corpses.

Their footsteps pounded down the tunnel as they raced for the portal. There was no point in trying to be quiet. The rock walls echoed every sound, even their breathless panting.

The slope dropped twenty steps down, and Del stumbled.

Thank God Jake was right beside her or she would have fallen down at least sixteen of them.

As they rounded the next corner, Hawk slowed to a halt in front of a row of lockers.

Del ran back, grabbed his arm. "What are you doing? Come on!"

"You go ahead. I'll wait here for Gary."

"I'm afraid Mr. Ingram won't be joining you…"

✟WENTY-FOUR

He had an appointment…with a bullet."

Del froze.

A man stepped from the shadows, a gun in one hand.

Hans VanBuren.

His icy eyes sparked with anger, and his face was flushed, damp with perspiration.

Del's eyes drifted lower and she swallowed hard.

The front of VanBuren's blue dress shirt was stained with large splatters of something dark and wet.

Blood—Gary's blood.

Her heart plummeted.

The man grabbed her father and pressed the gun to his head.

"Hans, I should've known we'd see you again," her father said bitterly, dropping his gun to the floor. "I'm surprised you didn't just wait for us to self-destruct."

VanBuren's cold eyes narrowed in unbridled fury. "The rogues haven't been activated yet. There are a few things I want first. One of them is your daughter."

Del sucked in a sharp gasp. As the blood drained from her face, she clenched her fists. She understood what he wanted, and the thought made her sick. There was no way in hell she was going to let him touch her. Not without a fight.

Shivering, she remembered Francesca.

VanBuren smiled at her, his lustful gaze stripping her bare.

"We have unfinished business, Delila."

She swallowed the burning rise of bile that crept up the back of her throat. She felt dirty, contaminated, like the Nahanni River water she had ingested.

"That's what you remind me of," she seethed.

"What's that?"

"*Giardia Lamblia.* A goddamn parasite."

The man actually winced.

"How'd you get here ahead of us?" TJ demanded.

VanBuren indicated the lockers with a nudge of his head.

"Pull on them."

The entire section of lockers moved. It was hinged on the left side, and behind it was an elevator door.

"Goes right to the Director's office," VanBuren said. "Only Vance and I know about it. And the Director, of course."

Jake stepped forward, his gun raised. "Let Lawrence go."

"Nice try, Doctor Kerrigan. Hawthorne'll be dead before you even pull the trigger. Drop your weapons. All of you."

Without a second thought, Del let the rifle slide to the floor. It clattered at her feet, useless. There was a brief hesitation, then TJ and Hawk dropped their weapons.

"Jake!" she pleaded. "He'll kill my dad"

Jake gritted his teeth, tossing his gun toward the wall.

"You don't want to kill me, Hans," her father said calmly.

VanBuren's head twitched. "Why is that?"

"Because I have the serum."

"I have my own stash, thank you."

"But I have what the Director is after. A serum with no half-hour, painful side effects. One full dose and you never have to worry about it again. You'll live forever, at the age you are now."

VanBuren's mouth dropped. "You're lying!"

"I'll get it. It's in my pocket."

Her father moved cautiously and withdrew a capped syringe filled with a golden liquid. Then he pulled out two crimson syringes.

VanBuren eyed them suspiciously, reading the labels. "*Hypnos* and *Thanatos?* Which one is the serum?"

"Let the others go and I'll tell you."

Del could see the flicker of uncertainty in VanBuren's eyes, but she could also sense his hunger.

The gun in his hand wavered, then he lowered it, just a bit.

"Give me the serum, Hawthorne."

"Let them go first."

"What!" VanBuren said bitingly. "You don't think I'm serious?"

Without hesitation, he leveled his gun at Hawk, and before Del could move, the muzzle flashed and a shot rang out in the closed space of the tunnel.

"*No!*" she screamed.

A small bullet hole pierced Hawk's forehead. He slumped to the ground...lifeless.

In sickened disbelief, she tried to run to him but Jake held her back.

She struggled, oblivious to the flood of tears that streamed down her face.

Jake pulled her close. "Stay still!"

"Which one is the serum?" VanBuren snarled.

"Let them go and I'll give you the file too," her father said, his voice shaky. "It'll make you a very rich, very powerful man, Hans."

There was a long, tense moment of silence.

Finally VanBuren shrugged. "Fine. They can go."

Jake was the first to move. He carefully reached for his gun.

"Leave it!" VanBuren ordered, rolling up his sleeve. "Just go!"

Del choked back a sob.

She couldn't leave, not without her father.

VanBuren held out his hand. "The serum, please."

Mutely, her father passed him the *Hypnos* serum.

"You must think I'm a moron. I knew you'd try to trick me."

Before anyone could say a word, VanBuren snatched the *Thanatos* syringe, ripped off the cap and plunged the tip of the needle into his arm. Then he emptied the syringe and tossed it on the floor.

Seconds later, he smiled. "You were right, doctor. There's no torturing pain. I feel...great. You couldn't fool me. I knew that *Hypnos* meant *hypnotize* or something like that."

"Sleep," Del whispered.

But Thanatos means death.

"Now I'll live for—"

VanBuren gagged, then doubled over. A long, piercing scream issued from his mouth. He threw aside his gun as if it were burning him, then he slumped to the floor, writhing in agony.

"You bastard! You said no side effects!"

He rocked on his knees, head bent, clutching his stomach.

Her father shook his head. "There aren't any. Not in the real serum. Unfortunately, I don't have any on me at the moment. Oh, and you're right. I *do* think you're a moron, Hans. I knew you'd think I offered you the wrong one."

VanBuren raised his head. Blood oozed from every orifice of his body. Thick and crimson, it poured from his eyes, ears, nose and mouth. It dripped down his face, into his white hair, his white clothes...staining the crotch of his pants.

The stain of death.

VanBuren wiped a trembling hand across his drooping mouth and when he saw the gory trail it left, he whimpered.

"What have you done to me?"

Before their eyes, Hans went from thirty to sixty, to a hundred. He didn't just grow old, he grew *ancient*. His skin shriveled and blistered, with oozing cancerous sores that spread across his face. His eyes turned opaque and sunk deep into wrinkled, loose folds of flesh. Within seconds, he resembled a fossilized mummy. Twitching, he crashed to the floor and stared blindly at the ceiling as his body consumed itself.

"*Thanatos?*"

Del saw her father purse his lips.

"It means death, Hans. Instant death. Too bad you weren't versed on mythology, or you would have known which serum to choose. Your body has been infected with hundreds of self-destruct nanobots—not just one. And they're all activated."

An agonizing spasm gripped VanBuren's body.

"*But I...want to live...forever.*"

Del stared down at him. "Longevity is overrated."

VanBuren shuddered and his head lolled.

Dead.

"Poetic justice," Jake mumbled.

She was about to comment when the elevator groaned.

"Someone's coming!"

Jake grabbed his gun from the floor. "It's either Paughter or the Director."

"Whoever it is," her father said. "We have to kill him. Gary said it'll take forty-two minutes for all of us to cross."

"It's less now," Jake murmured. "Maybe thirty minutes...without Gary and Hawk."

"We could be dead before then," Del said.

Her father's eyes swept over her. "If it's Paughter, he has the self-destruct code for the rogue bots. A push of a button on his watch and..."

TJ grabbed his gun from the ground, then motioned the others to do the same. "We gotta spread out. There's no place to hide, but at least we can make it harder for him."

He edged back until he was pressed up against the tunnel wall, next to Hawk's body. Then he raised the gun and pointed it toward the lockers.

Spurred into motion, Del hoisted the rifle to her shoulder. But it was too damned heavy. If she didn't find a way to support it, the weapon would be useless.

She flicked a look at the lockers.

When Paughter steps out, he'll be looking straight ahead. Not up.

"Jake!"

He moved toward her, one brow arched. "What?"

"Help me up!"

He drew back, hesitating. "Del, I don't think—"

"We don't have all day, Kerrigan."

Tucking his gun into his waistband, Jake quickly hoisted her up.

Behind the lockers, the elevator shuddered and slowed.

"Let one of us take him out," Jake said, giving her the rifle. "We'll lead him away from the lockers, from you. I don't want you getting shot."

Her eyes softened, watching him move away. *Jake...*

The panel of lockers started to swing out from the wall and she gripped the edge tightly, praying that she wouldn't fall off.

Could she actually pull the trigger?

The rifle's barrel was cool against her cheek. Peering through its scope, memories assaulted her. Memories of computer games, playing Unreal with her father, killing off his computer character...

But this isn't a game. This is life...or death.

She shivered.

Killing a human being was something she never dreamed she'd consider. But hell, she had never been held prisoner before—with rape or death hanging over her head.

"Hi everyone!" Paughter called out cheerfully. "Don't shoot us!"

Us?

Del lifted her head slightly.

The kid she had known as Peter took two steps into the room.

She cringed, recalling the hours of tutoring she had spent with him, unaware that he was a murdering bastard.

A murdering bastard with a hostage.

Del recognized Kate O'Leary immediately.

The redhead cowered in the doorway to the elevator, her arms tied tightly behind her back and her mouth gagged with a strip of duct tape. Tears streamed from her wild, terrified eyes.

Del's heart raced.

Kate had good reason to be terrified.

Strapped to the girl's bulging, pregnant waist was a black belt.

Made of licorice-twist explosives.

Oh God! He's going to blow her up. And the baby!

Paughter dragged Kate into the middle of the tunnel.

"My, my," he said in an amused voice. "What have we here? I see you've taken care of one of my problems."

Del couldn't see his face, but she was sure that his eyes were trained on VanBuren's bloodied body.

She checked the scope.

Perfect. He was in her line of fire.

She flicked on the infrared beam, squinted through the scope and aimed it at the back of Paughter's head.

She bit her lip.

Peter's head.

"I recommend you lower your guns," Paughter said. "I have something on me you'll want to see."

He strode to the center of the tunnel, jerking Kate after him.

"Kate's fashionable belt might not look like much, but there's enough explosive in it to obliterate everything within a two hundred foot radius."

He opened his hand, revealing a detonator switch.

Del muffled a gasp.

If the bomb went off in the tunnel they would all be killed. Every last one of them. And she wasn't ready to die.

Not this year!

Suddenly, Paughter froze. "Where's your daughter?"

Her father shrugged. "She went on...*ahead.*"

No pun intended...right, Dad?

Her hands trembled, and the tiny red light jumped from Paughter's head to the wall.

Focus...

Paughter's body twitched, and Del swore under her breath.

The infrared light had caught his eye.

He peered down the tunnel to the cave, then twisted his head in the opposite direction. His gaze shifted restlessly, from the shadowed recesses of the cave to the men standing along the wall.

Then slowly, he lifted his head.

Del glimpsed the whites of his eyes staring directly at her, and she drew in a long, uneven breath.

Paughter's mouth curved into a smile. "Delila, do you even know how to fire one of those?"

When she remained silent, he laughed mockingly. "Bet you've never held a gun."

Her finger caressed the trigger.

"I could blow us all to hell," he reminded her, his thumb hovering over the detonator.

She gritted her teeth. "Or you can go by yourself."

The sniper rifle hissed.

Paughter's body dropped to the ground, eyes wide, stunned.

"Head shot!" she whispered, resting her forehead on the locker.

No one moved, no one spoke.

But the voices in Del's head roared.

You killed him! How could you? Murderer...

She wiped away a tear.

How can I live with this?

She lifted her head and her eyes swept across the tunnel, to Hawk's lifeless form. He had been a good man, with a kind heart and spirit. She would miss him.

Avoiding Paughter's body, she looked at her father who had been held hostage for seven years. A man forced to do dreadful things in order to survive, in order to keep his family safe.

A movement caught Del's eye.

She held her breath as Jake cautiously removed the bomb belt from around Kate's waist. He tossed it inside the elevator and pushed the *up* button. As the elevator made its slow ascent, he cut through the cords that bound Kate's hands. The poor girl was a bundle of nerves. As soon as her hands were freed, she peeled aside the tape and threw her arms gratefully around Jake.

Del looked back at Paughter's limp, dead body.

Could she live with his death on her hands?

Her eyes were drawn to the swell of Kate's belly.

Yeah, I can live with it.

She slid down the side of the lockers, and Jake grabbed her around the waist and lowered her to the ground. Cradling her face, he kissed her on the mouth. Hard and quick.

Behind them, TJ noisily cleared his throat. "The air in here is getting—"

He doubled over in a coughing fit.

Del rushed toward him. "TJ, are you all right?"

"Yeah…well, no. I feel weird."

Her father yanked TJ close to the lights.

Del stared in shock.

TJ's face was aging—not as quickly as Paughter had, but he was aging.

"What?" he demanded.

Following their eyes, he stared at his fingers. Tiny cobwebs of wrinkles appeared, racing over the tops of his hands and trailing up his arms.

"What's goin' down, dawg?" he asked, confused.

Del turned to her father. "What do we do, Dad?"

"There's nothing we *can* do. I'm sorry, TJ. It's too late."

TJ nodded slowly. "So I'm a walking dead man. How much time have I got?"

"Two weeks, maybe three. But it's painful at the end."

"Dad!" Del hissed.

She wanted to shake her father. Why was he telling TJ this?

"Someone's in the tunnel," Jake said, cutting in.

She heard it too. The soft pounding of footsteps.

TJ coughed and spat out a bloody tooth.

"Go on. I'll take care of anyone else who tries to follow."

"What are you talking about?" she demanded.

He opened his hand, revealing the small domed bomb he had taken from her in the weapon room.

"You have five minutes. Then I'm blowing the tunnel. Course, I'm guessing that the explosion'll take out this section only. Not the portal."

Del threw her arms around him. "Come back with us, TJ! We'll find a way—"

"No, Del," he said. "This is my chance."

She leaned her forehead against his. "Chance for what?"

"To make things right. I love you, Del. I always loved you. I made a stupid mistake, tried to do the right thing by Julie…"

He shook his head. "Run, Del!"

Jake and her father peeled her away from TJ.

"Run!" Jake yelled.

And Del ran. Faster than she had ever run before.

She followed Jake and her father, her feet pounding on the hard slate floor.

Time was running out.

They veered around a corner.

Down another set of steps.

Running…faster.

Six, eight…twelve steps lower.

Hearts pounding.

Toward the blue light.

Faster!

They ran for their lives.

Del's chest burned when they finally reached the cave.

A few feet away, the mysterious crystals emitted their soft blue light and buzzing drone.

All of a sudden, a loud explosion rocked the tunnel.

The thunderous boom shook the cave walls, and she was thrown into the air. She slammed down on top of Jake. Her father landed beside them. Chunks of rock fell from the ceiling, and Jake threw himself over her, protecting her. No one moved until the rumbling stopped and a tomblike calm filled the tunnel.

"Ok, let's make this quick," Jake said. "There are three of us. It'll take roughly sixteen minutes for all of us to go through."

Del let out a moan of relief. Time to go home.

"Wait," her father called. "I have something for both of you."

She didn't know what to say.

What could he possibly want to give them?

Her father hugged her tightly. "I love you, Del."

Then his arm snaked out, gathering Jake in. "You're the son I never had, Jake. Look after my daughter. She's my heart and soul."

Del frowned. "I don't need looking aft—"

A sharp pain pierced her thigh.

Startled, she jumped back, gasping in shock.

Her father was holding two empty syringes.

Hypnos…

Her mouth trembled. "Dad?"

Beside her, Jake rubbed his leg, scowling. "What the hell?"

Lawrence kissed her forehead. "Trust me, honey. *Hypnos* puts the rogue bot to sleep. Permanently. There will be no way for anyone from the Centre to activate it. Ever."

He sneezed loudly into his hand, then turned away hastily.

She narrowed her eyes. "Wait! What about your syringe?"

"There were only two samples. Get going now."

Turning, she stumbled shakily toward the buzzing light.

Pausing at the edge, she said, "Jake, I—"

Jake reached her in three strides, kissing her hard. His hands feverishly touched her, memorizing every line, every inch of skin.

He pulled away and his eyes captured hers. "Me too."

Moving between the crystals, she caught sight of her father.

He stood in the corner, his back to them, shoulders stooped.

"Go home, Del!" he barked. "Jake will be right behind you."

Her eyes burned, mesmerized by the droning hum and the strange twisting tentacles of light that crawled up her legs. The air around her began to shift and the cave walls yawned.

Staring at Jake, she raised a metallic blue hand.

"Do you believe in destiny, Jake?"

He mouthed something she couldn't hear.

"What?"

"I'll find you, Delila Hawthorne," he said, his voice distorted.

He held up his hand.

In it, he held the detonator for the bomb belt that he had shoved into the elevator. He must have pushed it, because somewhere high above a loud boom erupted. The ceiling began to crumble as chunks of rock and fragments of crystal broke away.

"I love you, Dad!" she cried. "I love—"

In a burst of blinding energy, she sensed her body splitting apart, disintegrating into billions of DNA molecules.

Dust to dust…ashes to ashes.

Delila Hawthorne died a billion deaths.

♀HE PRESENT

Jade Hawker stared out the window at the snow-covered streets of Québec City. Ducking her head, she allowed her straight black hair to fall forward as she slid a pair of sunglasses over chocolate brown eyes. She peeked around the room.

A businessman in a dark suit eyed her. His suit reeked of money, and with money came power. And with power came…

She shivered.

This was the first time in a month she had allowed herself the luxury of a steaming mug of Chai tea at a hole-in-the-wall café.

The place was packed. And that created a problem.

Someone might recognize her.

Jade glanced at her watch. Half an hour until her appointment.

The executive unexpectedly appeared at her side.

She kept her head bent slightly. *"Oui?"*

The man smiled. "Est ce que nous nous sommes déja rencontré?"

Have we met before?

She drew in a breath, shook her head. *"Non."*

Apprehensive, Jade took a sip of tea. A long sip.

The man's eyes lit upon the simple wedding band she wore.

"Je m'excuse, mademoiselle…uh…"

"Please, leave me alone."

Jade rose swiftly.

It wasn't safe to be out too long in public. Someone might discover who she really was—although some days she had to question that herself.

Jade Hawker worked in Québec City, in a quaint privately owned flower shop, *Le Fleuriste Duchesne.* Jade had no family, no close friends…no husband. She was a loner who rarely went out—unless she *had* to. Like today.

Jade Hawker was a combination of two names. Hers and Jake's.

It had taken Del two weeks to come up with it. Before that she had been *Diana Smith*. Before that, *Debbie Hampton*. But each time, *they* had found her. And each time, she had escaped by sheer luck.

She was learning though, getting better at changing her identity and blending in. This time she had grown her hair past her shoulders, dyed it black and bought brown contact lenses. And she had gained some weight, about fifteen pounds. She doubted that anyone would recognize her now. And they certainly wouldn't think to look for her in Québec. They were probably still searching Alberta, maybe even the Northwest Territories.

The thought made her chuckle at first, then she grew sad.

It seemed like an eternity had passed since eight near strangers had first stepped foot on the shores of the South Nahanni River. A river brimming with life—and cursed by death.

Miki, Francesca, Gary, Hawk, TJ...none of them had made it.

Neither had her father.

She had heard his hoarse, labored cough and had seen the wrinkles rippling in his face before he turned away.

She thought of Jake.

For a week, she had waited for him, searching the river's shores around The Gate. Looking for a footprint, a sign.

But he never appeared.

It was Hawk's partner, Henry McGee, who had found her wandering mindlessly on the banks of the river. He had been out on his weekly walk, searching for all the lost souls who had gone missing, including his partner and friend.

At first McGee hadn't believed her story.

Who would? It was an insane story, an impossible one, filled with images of time travel portals to the future, microscopic nanobots and fountain-of-youth serums.

She showed him the memory stick that her father had dropped into her pocket right after he had stuck her with *Hypnos*. McGee still didn't believe her. Not even when she showed him the strange ankh key—the one that Blackwell had given her. Unfortunately, the technology of it was so advanced there wasn't a computer designed yet that could read it.

Frantic to convince McGee that she wasn't insane, she had grabbed a knife and sliced open her arm. It was probably the most insane thing she had ever done.

But when it healed before McGee's eyes, he finally believed her.

Henry McGee, with his grizzled old face, had been a godsend. Especially when he noticed the strange aircraft flying over the area. He had rushed to warn her, then he had moved her out of his cabin and helped her find Hawk's cave after she refused to leave the area.

She couldn't leave. Jake was coming for her. He had promised.

One day, McGee accompanied her on a walk and she tearfully told him how Hawk had died. Without a second thought, she took out a pocketknife and lopped off a blond curl. She placed it on a flat rock, then piled three smooth stones on top.

"The land provides all things for us," she murmured. "Hawk was provided for me when I needed him so I leave the land a token of my gratitude."

McGee had stared at her for a long time. Before he broke the connection, she caught a glimpse of tears in the old man's eyes.

A week went by.

There was still no sign of Jake, and McGee was worried. He had heard rumors that some influential people were searching for her. A few had shown up at Fort Simpson, when she was registered in a hotel as *Debbie Hampton*. McGee had helped to smuggle her out.

A few days later, *Diana Smith* made it to Vancouver and gave the taxi driver an address a block from her house. He drove past it and she gaped in shock.

The bald guard from the Centre for Enlightened Living was sitting in a lawn chair in the garden. Kayber was curled up on his lap. Lisa was nowhere in sight.

The following day, Del came across a brief article in the archives of the *Vancouver Sun*. A few weeks earlier, Lisa Shaw's body had been pulled from the rubble of an art gallery explosion. She had to be identified by her dental records.

Gulping down the last of her tea, Del wiped away a straying tear and stared out the café window.

If it wasn't for Phoebe, I'd be dead too.

The men from the Centre had hunted down *Diana Smith*, and she barely managed to escape without being shot. Desperate and terrified, she turned to the one person she didn't think they would connect her to. Phoebe gave her a small fortune, money that she had stashed away for a 'rainy day'.

She smiled, remembering Phoebe's insistence.

It ain't raining, honey. It's a goddamn flash flood!

Del flicked another look at her watch.

Time to get going.

She walked across the street, her feet dragging tiredly. She stepped into the medical centre, stopping at the receptionist's booth where she filled out a form. After her name was called, she followed a woman into a tiny room and sat on the examining table.

Since her return from the Nahanni, she had been experiencing some unusual symptoms. Not quite the same as her normal MS exacerbations. Overall, she felt good. She suspected she was in remission. But at times, she felt drained and sometimes her legs ached. It was just…different.

Dr. Massé entered the room. In his hands, he held a folder—Jade Hawker's medical history. Of course, most of it was falsified, thanks to one of Phoebe's contacts, but Del couldn't conceal the MS.

The doctor greeted her with a hesitant smile.

"We have your tests results back. But I am a bit confused."

She was taken aback. "Why? I just need a prescription refill."

Dr. Massé walked toward a small cabinet. "Because of your MS?"

She nodded, even though he couldn't see her. "Yes."

The doctor turned, handed her a paper gown.

"Mademoiselle Hawker, you know what your problem is. And it isn't MS."

He studied her so carefully that she had an awful thought.

What if he is linked to the Centre?

Dr. Massé left the room and she quickly stripped off her blouse and slacks. Fighting with the paper-thin hospital gown, she twisted sharply, trying to tie the laces. She made it to the top before realizing that she had missed one on the left.

With a nervous sigh, she started again.

The doctor knocked on the door. "This way, please."

She followed him to a room at the end of the hall where she was greeted by a friendly, blond-haired technician.

"Make yourself comfortable on the examining table, please."

Within minutes, Del was staring at something inconceivable.

"But I don't understand…"

The technician eyed her oddly. "What's not to understand?"

"I-I'm…it's not possible."

"What are you saying, mademoiselle?"

"I'm saying this can't be right!"

The technician nodded slowly.

Hot tears flooded down Del's cheeks.

Oh…my…God!

Delila Hawthorne—aka Jade Hawker—was pregnant.

She could make out the head, the tiny fingers and feet. And the heart. She heard it beating, strong and fast.

Blip-blip, blip-blip…

She was floored.

For years, she thought she couldn't get pregnant. A surgeon had made sure of that. The only explanation she could think of was that the injection of Ankh serum had healed her previous surgery. Her father had said that he had healed after a bullet wound.

"Do you believe in destiny?" Miki had asked an eternity ago.

Del gaped at the tiny baby—*Jake's* baby.

A baby conceived in 2031, but who would be born in 2006.

I believe in life. Not eternal life—just life.

"Is your husband here?" the technician asked, interrupting her thoughts.

"He's…away. On a trip."

Blip-blip, blip-blip, blip-blip…

Suddenly, Del scrunched her face.

Something flashed near the baby's head.

There!

A thin vein of pale blue light flickered over the baby's body.

"Something's wrong! I saw a light."

The technician moved closer to the monitor. "Everything's fine."

Del looked again, searching.

The light was gone.

What the hell?

She had a sudden flash of memory—something Schroeder and her father had said. Only one person could cross back at a time…*one* set of DNA.

She stared at her stomach, terrified of what that meant.

"You're finished," the technician said, moving to the door.

Del's head jerked. "Wait! What about my MS medication?"

Frowning, the woman picked up the folder, opened it. A minute later, she beamed a huge smile. "You don't have MS."

Del's brow furrowed in confusion. "I'm in remission?"

"No. You don't *have* MS. You're perfectly healthy."

The woman whirled on one heel and left the room.

Shocked, Del got dressed and grabbed her belongings. Outside, she slipped on the sunglasses and breathed deeply, dazed by the technician's words.

Somehow, miraculously, her MS had disappeared.

And she was pregnant.

Deliriously happy, she weaved her way through the throng of tourists that swarmed the city for Carnaval de Québec. Strangers surrounded her, passed her, jostled her. She hid behind the glasses studying their faces as they passed by, searching for the one she waited for—the one she ached for.

Jake…

A cold wind sent shivers up her spine.

She flicked a look across the icy street at an electric billboard three stories up. Bio-Tec Canada's new DNA ankh logo dominated the screen.

She looked away, trembling.

"How does that saying go?" she muttered to herself. "The past is history, the future is a mystery, and the present is a gift. That's why it's called…*present*."

Well, the future wasn't such a mystery to her anymore. She had to forget it. Forget everything she knew and focus on the present.

A face in the crowd drew her attention and she hissed in a breath.

Wait! Is that…?

The face vanished, melting into the background…a ghost.

Impossible!

She shook her head and smiled sadly, losing herself in the mob.

She was once haunted by shadows of people who flitted in and out of her life. Now her life was haunted by a river.

A river of ghosts.

References:

Besides months of research on the Internet, I found the following books or papers vital to the realistic authenticity of *The River*:

Robert A. Freitas Jr., *Exploratory Design in Medical Nanotechnology: A Mechanical Artificial Red Cell*, *Artificial Cells, Blood Substitutes, and Immobil. Biotech.* 26(1998):411-430.
www.foresight.org/Nanomedicine/Respirocytes.html.

Robert A. Freitas Jr., *Nanomedicine, Volume I: Basic Capabilities*, Landes Bioscience, Georgetown, TX, 1999. www.nanomedicine.com.
K. Eric Drexler, *Engines of Creation:* The Coming Era of Nanotechnology, ©1986

Kathleen Meyer, *How to Shit in the Woods: An Environmentally Sound Approach to a Lost Art*, ©1994

R.M. Patterson, *Dangerous River: Adventure on the Nahanni*, ©1989

Peter Jowett and Neil Hartling, *Nahanni River Guide*, ©2003

Nahanni River Adventures, *Nahanni River Adventures: Headless Creek Cooks Manual*, ©2003

To Book A Nahanni Adventure:

Nahanni River Adventures
Eco-River Expeditions From Alaska to Nunavut
P.O. Box 31203 Whitehorse, Yukon Territory
Canada   Y1A 5P7
Reservations: 1(800) 297 - 6927
Phone (867) 668 - 3180   Fax (867) 668 – 3056
www.nahanni.com
info@nahanni.com

Book 1 in the Divine series by Cheryl Kaye Tardif...

Divine Intervention

CFBI agent Jasmine McLellan is assigned a hot case—one that requires the psychic abilities of the PSI Division, a secret government agency located in the secluded town of Divine, BC.

Jasi leads a psychically gifted team in the hunt for a serial arsonist—a murderer who has already taken the lives of three innocent people. Unleashing her gift as a *Pyro-Psychic*, Jasi is compelled toward smoldering ashes and enters the killer's mind. A mind bent on destruction and revenge.

Jasi's team, consisting of *Psychometric Empath* and profiler, Ben Roberts, and *Victim Empath*, Natassia Prushenko, is led down a twisting path of dark, painful secrets. Brandon Walsh, the handsome, smooth-talking *Chief of Arson Investigations,* joins them in a manhunt that takes them across British Columbia—from Vancouver to Kelowna, Penticton and Victoria.

While impatiently sifting through the clues that were left behind, Jasi and her team realize that there is more to the third victim than meets the eye. Perhaps not all of the victims were *that* innocent. The hunt intensifies when they learn that someone they know is next on the arsonist's list.

The case heats to the boiling point as Jasi steps out of the flames...and into the fire. And in the heat of early summer, Agent Jasi McLellan discovers that a murderer lies in wait...*much closer than she imagined.*

ISBN: 9781412035910 (trade paperback)
ISBN: 978-0-9865382-2-3 (ebook)

Available at various retailers, including Amazon, Chapters and KoboBooks

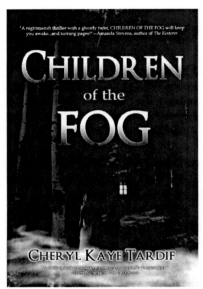

In the tradition of Stephen King, The Twilight Zone and The Hitchhiker, comes a terrifying collection of short stories in...

Skeletons in the Closet & Other Creepy Stories

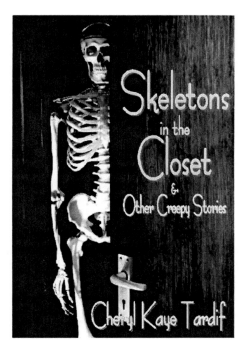

Thirteen stories take you from one hold-your-breath chapter to the next.

Enter the closet...

A Grave Error
The Death of an Old Cow
Maid of Dishonor
Atrophy
Picture Perfect
Sweet Dreams
Separation Anxiety
The Car
Deadly Reunion
Remote Control
Ouija
Caller Unknown
Skeletons in the Closet

ISBN: 978-0-9866310-2-3 (ebook)
ISBN: 978-1-926997-05-6 (trade paperback)

Cheryl Kaye Tardif is an award-winning, bestselling Canadian suspense author. Her novels include Children of the Fog, The River, Divine Intervention, and Whale Song, which New York Times bestselling author Luanne Rice calls "a compelling story of love and family and the mysteries of the human heart...a beautiful, haunting novel."

Her next thriller, Divine Justice (book 2 in the Divine series), will be published in spring 2011, in ebook and trade paperback editions.

Cheryl also enjoys writing short stories inspired mainly by her author idol Stephen King, and this has resulted in Skeletons in the Closet & Other Creepy Stories (ebook) and Remote Control (novelette ebook).

In 2010 Cheryl detoured into the romance genre with her contemporary romantic suspense debut, Lancelot's Lady, written under the pen name of Cherish D'Angelo.

Booklist raves, "Tardif, already a big hit in Canada...a name to reckon with south of the border."

Cheryl's website: http://www.cherylktardif.com
Official blog: http://www.cherylktardif.blogspot.com
Twitter: http://www.twitter.com/cherylktardif

You can also find Cheryl Kaye Tardif on MySpace, Facebook, Goodreads, Shelfari and LibraryThing, plus other social networks.

IMAJIN BOOKS

Quality fiction beyond your wildest dreams

For your next ebook or paperback purchase, please visit:

www.imajinbooks.com

CPSIA information can be obtained at www.ICGtesting.com
Printed in the USA
LVOW031633041111

253593LV00009B/154/P

9 781926 997179